BROTHERS OF THE SEA

BOOKS BY D. R. SHERMAN

OLD MALI AND THE BOY

BROTHERS OF THE SEA

BROTHERS OF THE SEA

by D. R. Sherman

Little, Brown and Company • *Boston* • *Toronto*

To Clarice and Dorothy Clayton,
my grandmother and my aunt

BROTHERS OF THE SEA

THREE concrete steps led from the doorway of the small wooden-shuttered porch to the ground outside. Seated on the topmost step was a man, his left leg stretched out awkwardly in front of him. It was cased in plaster, from the foot to halfway up his thigh, and the white color of the plaster was no longer white but a dirty gray, and in places it was splotched and stained with other colors which had come from all the different things which had been a part of living since he had broken the tibia of his leg.

For a long while the man did not move. He sat motionless, the palms of his hands flat on the concrete behind him and his arms straight and taking most of the weight of his upper body which was inclined backwards. The veins in his stringy muscled arms stood out like cords under the dark skin which had been burned even darker by the tropic sun.

He wore a pair of faded shorts and nothing else. They were frayed and patched in places, and they were so old and worn with washing that now the patches were the only parts with any true color left in them.

The man moved suddenly. He eased the weight of his body forward and then brought his hands round in front of him and rubbed the palms together briskly. When he felt the blood coming back into them and the cold tight tingling left the flesh beneath the calloused skin he leaned back again and took up his former position, which was the way he had grown to like most since his leg had been broken.

He stared out to sea again, watching the water break on the reef. It was a dull sea, reflecting the color of the clouds which blanketed the sky, and he knew from the way the small waves broke and tumbled that the shoal waters would be murky with sand.

It is not a good way for the sea to be, he thought, because there is much food in it and the fish will not be bothered to take a man's bait.

From where he sat he could see the humpbacked shape of Praslin Island lying far across against the horizon. It was twenty-five miles away, and the weather and the distance combined to make it dark and featureless. It was not the way the man liked to see it. He liked it in the late evenings, when the sun was going down, because then the patches of red soil that the rain had laid bare showed like raw orange scars against the green of the trees. It looked good to him, the bright orange with the dark green, and looking at it always made him feel good.

He watched the restless water a little longer, staring down on it from the side of the mountain where he lived. He did not see it as an unbroken stretch. Tall casuarinas and fat-leafed takamakas hid it in parts from his view, and the coconut palms which grew more thickly on the narrow belt of flat land which bordered the sea spread their green rustling fronds in a dark umbrella which obscured all but patches of the golden-white coral sand of the beach.

He switched his glance suddenly to the leg which was stretched out clumsily in front of him. He regarded it impassively, feeling neither regret nor annoyance that this thing had happened to him. It had been his own fault, for not going down the mountainside carefully enough, but it was hard to walk with caution and without haste when the early morning was fresh and bright and when the sea was smooth and full of fish that you hoped were going to bite. It had happened, and that was all there was to it, but he had wished many times that he had been more careful, because it was more than a month since he had fished and now there was no money for rice or sugar or tea and all the other little things which made life sweeter and more bearable.

He began to think of his son then, and he knew that without him this last month would have been even more difficult. He caught the fish for their food every day now, sometimes with a line but most of the time wearing the glass mask and using the harpoon gun he had been given for his last birthday just over six months ago. He carried water from the stream, the weight of the brimming bucket making his ever-present limp even more pronounced, and he foraged far and with great stealth to bring back bananas and pineapples and sometimes even a huge jackfruit.

Oui, the man thought, though he is not the son of my own flesh, I do not think I could have made a better boy myself.

Then in his mind he went back again to the night which had brought them together. It was a long time ago, but the memory of it was as fresh as if it had just happened. He was lying in bed, awake in the dark, flinching at the ear-shattering thunder which followed every crackling bolt of lightning. Once the lightning struck very close, and the whole house rattled and he saw the searing flash of brilliance through the crack between the wooden window and its frame. In the awful silence which followed the thunder he heard a sudden clamorous banging on the front door. His scalp prickled, and his hair stood on end. He sprang out of bed and lit the lamp. He lifted it high in his left hand, and with his right hand he snatched the heavy killing harpoon off its bracket on the wall.

He padded out of the room and across the veranda. He paused before the locked front door. He altered his grip on the harpoon and with the same hand he began to slip the bolt. When it was free he braced the sole of his bare foot against the door to keep it shut, feeling the force of the gusting wind. He took a fresh grip on the harpoon. He put his shoulder against the door to hold it, and then he eased his weight a little and allowed the wind to inch it open.

He peered out cautiously into the ragged night. He saw nothing, and his hair began to stand on end once again. The small flame behind the glass of the lamp flickered and bent double and almost blew out. He wanted to cross himself, but his hands were full. He was putting the weight of his shoulder against the door to close it when he heard a strange, wailing cry. It came from low down and very close, and he almost jumped with the fright it gave him.

He stared fearfully into the darkness at the bottom of the steps, and what he saw in the dim glow of light widened his eyes with astonishment. He bent quickly and laid the harpoon and the lamp on the floor beside him. He opened the door wide and clipped it back. He ran down the steps and picked up the basket of woven palm leaf. It was lined with cloth, and lying naked on the cloth was a boy child, its eyes wide and intent in the turning, flopping head. The small hands which lifted towards him were clutched into fists.

He walked back inside with the basket in his arms,

just as the first large drops of rain began to fall again, wondering what to do. During the long stormy night while he stayed awake and watched over the child he made up his mind.

The man sat up once more and rubbed the circulation back into the palms of his hands. He closed his eyes, shrugging the mental cobwebs from his mind before opening them again.

It had, he remembered, taken him a whole week to find a woman in milk who was willing to look after his son and give him her breast while he was fishing the seas for their livelihood.

"A little over fifteen years ago," he murmured aloud to himself. "And I have fished the same seas and lived in the same house, and nothing has changed much since that day."

And what of the boy, he rebuked himself silently inside his head. Has he not changed?

"Yes," he said, answering himself aloud once again. "He has grown up well, and he is strong and quite tall, and it is a pity only that he has that one leg shorter than the other."

The man shook his head, fighting the sudden ache which filled him.

It is a good house that we live in though, he thought quickly, consciously changing the direction of his thinking to something that would give him happiness and not pain. The thatched roof does not leak during the heavy rains and it is not too far from the stream, and in the months of the wet heat it catches the breeze and is cool and more bearable than those big houses which the *propriétaires* build for themselves on the edges of the sea.

No, he thought, I would not change it for another.

It was then that he remembered the rent for the house. It was due at the end of the month, which was in another ten days, and because he believed in work and not in miracles he realized once again that he would not have the money to pay it.

The third month, he reflected, and we are living on charity, which is not a constant and dependable quality.

He shrugged abruptly, trying to push the whole thing from his mind, because there was nothing else that he could do about it. But the knowledge of the matter did not leave him so easily: it was a humiliating thing for a man to be unable to pay his way, and it was a situation for which he had no stomach.

I wish it were very near the time of my son's birthday, he thought suddenly, longingly, because then we should have the money to pay for all the rent which I owe.

Thinking about it now made him shake his head in wonder. It had happened fourteen times already, but he knew he would never get accustomed to it or be able to understand it. On the twenty-fifth of February each year he found an envelope containing two hundred rupees lying on the veranda just inside the closed front door. He always found it there in the morning, and always without any note or explanation.

The boy had been five years old when his curiosity and mystification got the better of him. In his superstitious heart he knew that what he contemplated would be tempting the fates, but even the thought of never again receiving the white envelope did not deter him.

The night on which it usually came he climbed into the jamalac tree which grew a little way from the front of the house. His muscles cramped with the waiting, and three times he had to fight an almost unbearable tickling inside his nose which made him want to sneeze. It was two hours past midnight when he heard the soft scuffle of approaching footsteps. He tensed, and with his eyes he strained to pierce the darkness of the night, and then just when he made out the vague outline of the figure which stole up the path his nose began to burn again. Before he could stop himself he closed his eyes and sucked a great breath of air in through his mouth and it hit the bottom of his lungs and came up again with an explosive roar that shattered the stillness of the night.

The figure on the ground below him froze. It remained motionless for a second, and then with a startled cry that rang with fear and despair it turned and fled down the side of the mountain and into the sanctuary of the distant darkness.

He swung himself off the branch on which he had been sitting. He hung full-length for a moment and then let go. He felt the rough bark scraping the tips of his fingers and then before he expected it he hit the ground with a bone-rattling impact. He stumbled, almost falling, but then he regained his balance and sprinted forward in pursuit. He had not run ten yards when he tripped and fell. He crashed headlong to the ground, and the force with which he landed knocked the breath right out of him.

He lay still for a moment, too stunned and bewildered to move. When he got his breath back he pushed himself up off the ground. He peered into the darkness. He saw nothing, and the only sound he heard was the noise of his own gasping.

He turned away, cursing silently, and it was then that he became aware of a faint and tantalizingly sweet fragrance. He moved in a small circle, head held high and sniffing at the air. He lost the scent for a while, but then it came back again, even more faint and elusive than it had been before. His nose twitched delicately, and his heavy eyebrows drew together in concentration as he tried to identify the source of it. There was the piquant sweetness of mountain flowers in the scent which he smelled, of ylang ylang and coffee blossoms, but he knew just as surely that it did not spring from any of these or the trees and plants which grew on the side of the mountain.

He started down, his head turning from side to side as he sniffed rapidly like a dog sampling in his nose the flavor of the air. He lost the scent completely for a moment, but then an instant later he caught it again. He took three more paces and then he halted suddenly. He sniffed tentatively once or twice, and then he drew in a great lungful of strongly scented air through his quivering nostrils. He breathed out with a sigh of understanding and satisfaction. There could be no mistaking its origin now: it was perfume, with the bouquet of it released and made even more fragrant by the pulsing animal warmth of a woman's body.

He stood in puzzled silence, and his heavy brows began to draw together again as he thought about it. He stiffened suddenly at the idea which came into his head.

Could she have been the conscience-stricken mother of his boy, he wondered, this woman who had run off into the darkness and left the perfume of her body to linger on in the airless night? And if she was, why did she leave the envelope on the same day every year and then steal away silently without so much as showing herself?

It occurred to him then that the money might be a birthday present for the boy, but he quickly rejected the idea with a shake of his head. To him his son had been born one stormy night on the eleventh of March. Over the years fact and sentiment had become helplessly mixed in his mind, and after a while he began to believe truly that it was the real day of his birth. He found it impossible to associate the twenty-fifth of February with his son: it was simply the day the money came, and nothing else.

If she is not his mother, he asked himself, who is she?

A sudden shiver passed through his lean body, and the cold of all unknown fear made his hair stand up stiff and straight on the back of his neck. He crossed himself quickly and hurried back into the house.

In the morning there was no envelope. That night he prayed that it would come once more, and he vowed solemnly that he would never again attempt to discover the identity of their strange and unknown benefactor.

There was no envelope that year, but it came again the next year and regularly each year after that. He prayed to his God and thanked him, and then after that he did not bother to pray again.

The man felt a numbness in his hands. He sat up straight to take the weight off them. He took a deep sniffing breath, and the memory of the perfume he had breathed that night long ago was rich and fresh in his nostrils.

Yes, he thought again, it would be a good thing if it were near to the time of my son's birthday.

But it was September, so he put the wish from his mind.

He glanced down at his belly. It was lean and flat, and his brown skin had a young healthy look about it, and only when he sat forward and the skin wrinkled was it apparent that the brown skin on his belly was no longer the skin of a young man. He studied his flat stomach affectionately. His thoughts began to wander, and he felt a sudden stirring warmth in his loins.

He remembered the last time he had lain with a woman, and the warmth between his legs grew as he remembered the softness of her belly and the way it had felt pressed beneath his own. He went back further in his mind, to the woman before that, and then he went further and further and in his mind he saw the different faces and the shapes of the different women with whom he had slept. Some of them were beautiful, and some of them were ugly, and all of them floated in that area of vision which was just behind his eyes. One of them had been truly fat and ugly, and he remembered it even though he had been very drunk.

His mouth curled in sudden distaste and he shook his head abruptly and exorcised the vision of it. He stared out to sea once again.

It is a strange thing, he thought, that I have slept with so many women and never loved one of them, and that I never slept with the woman I really loved.

It had been long ago, long before the night he had found his son, and she had run away with the captain of a three-masted schooner out of Mauritius. Something in him died after that, and though he had tried many times the fire in him smoldered but never burst into flame. Thinking about it he felt a moment of pain, but it did not last long: the memory of it was too far back.

It is a good thing to sleep with a woman, he thought, but when the strength and the fire have gone from between your legs and into her body there is nothing left but a terrible emptiness. It is not the way it should be.

His eyes lost their glazed expression and became thoughtful.

I wonder, he went on in his mind, what kind of seed is it that grows a strong love like the one I had so many years ago?

He thought about it for a while, but he could find no answer, and then he thought about the love he had for his son and in a sudden bursting moment of clarity he knew that there was no such thing as *love*, and that all of it was no more and no less than the great hunger inside a man to be needed and also to give of himself. And he had given away all of what he had a long time ago.

And what of the others, he thought, all the other women you have slept with but not loved?

He had given them something, and even though it had been without any real value it had been of himself. It had been accepted though, and he in his turn had accepted the gift of their bodies. He knew then that he had loved them also, not for long, but he had loved them just the same and just as truly in those brief moments before he had given away the little he had left to give. The knowledge made him feel less sad.

The man sat up and passed a hand across his eyes. There was pain behind them, and he knew it came from the intense effort of unaccustomed thought.

You are stupid, he told himself, thinking about such impossible matters and imagining such clever answers when you cannot even walk down the hillside without falling and breaking your leg.

I wish the boy were here, he thought, because then we could talk together and I would not be tempted into thinking all these foolish thoughts.

It is still early though, and he may not have been gone long, he reminded himself. The boy had already been gone when he woke in the morning.

"Be careful and make sure you are not caught," the man said aloud, thinking his thoughts of the boy. "And come back soon because I am feeling very much alone."

The first stillness of the morning is a hard time, he thought, because the quiet of it always starts a man thinking.

I wish I had tobacco for a cigarette, he thought, and he began to wonder whether the boy would bring any.

The echo of his softly spoken words was still alive in his mind when the boy stepped round the corner of the house and came limping up to the steps where the man sat. His left leg was two inches shorter than the right, and when he walked his right hip jutted backwards and a little way out to the side and the whole of his upper body rolled from side to side with each step he took. The shirt he wore had been patched in three places, and his shorts were no better than those of the man. He stopped in front of the steps and immediately dropped the weight of his body onto his left leg. He stood hip-shot, resting his right leg, because that was the one which always became tired when he walked any distance.

In his right hand he carried a whole stalk of bananas. They were *banane gabou*, long and pale green, and most of the bunches were ripe and ready to be eaten and the others would ripen in a day or two. He held his left hand hidden behind his back and out of sight.

He stooped and laid the stalk of bananas carefully beside the steps. "Breakfast," he grunted, speaking in the patois of the Creoles.

He straightened up and faced the man, his left hand still hidden behind his back. "I have a surprise for you, Papa," he said, and his face lit up with a sudden smile. "I do not think you will be able to guess what it is."

"*Tabac,*" the man replied quickly, and he began to taste again the raw sweetness of smoke in his mouth and the hot satisfaction of it in his lungs.

"Not today," the boy said, and the smile on his face grew wider.

The eager expectancy froze on the man's face and then drained away. He tried to hide his disappointment, but he did not manage to conceal it altogether. The boy did not miss it, and he felt a sudden tightness inside his throat.

"I will borrow some for you this afternoon," he said gruffly.

It meant getting right up to one of the thatched shelters where the coarse leaves were strung to dry out of the light of the sun. The shelters were erected close to the dwellings to discourage theft, and even at night it took a lot of care and stealth to be certain of getting away with a few choice leaves without being seen and chased and caught.

"But in the meantime," the boy went on brightly, hiding his distress, "see if you can guess what I have in my hand."

The man chuckled abruptly and eased the weight on his buttocks for a moment before settling back once again. "There are so many things which you borrow so well that it would take me all of the morning to go through the things which it might be."

"Do you give up, then?" the boy asked triumphantly.

The man nodded and bowed his head in mock defeat. "Yes, I give up," he said.

With a carefully restrained flourish the boy brought the hollow *bambou calou* from concealment. It was brimming with *calou,* which is the milky blood that is tapped from the *baba* of the coconut palm. The end of the *baba* or young shoot which bears the nuts is cut off before it flowers, and then it is bound firmly to prevent it from opening. It is shaved finely every day for about a week to make the sap flow more freely, and then after that a hollow bamboo is hung from the end of it. Sometimes for as long as six months it fills each day with the lifeblood of the tree, and twice every day the men who bleed it run the edge of a knife over the open wound and scrape it to make sure that it does not heal.

The man's eyes lit up. "And from whose tree did you pluck that excellent fruit?" he asked. "Was it one of the trees of Jean Morel?"

He knew it was straightforward theft, but he felt that it was perfectly justified. When a man was hurt and unable to work, or when he toiled and came away empty-handed because his luck had run out, then it was his right to do anything to survive. He did not particularly like any of it, but there was not enough charity in the world to enable it to be otherwise. When a man had sufficient to exist, but stole from cupidity, then only was it a sin, because it was an unnecessary violation. He had spoken to his son of his thoughts when first it had become a matter of survival. But this *calou* now, there was no real need for it: the light in his eyes died.

"It is not food, my son," the man said with gentle accusation. "You did not have to take it."

The boy was astonished, and then indignant: he had expected praise and not reproach. "And what of the tobacco I steal for you?" he asked angrily. "Is that food?"

The man stared unwinkingly at the boy, but then he dropped his eyes. He had been smoking since he was ten, and he was now forty-six years of age. It was the habit of a lifetime, and it was more than his life was worth to try and break it now. He knew he could not explain such a thing to his son. He consoled himself by thinking that not all of the food which people ate was necessary, but to go without it altogether was inviting death.

"You are right," he said, and he did not look up. "It is not food."

The shame and humiliation on the face of his father shocked the boy. To him, all of it was an exciting game, and there was no question of right or wrong. The knowledge that his angry words had wounded was unbearable.

"Forgive me, Papa," he said quickly, contritely. "It is only my quick tongue, making these words which are not true."

The man looked up, and there was sadness and resignation on his lined face. "But it *is* true, mon garçon," he said gently.

The boy fidgeted and looked away from the steadiness in the man's eyes. After a few moments of discomfort he brightened suddenly.

"I will throw it away," he said in a flash of inspiration. "And then everything will be all right."

"Oh no!" the man exclaimed. "That would make the whole thing even worse."

"Why is that?" the boy asked, puzzled.

"Because that would be a senseless waste, one more mistake on top of another."

"I could try and return it to the tree," the boy offered, but without much enthusiasm.

"No — that is too great a risk to take. You may be seen, and then no matter what you say people will not believe that you were returning it. If you were seen climbing with the bamboo hanging from your mouth they would swear that you were returning to the ground with it. And if they observed you descending empty-handed after returning it, they would say that you were climbing the tree to steal it."

"What is there to be done, then?" the boy asked.

The man was thoughtful for a while. He knew already what had to be done, but he was reluctant to bring it out into the open. With a little start of guilt he found that he was licking his lips in anticipation.

"I am sure," he said, and though his face was very solemn his eyes were twinkling, "that the only sensible thing to do is to keep it and drink it."

The boy stared at him in amazement for a moment, but then his face broke into a sudden smile. He stepped right up to the man, holding out the brimming eighteen-inch-long bamboo that was almost five inches in diameter.

"Will you drink some of it now?" he asked.

"Ah no!" the man exclaimed. "When it is sweet it is for young boys and little children. I will try it tomorrow and see whether it has enough strength for an old man like me, and if it has not, then I will wait another day."

"Well, if it is for young boys when it is fresh from the tree, I will have some of it now myself."

The boy lifted the bamboo in both his hands and put his mouth to the rough rim. He tilted it up slightly and drank deeply. He lowered the bamboo and smacked his lips together, savoring the effervescent sweetness of the toddy. He had drunk a two-day-old bottle of it once, but it was bitter and sour, and the whole of the next morning he had felt a great burning discomfort inside his chest from his throat right down to the bottom of his stomach. He had never bothered to drink it again.

He walked round the man and edged past him up the

narrow steps to the gloomy little shuttered veranda. He hung the bamboo by the twisted cord of palm fiber which was fastened to it through two holes at the top, looping and knotting the tough rope over a long nail which had been in one of the wooden uprights ever since he could remember. When he had finished he gave the bamboo a last tug to make sure that it was secure and then he walked back outside.

He broke two large bunches of bananas from the stalk. He gave one of them to his father and then sat down on the bottom step, being careful not to get too close to the leg which was broken in case he knocked against it accidentally.

The boy ate hungrily, peeling his bananas, wolfing the sweet fruit and then hurling the empty skin as far as he could down the side of the hill.

The man stopped chewing for a moment and spoke through his half-filled mouth. "You did not tell me yet," he said conversationally. "But was the *bambou calou* from one of the trees belonging to Jean Morel?" He peeled another banana and took half of it off with one bite.

The boy shook his head vehemently. Jean Morel had a daughter, and for some reason which he did not understand he could not bring himself to steal from him. He had seen her more times than he could remember, especially in the late afternoons when he and his father came home from the sea and sold their catch, but he had never spoken to her, and he had always seen her from a distance.

She was white, and she was very rich: unlike his father, he was also white, but certainly he was not rich. He knew all about that too, because the man had told him the story from the beginning. Sometimes he wondered about his real parents, but it never worried him or made him sad, because the man had done the work of both and now he *was* his father.

He stared at the man, a little defiant, not knowing why he should feel embarrassed. His eyes were gray-green, and when he was angry they became quite green, sea-green like the sea was sometimes when the clouds were high in the sky and only a little of the sun reached down to touch the water.

"No it was not!" he said quickly. "The *calou* is from the property of François Albert. I took it in the dawn and hid it away up in the mountain, and I returned across the side of the hill which is why it took me so long to get back."

"You did not take long," the man said decisively. "Not for the distance you have been."

He watched the boy finish his last banana and stand up suddenly, wiping his mouth with his forearm. He remembered wishing earlier that the boy would hurry home, and he felt ashamed of his thoughtlessness: his son had traveled far to get him the *calou*.

It is a pity only that he may not do it again, he thought gravely.

Hah! he exclaimed suddenly to himself, and the realization of his own duplicity made him smile.

You are a wicked man, he thought with laughter, and you get no better as you grow older.

"Why do you smile?" the boy asked.

"It is nothing," the man said, becoming grave again. "But you must steal no more *calou* for me, otherwise I shall be forced to drink it against my wishes."

The boy laughed delightedly. "No more, Papa," he agreed. "And now I will get my gun and see what the sea has for our lunch."

There were two rooms behind the small veranda, each with its own door opening on to it. They slept in one and ate in the other when it was raining and not possible to sit outside beside the fire or on the steps, and in the room in which they ate were stored the handlines of different lengths and thicknesses and also the gaff and the club and the hooks which gave purpose to their existence.

The boy went in through the door on the right-hand side. There were two beds inside the small room, each with a handmade mattress and pillow. There were no sheets or blankets. Between the beds was a crude table of native cedar. It was not painted or varnished. There was a small oil lamp on the table, and a few rusted hooks which the man had been working on, and on the side which was against the bed in which the man slept there was a small shiny tin can which had once contained beans but now served as an ashtray. There were no butts in it, only ash and stained pieces of brown paper. They had been dog ends yesterday, but they had been torn open since and plundered of their meager fillings. The box of matches beside the tin can looked somehow foolish and superfluous.

The boy walked over to his bed. His feet were bare, and the left foot made more noise than the right as he stumped across the hollow boards. He knelt at the side of the low bed, going down on both knees. He reached out with his left hand, but his groping fingers found nothing. His heart almost stopped beating. He dropped forward quickly, hardly daring to breathe, and with his cheek almost on the floor he peered into the gloom beneath his bed.

His frantic eyes caught the glint of metal. He blew the frozen breath out of his lungs in trembling relief.

He scuttled forward, nearer towards the head of the bed, and then he reached under it again and drew out his precious speargun and his mask.

He stood up, a smile of secret pleasure lighting his face, running a calloused thumb exploratively across the point of the harpoon which was locked in position on the gun. His father had bought it for his last birthday in one of the big shops in Victoria, and the money for the gun and the mask had come from the envelope that came once every year. He had promised him a pair of flipper feet the next time it came, and thinking about it now made his heart race. Wearing them he thought he might be as swift as a fish of the sea. It was one thing to catch them on a line, but to enter into their own domain and hunt them down was far more exciting. He walked out, the gun over his left shoulder and the mask dangling from his right hand.

"Quick!" the man said, as the boy came down the steps. "Take those bananas and put them inside the house."

"What is it, Papa?" the boy asked anxiously.

He heard the urgency in the man's voice, but he could think of nothing to warrant it. He had stolen the bananas, yes, but he was quite positive that he had not been seen.

The man pointed down the hillside without saying a word.

The boy turned his head and stared in the direction of the outthrust arm. He saw the bent figure a hundred yards down the side of the mountain, toiling slowly upward. Even at that distance there was no mistaking the identity of the man. He lost sight of him for a moment, but then he came into view again from behind a clump of giant ferns. He watched his unfaltering ascent in fascination. For all his great size and bulk he moved with the effortless grace of a cat, and as he drew closer the boy could see the huge muscles in his great black legs bunching and then flattening out as his weight swung from one leg to the other.

"It is only Pierre Vigot," he said, and then softly, as an afterthought and mostly to himself: "Whore of a mother, but he is the biggest man I have seen."

"The bananas," the man reminded the boy patiently, his eyes fixed on the approaching figure.

"But why?" the boy asked. "There is nothing he can say."

"Yes, but what of the things he is sure to think? He knows that I have not been fishing, and he will also know that you have had no real luck."

The boy nodded silently. He laid his mask and speargun on the ground, putting them down with the utmost care, settling the pistol grip of the speargun on a large stone and making sure that the well-oiled trigger mechanism was clear of the dirt. He picked up the stalk of bananas, swung it clear off the ground and then skipped up the steps. He laid it down in the far right-hand corner of the veranda and covered it over with a piece of old sacking. He prodded the covering a few times with his toe to camouflage its shape and then he turned and limped outside.

He retrieved his mask and slipped his left arm through the rubber headstrap, and then he picked up the speargun and cradled it against his body. He stood beside his father, watching Pierre Vigot climb the last few yards. He had taken a dislike to him from the beginning, ever since he had been old enough to see beyond a face.

"I wonder what he wants?" the man mused softly.

"It cannot be the rent, can it?" the boy asked.

"No, he never calls for it before the last day of the month."

Seconds later the great bulk of Pierre Vigot vaulted nimbly onto the small square of flat terrace on which the house stood.

"Bonjour, Roger," he said, ignoring the boy. He tapped his chest and shook his head depreciatingly. "It is becoming a longer climb for me each time."

Pierre Vigot was not even breathing heavily. The boy saw no reason for his remark, and the smile which accompanied it struck him as being quite false. The blue in the boy's eyes began to go green, and his fingers tightened unconsciously on the stock of the speargun.

"Bonjour, Pierre," the man replied. There was no expression on his face, but his eyes were watchful.

Pierre Vigot took a step forward and then squatted on his haunches. "How is the leg coming along, Roger?" he asked.

The man flicked his finger against the plaster: the noise it made had a brittle sound. "I cannot tell," he said. "But in another two weeks I will go to the hospital in Victoria and when they have taken off this terrible bandage I will be able to see the leg and try it out and then I will know."

"Quite so, quite so," Pierre Vigot rumbled soothingly.

The echo of his words was followed by an uncomfortable silence. He scratched at the dirt with the big toe of his left foot, pretending a great absorption with what he was doing. He glanced up suddenly, his eyes coming to rest on the boy.

"And how are you, Paul?"

"I am well," the boy replied, and his voice was without warmth or enthusiasm.

There was another uncomfortable silence. Pierre Vigot again scratched at the dirt with his big toe. When he looked up he spoke to the man once more.

"There is no pain in the leg now, Roger?" he inquired solicitously.

The man became suddenly irritated. He leaned forward, fighting his rising anger. It was one thing to be patronized by a greater fisherman, but Pierre Vigot had never been a better fisherman and now he never would be.

"Come, Pierre," he said dryly. "You yourself have said that it is a long climb. You did not come all this way to ask me about my leg and the pain in it."

Pierre Vigot stood up. He did it slowly, and there was menace in the way his whole body seemed to uncoil from the ground and come erect. His eyes narrowed, and there was a dangerous glint in the deep fluid blackness of their depths.

"We do not talk, eh?" he said softly.

"We do not talk about nothing," the man affirmed.

"Well then we will talk about something," Pierre Vigot said. He smiled with malicious pleasure. "It is a little matter of the rent."

"It is not due for another ten days," the man said quietly.

"That is so," Pierre Vigot admitted hesitantly.

He was a good actor. His face registered dismay and surprise, and then just when the other was beginning to relax he held up his hand abruptly. The smile on his face was one of cruel triumph.

"That is so," he smirked again. "But I am talking

about the rent for the *last* two months, of which you have paid nothing as yet."

"But you told me the last time that M'sieur Morel had agreed that I should pay it when I could."

"That is correct, but he has changed his mind since then." Pierre Vigot laughed, and the sound of it boomed from his chest. "M'sieur Morel," he said with grand formality, "has asked me to tell you that unless you pay him half of all the money which will be due him at the end of this month, he will be forced to have you removed, and he will find a tenant who is able to pay promptly."

"But it is sixty rupees!" the man said aghast. "Where can I find half of such a sum when I am not able to work?"

Pierre Vigot ignored the outburst. "M'sieur Morel further added that though it grieved him, he was not prepared to permit lazy fishermen to take advantage of his good heart."

The man was shocked. In his time he had been called many names by many men and many women, but no one had ever called him lazy. His face flushed with anger, and red blood darkened his brown cheeks. He started to rise, his eyes sparking, and he thought to himself that it was a long time since he had been in a good fight. His unwieldy leg reminded him instantly that he was not in a position even to stand up properly, let alone fight. He sank back, and the red mist in front of his eyes began to clear.

"I am not lazy," he asserted calmly.

"Then why have you not been able to pay your rent?"

"Am I to go fishing with a leg which I cannot even bend?" the man asked sarcastically.

"And what of the rent you did not pay in the month

before you broke your leg?" Pierre Vigot shouted angrily.

"In the *vent du sud-est?*" the man asked scornfully. "Even you who used to be a stupid fisherman know that the fish do not bite and that most of the time there is too much wind to take a small pirogue far out to sea where the tunny and bonito swim."

"So I used to be a stupid fisherman!"

"Yes, you were a stupid fisherman," the man said flatly. "And I think you are also lying."

Pierre Vigot almost danced with rage and astonishment. "Do you think I would come all the way up this miserable hillside if I did not have to do it?"

"It is true perhaps that M'sieur Morel wants his money," the man pointed out evenly. "Because that is understandable. But you are certainly lying when you say that he called me a lazy fisherman who wished to take advantage of his patience and kindness."

Pierre Vigot stiffened. "Are you really calling me a liar, Roger?" he asked quietly.

The seated man returned his stare insolently. He braced himself, getting ready to use his hands and his one good leg.

"You were always a fat pig of a man when you were a fisherman," he said. "But since you gave it up to become an errand boy for Jean Morel you have become much fatter, and what is more, you have also become a liar."

Pierre Vigot gasped. His eyes glared wildly, and then a second later he roared like a strangling bull. He shot one contemptuously estimative glance at the boy and then started for the man.

The boy snapped the heel of the pistol grip on the speargun hard in against his stomach. He braced the muscles of his belly and then hauled back on one pair of the thick circular rubbers which drove the harpoon. He jammed the wire tongue into the last of the three notches which were spaced along the top of the harpoon shaft and then swung the gun up and hooked the index finger of his right hand over the trigger.

"Wait!" he cried fiercely.

Pierre Vigot came to a sudden halt, not really knowing why he did. There was something about the shrilled command, about the tone of it, which did not make sense. He turned and stared at the boy. He saw the fury in his green eyes, and in that instant he realized why he had been puzzled. It was not what he had heard, but what he had been expecting and had not heard: there had been no fear in the boy's voice.

His glance dropped to the gun in the boy's hands. He took in the harpoon which was pointing straight at him and the tautly stretched rubbers which were still vibrating slightly. The blood left his face and the healthy black color of it changed to a brownish-gray.

"Mon Dieu, Paul," he breathed. "You — "

He tried to go on, but his throat shut tight and his tongue was so dry it seemed to be filling his whole mouth. He wrenched his gaze from the terrible fascination of the quivering rubbers and the barbed harpoon which had the barbs ringed flush with the head and waiting to spring open the moment it penetrated. He looked up at the boy's face, and what he saw made him even more afraid: there was an expression of indecent eagerness on it.

"Paul — " he whispered.

The boy lifted the gun a little. "You had better go," he said.

Pierre Vigot nodded shakily. He backed off warily, and when he reached the edge of the terrace he spun round quickly and jumped down onto the sloping hillside. He ran a little way, and when he thought he was out of the speargun's range he paused and looked back across his shoulder.

"You will be sorry for this," he called softly, and then his voice rose in sudden fury. "Both of you!" he screamed. He turned away, and then he did a strange thing. He crossed himself furtively and superstitiously as he went on down the hill.

Child of the devil, he thought fearfully, with his one leg shorter than the other.

"And you remember!" the boy shouted back at him. "There are still ten days to the end of the month!"

He waited for Pierre Vigot to go on down the hill, and then he turned towards the man. There was a look of shock on his face. He could still hear the words he had spoken ringing in his ears, and they were full of a rage and hate he had not known was in him. He unloaded the speargun numbly, doing it mechanically and without thought.

"My God, Papa!" the boy exclaimed softly. "He would have killed you!"

"Perhaps," the man replied calmly. "But even with my leg as it is I would have hurt him very badly."

"Are you mad, Papa?" the boy asked incredulously, angrily, and suddenly he felt his legs begin to shake with reaction. "He makes three men of your size."

"There are certain ways to almost kill a man with one single blow," the man explained to the boy. "I learned them as a young man long ago when I sailed for a while on the Arab dhows out of Mombasa, and I have never forgotten it."

Yes, he thought, I have never forgotten it, as I will never forget the sharp agony of a blow dealt to the throat by the edge of a man's hand, or the veiled women of Arabia with only their eyes showing above their veils, and all the terrible wet heat till we got down to Karachi and Bombay and Cochin where the women did not wear veils but smiled their brown smiles with the rice on their foreheads and the glitter of rubies set in their pierced nostrils. It was a long time ago, he remembered, and through all of it he could not forget her.

He came out of his reverie to see the boy shaking his head in disbelief. "It *is* so," he said. "Even if you do not believe it now, it is so."

"Will you show me when your leg is well?" the boy challenged.

"I will do it," the man said.

The skin under the plaster on his thigh began to itch maddeningly. He dug his fingers in under the cast and scratched furiously, and when he drew them out again there was dead skin embedded beneath his broken fingernails. He worked it out with the thumbnail of his right hand and then he brushed his hands off against his patched shorts. He looked up suddenly at the boy.

"It is a terrible thing, this, Paul," he said quietly. "I have lived in this house many years, and it is also the house in which you were born to me. I have many memories of it."

The boy stared silently at the man. He saw the sadness on his face, and far back in his eyes he saw the glitter of something which he had seen once in the eyes of a large tomcat. Its back had been up against a wall, and three snapping mongrels had been closing in on it. He watched the man, feeling a strange pain in his chest, and he could think of nothing to say.

"I think Pierre must have talked M'sieur Morel into doing this thing," the man said suddenly.

"But why?" the boy cried. "You have not had words with him, not until today."

The man rubbed thoughtfully at his gray stubbled chin. "That is true, but I have never liked him and he has known it." He compressed his lips suddenly and then went on in a grave voice. "I think perhaps he envies me, because I am still a fisherman with my own pirogue."

"Ahhh!" the boy breathed.

Even now this was something he could understand. When once a man had known the sea and fished it he was bound to it forever. When a man was no longer a part of it, through circumstance or even choice, there was always regret, and more often than not, envy of those who still belonged.

"Perhaps M'sieur Morel would change his mind if you explained our position to him," the boy said. He spoke without conviction, because he had seen M'sieur Morel, and he did not think he was a man who would change his mind when once he had made it up.

"No!" the man exclaimed, and he was suddenly proud and fierce. "I explained it to him the first time, and now it would be begging. I have never done it, and I will not do it now."

"Well — " the boy said uncomfortably.

"I wish that M'sieur Duvalier were still the *propriétaire*," the man said wistfully. "And I wish that he had sold his property to anyone but Jean Morel."

"Well," the boy said again, "I think it is time for me to go and shoot some fish."

"You will not take any line?" the man asked.

The boy pointed out to sea, waving his hand at the broken water with a gesture of futility. "It would be a waste of my time, I think," he said.

The man was thoughtful for a while, and then he nodded. "Take care though," he warned. "And do not go out beyond the reefs."

Like most fishermen he did not know how to swim. He cursed the sea, and sometimes he came very close to hating it, but it was only the hate that comes from the sorrow and despair of watching a loved one misbehave. He loved the sea for many things, for its fierceness and its gentleness, and for the fishes which it gave him, but the thought of entering the water itself was quite abhorrent to him. He gazed at his son with a pride that was tempered with awe.

"We have no more credit at the store, do we?" he asked suddenly.

He knew very well that they could no longer get credit at the store, but he felt, as before, that it was a necessary preliminary.

"Not any more," the boy answered. "Not even with that old thief of a bearded Chinaman."

"Then perhaps you could try the other store for some tobacco," the man said gravely.

There was no other store. The boy opened his mouth to protest, but then he became aware of the strange alertness in the man's eyes. He understood, and he felt a sudden sorrow and pity for his father.

"I will," he said, keeping up the pretense. "Perhaps they might oblige me."

He turned away and started down the hill, and he was thinking that he had learned many things about the man since he had broken his leg which he had not known of before.

"There is one thing, Paul," the man called, and then when the boy paused he went on again: "I think I must thank you for my life. If Pierre Vigot had not taken it, he would have hurt me badly, perhaps so badly that I might never have fished again."

There, it was out, for all his earlier show of foolish bravery and defiance.

"It was nothing," the boy said gruffly, trying to hide his embarrassment. "You did more than that for me when you gave the life in my body your name."

He stared blindly past the man. He saw the small house perched on a ledge of the hillside, and beyond it he saw the green of the mountain going on for as far as he could see till he could see no more through the trees which grew thick and green against its side. He turned away silently and started down the hill again.

And a purpose to my life, he thought, because already I am a good fisherman.

"Perhaps you will be lucky and spear a big fish," the man called after him. "One so big that we can sell its meat for more than sixty rupees."

He did not believe it, because even on a strong line it took a long time and much sweat to boat a fish that would sell for that much money. He knew it was really impossible, but he thought about it for a long time, even after the boy was no longer in sight.

Such a boy, he thought, and then he pushed himself up off the steps, his left leg stretched out stiffly at an awkward angle as he rose. He stood for a moment, looking down the hill, and then he turned and stumped across the veranda and into the room which he shared with the boy. He saw the ends of his crutches sticking out from under the foot of his bed, and he felt glad that he had learned to walk without them. He walked over to the table, and even though he knew the tin ashtray was empty he could not help himself from peering into it with a little flutter of hope.

The boy limped along the winding, well-trampled path which snaked round huge boulders and tall trees and all the way down the side of the hill. In some places it was very steep and slippery from the rain, and he turned side-on, so that the right side of his body with the longer leg was forward and then he slithered and slid taking short quick steps till he could walk normally once again.

As he worked his way down the side of the mountain he was thinking of the things which had just happened, and he remembered what he had said to his Papa when the man had spoken that foolish nonsense about saving his life.

It was nothing, he told himself, because you have given me more than my own mother and father gave me.

For a brief instant he hated them, that unknown man and woman, but then he pulled himself together. The emotion in him was fierce, and the strength of it made him tremble.

I am Roger Paul Mistral, he thought defiantly, and there was anger and pride and happiness all mixed up in his thoughts.

"Roger Paul Mistral!" he whispered aloud, sounding the names experimentally.

When he realized what he had done he glanced round with a nervous start of guilt. But he was quite alone and, sure of his privacy, his embarrassment vanished. He tried it out again.

"Roger Paul Mistral!" he said, his voice ringing loud and confident on the lonely side of the hill.

He walked on, drawing great comfort from the sound of his full name, and then suddenly he wondered what it would be like to be able to say *Maman*. He had never

34

used the word though, and because the man had been his mother as well, the thought was not with him for long.

Passing a cinnamon bush he tore off a green sprig and began chewing on it. The smooth bark was still wet with the rain of the night. He came to the bottom of the hill, running the last few yards. He walked on, and a little farther he crossed the sandy road and continued across the flat land which sloped gently down to the sea on the other side.

Through the thickly clustered coconut palms he caught glimpses of the big house of Jean Morel. It was about a hundred yards to his left, on a high grassy clearing which overlooked the beach.

He wondered whether he would see the girl. He had seen her yesterday, for the first time in a long while, but that did not mean that he would see her today. He remembered then that it was the time of the school holidays, and his heart began to beat a little faster. He wondered whether she would be sitting on the seawall where he had seen her yesterday, or whether she would be inside the house and out of sight.

His father's pirogue was anchored where he had left it yesterday, in the shallow tidal waters fifty yards beyond the highwater mark. If he had walked on in the direction he was taking he would have come out on the beach right opposite it. Without consciously changing his direction he started angling off to his left. When he realized where he was going a few seconds later he halted suddenly. He thought about it for a while, and then he straightened his shoulders abruptly with a shrug of defiance.

He walked on a little bit farther, and then through the trees he saw the high land of the open clearing and the seawall which had been built up ten feet tall from the beach and three feet above the level of the land. The girl was sitting on it.

He halted, undecided and unsure of himself now that he had actually seen her. The nervous tempo of his pounding heart increased. He studied her for a moment longer, and then he made up his mind abruptly. He turned and ran straight down towards the beach, dodging in and out among the coconut palms, fearful now that she might decide suddenly to move.

He broke through the grove of coco palms fifty yards to the right of where she sat. He vaulted the low seawall without breaking his stride, landing on the soft damp sand on the other side. He stood breathlessly still for a moment, watching her and hoping that she had not noticed him. His toes curled unconsciously and dug into the moist sand.

He started forward and then halted again, and for one petrifying moment he was so nervous and appalled by what he was contemplating that he almost turned back. He had never spoken to a girl before, not at any rate with his mind full of the vague and unformed longing that was now making his head spin. He took a deep breath, and holding it for a while steadied him. He glanced down at the speargun in his hand, and the sight of the beautifully pointed harpoon sent a surge of confidence through him. He tossed his head, feeling angry and full of contempt for his cowardice.

He limped forward again, forcing himself to breathe more slowly, but before he had covered half the distance to her his breath was once again coming in short little gasps. He hugged the seawall, and twice he splashed through little pools of water which the tide had left behind in shallow depressions against the wall.

He was fifteen yards from her when she turned abruptly and caught sight of him. She started suddenly, but then she masked her surprise with a practiced ease. She stared down at him coolly for a moment, and then with a haughty toss of her head which flung her long golden hair across the side of her face, she turned away from him and stared out to sea once again.

The boy faltered and almost came to a halt. He began to wish that he had never come. He clutched his spear-gun more tightly and with a great effort of will forced his legs to keep moving.

It was foolish of you to think she would take notice of you, he told himself, and for the first time in his life he became conscious of the bright patches on his faded shorts. He halted directly below her.

For a while the girl ignored him completely, as if she were quite unaware of his presence, staring seaward with a feigned preoccupation. She too had seen him before from a distance, and she knew who he was and all about him. In her mind she thought of him as "Limp-leg." The fact that he was illegitimate meant nothing, not here on the islands.

When she believed that she had kept him waiting for the correct length of time she lowered her gaze with a studied air of cool detachment. She found herself look-ing squarely into his exquisitely shaded eyes, and some-thing about them made her heart lurch. She took in the deep golden-brown color of his skin, and she saw the way his shoulders tapered down into the narrow flatness of his waist and stomach.

But he's beautiful, she thought incredulously, except for that limpy leg of his.

Startled at the audacity of her thoughts she shut her mind to him hastily. Desperately she sought an avenue of escape. She became aware of his patched shorts and retreated thankfully. Her lip curled in delicate distaste: it was a really perfect imitation of the sophistication she had come to know from the films which were publicly screened once a month in the hall of the convent where she went to school. She was almost thirteen and a half years old.

"Yes?" she inquired, and she was immensely gratified to hear the little touch of polite disdain she had injected into her voice coming out so perfectly.

The boy gazed at her and fidgeted. He was shy and nervous, and he completely missed the contempt in her voice. He *had* expected her to be pretty, because long ago he had made up his mind about that, but he had never dreamed that any girl could be as lovely as she was. He stared at her face entranced, and from where he stood he could not help but notice the thrust of her small breasts which tightened up the front of her dress. He dropped his eyes in confusion and looked down at his feet, and as he did so he caught a fleeting glimpse of the curved softness of her touching thighs. He wanted to look again, tantalized by what he had already seen, but he thought that if he looked again she would know what he was doing and become angry. He began to wonder about the mysteriously thrilling secrets he would discover if he did look. He lifted his head suddenly, resolutely keeping his eyes on her face and refusing to let them stray.

He stared at her dumbly, unable to think of anything to say. It was terrible. For a moment he was tempted to turn and run back the way he had come. He fought the desire with a stubborn obstinacy. He had made up his mind that he was going to speak to her, and nothing was going to move him until he had done it. His face began to redden with the shame and anger of his own inadequacy.

The fingers of his left hand began to ache. He glanced down at them in puzzled surprise, and he saw that he was clutching the speargun so tightly that his knuckles looked like four bleached seashells lying in a line across his brown skin. He had forgotten about the gun, but becoming consciously aware of it gave him a sudden idea. He swung the speargun up and gestured with it, and he was glad then that he always kept the metal bright and clean and the harpoon point glisteningly sharp. It was the most expensive thing about him.

"I — I thought," he blurted out, "that I would ask if you would like to come fishing with me."

He held his breath as he watched her, but then he breathed out shakily. He felt suddenly old and tired. He wanted to turn and walk away quickly, but he waited on, fascinated and stricken by the look which was coming to life on her face.

The girl leaned forward eagerly. "I would — " She checked herself abruptly, but she could not stop the words from going through her mind.

I would love to go fishing with you, she thought, looking into his strange-colored eyes, but she did not say any of it.

She tossed her head insolently, and her long hair flew across her face again. She timed and executed the gesture so skillfully that it appeared to emphasize her momentary pause.

"I would," she repeated haughtily, "never think of going fishing with *you*." She spoke in pure and uncorrupted French.

The boy had to concentrate hard to understand her. He blushed painfully, but still he was unable to tear himself away. He stood his ground stubbornly, wondering at his own obstinacy.

"But why?" he asked. "I have a good speargun, and I will let you use it first."

He felt a momentary shock when he realized what he had said, and he began to wish he had not spoken. In his mind he could see her firing it and missing and blunting the beautiful point of the harpoon on some great boulder of coral. And then pursuing the nightmare to the deeper water on the edge of the reef he saw her dropping his precious speargun and then he saw its wavering descent as it sank and vanished into the ever-darkening blue which sloped down the great hill on the seaward side of the reef.

"I have a better one," the girl replied scornfully. "It is worked with air and not with those silly rubbers which you have to keep stretching all the time."

"Even so," the boy said doggedly, "I think I could still shoot more fish than you with my gun."

The girl swung her legs off the wall and stood up. She glared down at him angrily. "You could not!"

The boy felt strangely calm and confident now. He understood the meaning of her anger, and it brought a smile to his face.

"Bring your own gun," he said easily. "And we will see who can shoot more fish."

"I will do no such thing!" the girl snapped indignantly.

She cast around in her mind for a plausible excuse to evade the challenge and crush the gentle mockery in his eyes. She was becoming desperate when his patched shorts drew her attention once again.

"You have no proper bathing suit," she said tauntingly. "Do you expect me to swim in the water with you when you are dressed like a poor little black boy?"

"Why not?" the boy answered calmly. "We are going to spear fish, and the fishes will not concern themselves with what we are wearing."

He smiled slowly and ironically, because he knew her sneering remarks were only a means of evading his challenge, but he smiled also to hide his own pain and humiliation.

"When you can get a proper bathing suit to wear," the girl said sarcastically, "I might change my mind and go with you and teach you how to shoot fish."

"I think you speak as you do only because you are frightened of being beaten in such a contest," the boy said, and he felt his face begin to hurt with the smile that he was keeping on it.

"It is not true!" she cried desperately, angrily.

For one incredulous moment she stared at him. His eyes were level and steady, and there was a green tint in them which she had not seen before. She wondered if he could read her thoughts. She began to feel naked and quite exposed. Her mind fluttered like a dazed butterfly for a few seconds, but then anger and resentment came to her rescue.

"I will never go fishing with you!" she shouted.

She turned on her heel and flounced away. She took three steps and halted. She glanced hesitantly and warily over her shoulder, and then she jerked her head to the front as if she had been stung. He had been standing quite still, watching her, his body leaning a little to one side. His face was without expression, but his eyes were alive with pain and bewilderment. For some reason it made her furious.

"*Jambeclopante! Jambeclopante! Jambeclopante!*"

she screamed, and she started running across the lawn towards the front of the big house, the anger and cruel laughter blending together in a sound that was sickening to hear.

She had almost reached the glass-enclosed veranda when her mother pushed the door open and came down the steps onto the lawn. She moved with an easy grace. She was still a beautiful woman, and only on closer inspection could it be seen that her beauty was also the product of sorrow and resignation which had touched her gentle face.

"Who were you calling to, Danielle?" she asked.

The girl turned, and from where she stood she could just see the bobbing head and shoulders of the boy. As he walked farther out to sea more and more of him gradually became visible, and then finally she saw all of him and the little splashes of his feet as he waded through the water and out towards where the rocking pirogue lay anchored. She pointed silently.

The woman nodded, as if in confirmation of something she had really known all the time but was unwilling to admit. She brushed a hand across her forehead, pushing at a tendril of windblown hair which kept falling across her face.

"And did I hear you call him Limpleg?" she inquired softly.

"Yes," the girl said defiantly. "I called him *jambe-clopante*."

The vehemence in her voice startled and surprised the woman. She studied her daughter, an expression of troubled curiosity on her face. She brushed again at the wisp of pale hair which kept falling across her face.

"That was not a nice thing to say, my child," she rebuked the girl gently.

42

"But he is a limpleg!" the girl cried.

The woman's eyes flashed angrily for a moment, but then once again they became gray and mild. "Yes, my daughter, and it is a great enough burden to have, without you reminding him about it. I think you should apologize to him when he comes back from the sea."

"No!" The girl tossed her head and stared defiantly at her mother, but then her anger melted at the reproach and sadness which brimmed suddenly in the woman's eyes.

"He said he could shoot more fish than me," she burst out. "And then when I said he could not he challenged me to go with him and see who could spear the most fishes."

A look of alarm crossed the woman's face. She took in the swelling roundness of her daughter's hips and the impatient thrusting of her young breasts. It shocked her a little to realize that her daughter was maturing so fast. It seemed only yesterday that she had been a little girl, and there had been no evidence then to indicate the startling changes which time would bring about in her awkward body. She shrugged mentally, and her face regained its tranquillity. The girl was growing up, and there was nothing that could be done about it.

On the contrary, she told herself. Since it is here now, it is a thing to be encouraged, and the force of it must be channeled in the right direction.

"Why did you not accept his challenge?" the woman asked, regarding her daughter with sly amusement.

"But Maman!" the girl protested. "He didn't even have on a proper bathing suit." She sniffed, and the little snuffle sounded very superior. "Only a pair of patched shorts."

"Did you tell him that?" the woman asked.

"Yes, and I told him I would not go fishing with him unless he wore a proper suit, and he said that it was only an excuse because I was afraid to accept his challenge, and that the *fishes* would not care about what he was wearing."

The woman laughed at her daughter's indignation: it was a bright tinkle of sound, and it rang clear and true like the chime of a bell.

"I'm sure I would agree with him about the fish," she said, and then abruptly she shed her bantering lightness and her face became grave. "But tell me, Danielle," she went on quietly, "do you think it is right to call his attention to his poorness and to use it as an excuse because you *are* afraid to accept his challenge? He might be poor, but from what I know of him he is a good boy, and he is a good fisherman like his father, and it is not his fault that he is poor. It is a hard life he leads, but he does not flinch from it, and this is a thing of more consequence than the clothes he wears on his body."

"Perhaps it is," the girl retorted. "But I do not care."

"Or is it that you care too much?" the woman asked slyly.

The girl started, and then she blushed with embarrassment. The woman laughed softly and triumphantly, and there was gentle amusement in her eyes. Seeing it, the girl stamped her foot furiously. The force of the impact made her small breasts jump.

"I hate him!" she shouted. "I hate him!"

"Perhaps if you went fishing with him you would begin to change your mind."

"I will never go fishing with him!" the girl cried, and there were tears of temper and humiliation in her eyes as she turned and ran into the house.

The woman smiled tolerantly after her daughter.

After a while she turned and looked out to sea. The boy was already poling the pirogue through the shallows, and as she watched him the sun burst suddenly from behind the clouds and the drops of water which fell from the long bamboo sprayed from the end of the pole like a glittering necklace of seashells.

She turned away, and as she started for the house her forehead wrinkled in a frown of worry and her light gray eyes seemed to darken with a brooding sadness.

F OR a long time after the girl had run off the boy stood and stared silently after her. He stood without moving, and nothing inside his mind moved either. His shoulders sagged suddenly. He breathed out harshly, and that was when he felt the terrible agony of a nameless pain come alive inside him. It hurt and cut like a knife, and it was so vast and overpowering that he felt as if he were suffocating. He turned slowly and started trudging down the beach and out towards the sea.

Jambeclopante, he thought chokingly, and the word echoed and reechoed inside his head with a frightening, rhythmic regularity.

Limpleg . . . limpleg . . . limpleg.

His fingers tightened round the stock of the speargun. He squeezed with a sudden fierce release of strength, and he went on squeezing till the pressure of his effort was so great that his whole arm began to shake. He stopped it then and straightened up, and he tried to walk without limping, coming down on the toes of his left foot instead of placing the foot flat on the ground. But the sand was too soft, and his toes sank into it, and the unaccustomed method of walking put him right off balance. He gave it up, walking on with his rolling limp, and then in a sudden burst of angry retaliation he began to limp even more heavily, exaggerating it till it became a comical travesty of his afflicted walk.

He glanced back across his shoulder, but she was out of sight on the high ground beyond the wall, and all he could see were the glass windows on the second story of the big house. He resumed his normal walk, feeling better somehow for his spiteful little pretense at indifference. It did not worry him that she had not seen it: he was definitely feeling better, even though the pain had not gone away altogether.

He walked on, and into his mind there came the memory of the first time he had worn his mask and gone into the sea. He had been under the water hundreds of times before, but everything had been dull and blurred and he had not been able to see clearly. And then there came the day when he put the mask on and slid beneath the surface of the sparkling sea, not really knowing what to expect, a tremulous and almost fearful anticipation bubbling up inside his throat. The crystal beauty of what he saw astonished him: he had never dreamed that it existed.

Thinking about that first time took his breath away, and even now, which was months later, he had not got over the startling difference, and sometimes, to intensify his pleasure, he first opened his eyes underwater without the mask, and then immediately afterwards, nonchalantly pretending to himself that he did not know what was in store for him, he would tug on the mask and float himself off into the water with his head held high and then jackknife suddenly, clawing his way under and deep down with one powerful sweep of his arms. It was like being born again every time he did it, and there were some days when he wondered whether the world in which *he* lived had seemed to him as beautiful when he saw it for the first time. He did not think so, even though he had no recollection of the first time, because certainly there was nothing special to it now, and he knew it could not have changed all that much since the day he had been born.

He moved diagonally across the beach, heading straight for where the pirogue lay in the shallow water thirty yards inside the deep channel which ran between the mainland and Île aux Cerf. The island was small and rocky, rising steeply from the sea, the beaches strewn with boulders. To the right of it the water broke in a foaming white line across the coral reef which had grown to within a few feet of the surface of the sea. On the other side there was no indication of the reef. He knew it was there though, and as he limped along he pictured it in his mind. The top of it was forty feet down in some places, and it sloped steeply on the seaward side and fell away abruptly and ran down, vanishing into the dark blueness of the sea.

He splashed through the tepid water of a tidal pool. Before he had gone far his quick eyes caught the flash of silver in the water. He froze instantly, and when the ripples had subsided he made out the shape of the small fish which lay unmoving at the far end of the shallow pool, its silver belly flat against the sand. He took a step forward, and then another, moving his feet through the

47

water slowly so as to cause as little disturbance as possible. He pressed the trigger on the speargun, unlocking the harpoon. He began to slide it out, keeping his eyes on the motionless fish. When he had run it all the way out through the guides he slipped the mask off his right arm and took hold of it with his left hand. He gripped the harpoon in his right hand and lowered the point slowly towards the water. It was still attached to the muzzle of the gun by the nylon line which was secured to the sliding ring on the shaft.

He tensed himself for the thrust, and in that instant before he plunged the sharp point of steel into the water the little fish darted forward and flashed past his legs.

He felt quite foolish, but then after that he began to feel cheated. He turned round, searching for the fish in the sand-speckled water. He spotted it after a moment, at the edge of the pool, its belly flat against the white coral sand.

The boy slid his left leg forward, moving it cautiously through the water. When it had traveled fifteen inches he set his foot down gently, careful not to disturb the sand. He was about to take another step when he froze. He stood motionless for a moment, a peculiar expression spreading over his face, and then suddenly he threw back his head and laughed. He kicked his foot through the water, still laughing, and he lost sight of the little fish in the splashing turbulence.

He lifted the harpoon with an abrupt gesture of dismissal and ran it through the guides on the speargun. He turned and splashed through the pool and out onto the rippled sand. He walked on, chuckling softly to himself, thinking about the fish in the pool of water he had left behind him.

It was a little fish, and even though the pool was no

more than six feet in diameter he knew it might have taken him half an hour or more before he finally managed to spear it. He remembered doing it many times in the past, using a pointed stick. But that had been years ago, and it had been the game of a child. He waded into the sea, dismissing the fish from his mind: there were other more important and valuable fishes waiting for him in the deep water of the channel.

The sand settled in the pool on the beach. The little fish finned its way lazily through the water, pausing now and again to gobble up a mouthful of sand which it spat out a second later. It browsed contentedly, the fear of a few moments before already forgotten.

The boy waded steadily through the water. It was knee deep when he reached the pirogue. He laid the speargun and the mask on the planking of the boat, and then he pushed it forward till the bow was almost over the large stone which served as anchor. He steadied the pirogue, and then he bent quickly and reached down into the water with both hands. He got a good grip on the stone, and then with a sudden heave he lifted it up clear and dripping wet with water and over the bow and into the boat. He jumped nimbly into the pirogue, and while it still rocked alarmingly he coiled the short fifteen-foot anchor rope.

He stepped aft and picked up the long bamboo pole which lay beside the oars and was as long as the pirogue itself. He swung it up, holding it with both hands at the thin end about four feet from the top and with his hands about eighteen inches apart. He dug the other end of the pole into the water, and then when he felt the end of it bury in the sand he bent a little at the waist and threw all of his weight down on the pole. As the boat began to move forward he slid his hands up the bamboo and bore down again till the boat had moved forward the whole length of the pole. He jerked the bamboo free of the clinging sand and then swung his body around and plunged the pole into the water on the opposite side.

He worked mechanically, without having to think of what he was doing, and though it was a difficult art to master it seemed quite easy the way he did it. The boat gathered speed as he drove it out to sea.

I wish the sun would come out, the boy thought suddenly.

He looked up, sweeping his gaze across the clouded skies, searching for the brightness behind the clouds which would tell him just where the sun was hidden. He found it after a moment, and beside it he saw a narrow slash of blue which widened in the sky even as he watched.

"Come on, sun," he murmured aloud.

He stared anxiously at the rift in the clouds, never once breaking the smooth rhythm of the driving pole. He liked it when the sun was shining, especially when he went into the water. It did not really matter at other times, but when he dived wearing the mask he liked the sun to be shining because then all the beautiful things under the sea came alive and shone their bright colors back at the sun.

"Come on, sun," he said again.

He began to think of the little fish he had left behind in the pool. He knew it would die before the tide came back, because all the water would have soaked away into the sand by then. He was wondering how long it would take for the water to seep away when the clouds peeled back from the edge of the sun and allowed the first shafts of light to come bursting through. He felt an immediate spurt of happiness, but then he thought of the little fish again and he felt very sad. It would have even less time to live now, with the sun also sucking on the water.

He began to wonder if it would stay out for a long time. He thought of the bigger pools which the tide-water left behind in the sand which it hollowed out. He remembered how warm the water in them became, and how it was good to come and lie in the water and feel the warmth of it soaking into the flesh after the cold of the deep reef water. He forgot all about the little fish, and he hoped the sun would stay out and warm the bigger pools for when he came back cold from the sea.

Before he reached the channel the water became too deep to continue using the pole. He shipped the bamboo and sat down on the stern thwart, facing the mainland he had just left. In actual fact it was the island of Mahé, approximately seventeen miles long and with a width of seven miles at its widest point. But to the boy it was the mainland, partly because he lived there, but also because it was the largest island of the Seychelles group. It was not something he had learned at school: his father had told him that it was so.

He reached behind him and picked up the two thole pins lying on the planking. They had been whittled from wood, and they were five inches long and three-quarters of an inch thick, and tied to each one was a small loop of plaited palm fiber. The boy pushed the wooden pins into the holes in the gunwale. He hammered them home with the heel of his right hand and then lifted out the oars. He fitted the handle of each oar through the plaited loops on the thole pins and then he braced his bare feet against the sides of the pirogue. He bent forward a little, dropping his wrists, and then as the oars dipped splashing into the water he lifted his wrists and pulled back hard. The muscles on his arms and on his back leaped and stood out for a moment before sinking back into the flesh from which they had sprung.

The boy looked up at the sky, and a smile creased his face. There was a great blue patch up there now, and the sun was right in the center of it. The color of the sea was changing also, beginning to turn blue, but it was not uniform in shading. Where the white coral sand reflected the sun from under the water the sea was shaded a light turquoise-green, and where there was only weed and dark unbroken coral the water was colored like the night sky when there was blue and purple mixed in with the growing darkness.

The boy rowed on into the channel till he was close to a patch of sea that was a deep dark blue. He backed water and brought the pirogue to a halt. He freed the oars and laid them down across the thwarts against the side of the boat, and then he crawled forward into the bow. He undid the anchor rope from the wooden cleat bolted to the inside of the stem. He gave it another five fathoms from the coil and then retied the lengthened rope to the cleat, securing it with two half hitches.

He stood up in the bow and tossed the anchor overboard. The heavy stone sank quickly, wobbling a little as it went down. It struck bottom at four fathoms, and the bubbles were still coming up as the pirogue began to swing broadside on in the gentle current. It went astern a few feet and then steadied on the rope.

The boy tested the half-hitches he had put round the cleat. He sat down and picked up his mask, and then leaning over the side of the pirogue he trailed it through the water, holding it by the strap, dragging it backwards and forwards till he was satisfied that the glass and the rubber of the mask had been made properly wet. He lifted it from the water and inspected it.

In the beginning he had taken great care to keep the inside of the mask dry. It always leaked, and the glass always steamed up, and then one day he dropped it in the sea accidentally and got it wet inside. He shook the water off and wore it as it was, and he never had trouble with it again.

He wondered suddenly whether the girl knew about this little trick of first wetting a mask thoroughly before wearing it. He did not think she would know about a thing like that. Thinking about it he felt a smug complacence, but then abruptly he remembered what she had called him. It took all of his satisfaction away.

He jerked the strap of the mask over his head and fitted it into place. He snatched up the speargun and got to his feet. Sixty yards to his left and a little farther out he saw another pirogue. It was heading for the open sea, its patched sail almost bursting with its load of wind and its sharp black bows knifing jerkily through the steep little waves. The boy lifted the speargun high and waved it slowly in greeting. A second later a black arm lifted momentarily in acknowledgment of the salute.

The boy watched the pirogue driving out to sea and he began to shake his head. It was not the weather in which to take a small boat to the far banks, when the monsoon winds were in the air, not even if a man had to fish for his living. Doubt and anxiety made his forehead wrinkle, but the lines did not stay there for long. If anyone could sail a pirogue, old man Rousseau could. What was more, he seemed to know where the fish hid themselves, even in the time of the *vent du sud-est,* and it was his boast that he always fished something from the

53

sea, even if it was only a single mackerel. Not every fisherman could say the same thing. The boy laughed suddenly, happily, and he felt a burst of pride in the other's courage. He too was a fisherman.

He turned and stared at the mainland. He saw the big house with the sunlight shining brightly on the windows, and beyond it the great green bulk of the steeply rising land. His gaze moved quickly up the side of the mountain, and through the trees he glimpsed the house which was his home.

He pressed the mask more tightly to his face, and as he forced a little more air out he felt the bite of its suction against his skin. He stared a little longer and then turned away, his body moving easily to the motion of the rocking pirogue. He did not like the sight of the mountains in the daytime. It was just an ordinary mountainside, with many different trees and bushes growing on it, and even when the topmost peaks were veiled in swirling mists it did not look as beautiful as it did in the late evening just after the sun had gone down on the other side of the island. That was the time that the boy liked to look at the mountains, when he was still out at sea or just coming in. There were the lights of many fires winking in the darkness, and if it was not too late the mountains sometimes took on a deep mauve color while the peaks were edged with the red fire of the setting sun and the line of flame stretched from one end of the island to the other.

It was all very beautiful, and it was very sad, and when he watched it his heart ached and he felt the same as the lonely mountain, because there was a great sadness and loneliness in him too.

The boy moved up into the bow as far as he could go and then he sat down on the gunwale. The pirogue listed sharply, and as it did so he swung his legs up and over and slipped over the side, holding the mask pressed to his face. He felt the pirogue kicking back as his weight left it, and then the water closed over him.

Three feet below the surface and still in an upright position he paddled himself round in a tight circle, alert and on guard. He did not really expect to come across a shark in the waters inside the reef, but it was a precaution he always took. He saw nothing to alarm him, and he kicked out for the opaquely shimmering surface, blowing a stream of bubbles from his mouth.

The moment he surfaced he gulped a quick breath of air and submerged again. He placed the pistol grip of the speargun against his belly, and drawing his knees up and rolling forward in the water to give himself balance and solidity he tensed the muscles of his stomach and then quickly one after the other he strained back on both pairs of rubbers and slipped the wire tongues into the last and second-last of the three notches which were cut into the top of the harpoon shaft.

He transferred the speargun to his right hand and then straightened out his legs. He surfaced, gulped air two or three times and then swam off with his face down, kicking with his legs and pulling with his left arm which was free. The speargun nosed through the water in front of him at the end of his fully extended right arm, and the fifteen-foot nylon line which was attached to the harpoon from the muzzle of the gun trailed beneath him in a twisted figure eight.

The boy swam out till he was directly over the patch of weed and coral, turning his head to the side now and again to draw a quick breath. He felt a sudden bursting elation. He always did when he was in the water. It was a free element, and here it did not matter that he had one leg shorter than the other. Though he did not think consciously of his release in terms of freedom, he knew he was a free man just the same.

Out of the corner of his mask he saw the slender eighteen-inch shape that was not much thicker than a pencil. It hung motionless in the water less than a foot below the surface, its cold unwinking eyes fixed on him. He turned towards it, remembering the first time he had seen a needlefish.

It had been in the days before he had the mask, when he could not see anything clearly under the water. He had been swimming in the shallows on the edge of the channel, and when he saw that five or six of them had gathered round him his first thought was that they were young barracuda. He had seen the sharp teeth of that particular fish, and as young as they were he knew that they could hurt him badly. And with his blood in the water there was no telling what the great hammer-heads and grays outside the reef might do. He felt a great knot of fear inside his belly, and he struck out for the shore with all the furious strength that it had given him.

When he told his father about it later the man had laughed. They did not frighten him any more, but remembering the first time, their presence somehow always made him uneasy.

He turned towards the motionless needlefish. It was so slender that he knew it would really be a waste of time firing the speargun. Even if he were lucky enough to hit it, the harpoon point would slide off the armor of its dark-colored scales unless it struck absolutely square. He had fired at them quite often, when he had been able to get close enough, but he had not as yet ever managed to get one.

He swam towards it slowly. When the point of the harpoon was about eight feet from the motionless fish he steadied himself and brought the speargun up. His finger was tightening on the trigger when the fish darted away. It flashed off fifteen feet to the right and then froze. It hung in the water, watching him, quite still. The boy turned away: he knew it was a game which could go on for a long time without his once getting the chance to shoot.

A red flash of color below him caught his attention. He took a quick breath and dived, pulling himself down with his left arm and kicking his feet like a frog. At fifteen feet he swam past the top of a great boulder of brain coral. Pink damselfish, striped hawkfish and angelfish and many other gaudily plumed varieties scattered in wild confusion. But they were all little fishes, and he paid them no heed. He went down another six feet and then leveled off and started swimming round the coral boulder. An instant later he saw the large red snapper. It was finning its way lazily along the coral face about eight feet in front of him, quite oblivious to his presence.

Bourjois, he thought, and his heart began to race.

He kicked out after it. The snapper wriggled its caudal and pectoral fins a little faster and maintained the distance between them.

Son of a pig, the boy said in his mind.

There were not many good-sized fish in the channel these days, and those that remained were very wary. They had been hunted too many times before and disturbed too often by the passing of pirogues. It was all very annoying.

The boy kicked out desperately, burning up his reserves of air in a last furious burst of speed. He felt a clamoring excitement as he gained on the snapper, but at the same time he felt a rhythmic and painful thudding in his ears and he knew he would not be able to stay down much longer. He began to swing away from the fish, so that he could get in a broadside shot. He lifted the speargun, and his legs bent at the knees and doubled up as he steadied himself in position. He did not use the sights on the gun, because he had found them to be too exacting in use, and so ineffective. He extended his right arm to its full length instead, lining the speargun up with an automatic and practiced ease. He dropped his wrist a fraction and squeezed the trigger.

The boy felt a slight kick against his hand as the harpoon shot out of the gun. The sudden contraction of the four heavy rubbers made the water swirl and boil in front of him. For a moment his vision was impaired, but then the turbulence subsided and he saw the harpooned snapper. It was spinning round and round like a propeller, all equilibrium destroyed, and the protruding harpoon revolved with it.

He took one last look at the dying fish and then struck out for the surface. His lungs felt on fire and ready to burst, and there was a strange thudding noise inside his head. It seemed to him as he thrashed his way up that he was getting no nearer to the surface. It looked leaden and dull from where he was, and it reflected like a mirror. He could see nothing beyond it. He began to wonder whether he would ever reach the surface.

The rippling mirror above him began to reflect more brightly. He knew he was almost there. With a final frantic effort he kicked out again and swept his arms down through the suffocating water. He could feel the weight of the trailing harpoon and fish, and it acted as a drag. He kicked out again, and then suddenly, miraculously, the mirror above him shattered.

The pent-up breath exploded from his lungs the instant he surfaced and the force of its exit made spray of the seawater which sought to enter his open mouth. Turning onto his back he sucked in great mouthfuls of sweet air, gulping them in and blowing them out again as rapidly as he could. After a while the pounding inside his head stopped. He rolled over and struck out for the pirogue.

Thinking about the fish on the end of his harpoon he felt an immense satisfaction. He realized he was grinning only when the mask began to pinch against his stretched skin. He would have been a little shocked if he could have seen the expression on his face: there was elation in it, but there was also a baying kind of cruelty.

He swam up alongside the pirogue. He caught hold of the gunwale with his left hand. He pulled himself up a little and then reached over with his right arm and laid the speargun down carefully on the planking. He pushed off and swam round to the bow, and then with a strong heave he pulled himself up out of the water and scrambled into the boat. He had almost capsized it once, trying to climb in over the side, and that was why he now always got aboard over either the stern or the bow.

He pushed the mask up onto his forehead and hauled on the harpoon. He watched it coming up through the water, and the fish on the end of it seemed to grow bigger and bigger. When the top of the shaft was still a foot below the surface he leaned out over the gunwale and plucked the harpoon from the sea. The pirogue listed dangerously, but it did not alarm him. He knew to exactly what extent he could abuse it with impunity.

He unscrewed the harpoon head, knocked the fish off

the shaft and then screwed the head back on again. He compressed the sprung barbs and secured them, and then he slid the harpoon back into the speargun. He pulled the mask off his head and rinsed it over the side. Before slipping it on again and going into the water he looked seaward. He saw that old Rousseau's pirogue was already far out to sea. It looked very small and vulnerable in the distance, a lonely black spot on the dancing sunlit wavetops.

In the next hour he shot only two more fish. One of them was a striped *papillon,* or angelfish. The other one was a *cacatois,* and the blue fire which had pulsed and throbbed within its sapphire-colored scales seemed to fade and die out altogether when he brought it to the surface with the harpoon through its gills. Both of them were much smaller than the snapper, and the red *bourjois* had only been a little over a pound and a half.

He remembered the great grouper he had speared a few months ago. It must have weighed at least eighty pounds, and it was too big and powerful for him to halt. When it started moving off with him under the water he experienced a moment of pure terror. His brain went numb, and for the first few seconds he was unable to think at all. He realized vaguely that he would have to either let go of the speargun or drown. But he did not want to do either. He hung on, his desperation mounting, and the big fish continued to tow him slowly through the water. The pressure in his lungs became intolerable, and in that instant he realized finally that if he did not want to drown he had no other alternative. The knowledge that he would never again see his precious speargun and harpoon filled him with a terrible rage and hate for the fish. He went after the big grouper with murder in his heart. He pulled himself towards the fish, going hand over hand along the thin nylon line, taking a bight of it round his fingers each time so that he could grip it properly. When he reached the end of the line he grabbed the shaft of the harpoon. He jerked at it, trying to tear it free, but it had gone in deep and the barbs held it firm.

He felt a moment of utter despair, but after that a raging madness took hold of him. He bore down on the harpoon with a sudden savage thrust and turned the swimming fish towards him. The fierce bulging eyes of the grouper rounded on him, and it seemed that the huge mouth opened in a silent scream of agony. He stabbed out with his right hand and drove his stiffened fingers through the gill-slit and then drove them deeper and deeper till his groping fingers found the gills. He tore out the blood-red hoops with one furious wrench, and the green sea darkened as the blood of the fish poured smoking from the ruptured vent.

There were black spots edged with luminous silver dancing in front of his eyes as he turned the grouper once again. He levered it round with the harpoon and tore out the other set of gills and then struck out for the surface twenty feet above him, wondering if he would make it before his lungs burst.

The boy swam towards the reef, thinking of the bigger fish that were to be found there, the memory of the big grouper filling him with a glow of warmth. It was the biggest fish he had ever speared, and though he wanted very much to shoot a bigger one he knew it would not be advisable. He wished he had a good sharp knife, one with a sheath that you strapped to your leg. He had seen such a knife once, with a cork handle that made it float if you dropped it accidentally. But it had belonged to a tourist, and so obviously it must have been very expensive. With a knife like that on his leg he did not think he would be uneasy about any fish, unless of course it was a shark or a barracuda or one of the great fishes that drove through the water with a sword attached to its head.

He swam on, kicking his feet like a frog, his left arm rising and falling and splashing into the water. He crossed the deep channel and the water began to get shallower. A little farther on it began to get deep again, and he knew he had reached the beginning of the broad reef. He glanced back across his shoulder. He saw that the pirogue was about fifty yards away. It was not far, but it was still quite a distance. He had thought about rowing the boat out to the reef, but that would have meant hauling up the anchor and lengthening the rope on it. He began to wish that he had not been so lazy.

The seabed was now five fathoms below him, and the coral grew in wild confusion on the rocky bottom. In places it lifted in steep banks and fell away in tangled slopes, and in some parts it made archways which looked like those carefully trained creepers which some of the rich people liked to grow above their garden gates.

The boy scanned the jungle beneath him, looking down on it through the faceplate of his mask. He saw many fishes swimming about their business, but all of them were small. Just as he was about to turn his face and snatch a breath of air he saw the big porgy. It glided out from behind a wall of millepora and then hung motionless in the water a few feet off the bottom. It was white with parallel blue stripes running horizontally along the entire length of its body and head, and its dorsal and caudal fins were bright yellow with markings like a cheetah in a deeper shade of blue which was so dark it looked almost black.

The boy allowed his feet to sink slowly to a vertical position and then he began to tread water. He took two deep breaths, filling his lungs to capacity and exhaling with a measured control. It was a long way down, and a longer way back, and he wanted his lungs clean before he took the final breath that he would have to hold all the way there and back.

He sucked in a great lungful of air and jackknifed. He went down, kicking slowly. The sight of the beautiful porgy made him want to increase his speed, but he fought the temptation, because he knew it would only burn up and waste his air, and working at these depths every little bit of it was precious.

He swam towards the striped fish at an angle of forty-five degrees. He took in the wavy wall of millepora, and his mind warned him automatically of the small stinging barbs. At fifteen feet he felt a sudden and intense pain shoot through his ears. He swallowed quickly, forcing his tongue against his palate and contracting the muscles of his throat, and after that the pain went away.

He began to align the muzzle of the speargun, pointing it at the gill-slit just in front of the left pectoral fin. The pressure in his lungs increased. From experience he knew he did not have much time to waste. He consoled himself with the knowledge that it was much worse farther out, on the edge of the reef which was at fifty feet. You had barely enough air to get down, and you had to shoot the moment you were there and then claw your way back to the surface before your head burst.

He was on the point of squeezing the trigger when the porgy swam off with a flick of its tail. He swung the muzzle of the gun, his heart beating wildly with excitement. He wanted to shoot, but he did not think he would hit it. He hesitated uncertainly for a moment, wondering if it was now too late to squeeze the trigger, and then in the next instant he knew that he had waited too long and that it was already too late. He kicked out furiously, driving himself after the fish which swam so easily through the dark blue water. He chased it a little way, burning up the last of his air, but the distance between them lengthened.

He changed direction quickly, swooping upwards and striking out for the glimmering milkiness far above him. He felt sick with disappointment, because thinking about it as he swam up he felt certain he would have got the fish if he had pulled the trigger instead of being so cautious. He began to feel angry with himself at having missed such an opportunity when the terrible pressure inside his chest drove everything from his mind except the frantic cry for air.

He burst through the surface and rolled over onto his back. He lay there for a few moments, gasping and blowing, kicking his legs lazily to keep himself afloat. When he got his breath back he flipped over and scanned the scene below him. His eyes glowed with an impatient expectancy, but after a few moments the fire in them went out and they grew dull with resignation.

He started swimming again, going farther out to sea. The formation of the reef below changed gradually. At six fathoms it was an almost level bed, with sprouting antlers of coral reaching up through the foggy blue. He swam slowly, twisting his head from side to side as he searched the water. He was about to turn back when out of the corner of his mask he saw a splash of mottled yellow that caught his attention instantly.

He turned toward it, knowing already that it was a porgy. It looked very big from where he was, but in his mind he made reservations about its size because he knew that all fishes looked much bigger than they actually were, when you looked at them under the water. It was finning its way slowly in and out between the branches of a gray-looking coral, drifting through a cloud of tiny, brightly colored fishes which shared the same coral and paid it no attention. He wondered if it was the same porgy he had chased a little earlier on.

The boy cleared his lungs and dived. He went down a little bit faster this time, because he knew he would not have the air for a chase at such a depth. He did not swim rashly though, using all of his power. He knew of the effort required to reach the surface again, and he used his strength accordingly.

When the pain came into his ears he cleared it by swallowing. He went down vertically into the silent blue world, and as he approached nearer and nearer to the beautiful fish he hoped fervently that nothing would attract its attention within the next few seconds and cause it to swim off.

He was lining up the speargun when the fish waggled its fins and swam clear of the spreading coral. He expected it to turn back again, but it did not. He changed direction slightly and spurted after it, and there was a hot emptiness at the bottom of his belly. The distance between them increased slowly. His chest began to hurt. He was about to start up when the fish veered suddenly in the still blue silence of the water and came back towards him.

He swung the gun a little and squeezed the trigger. The water flurried, and through the swirl he saw the harpoon strike. The fish darted away with the barbed head of the harpoon sticking out on the other side of its round belly.

The boy floated himself into an upright position. He

straightened his legs cautiously, and when he felt a coral branch beneath his feet he stretched upwards and pushed off. The coral snapped beneath his thrusting weight. It broke silently. The boy kicked out for the surface, the hard skin on the soles of his feet tingling with the retained impression of abrasive roughness.

The struggling of the harpooned fish communicated itself to him over the almost invisible length of nylon line. He felt the speargun jerking in his hand, and each time it did his fingers tightened protectively round the pistol grip.

He surfaced, took a few gasping breaths and then plunged his head under the water again. He knew the fish was still on the end of his harpoon, because he could feel the heaviness of it. He wanted to see it though, with his eyes, so that he could be certain.

He saw the fine fat fish, swimming weakly now, killing itself as it swam round dragging the weight of the harpoon with it. He started grinning, thinking about the stupid fish, and then, just as he began to haul the line in, the grin froze on his face.

In the blue haze sixty feet away he saw the hammerhead. It was coming straight up towards the harpooned fish, and it came from the deep water on the other side of the reef. The big shark closed the distance rapidly, and its dorsal fin stuck straight up in the water.

Fear gripped the boy. As the shark came in closer he measured its length with his eye, and the cold around his heart bit a little deeper. It was all of nine feet long, but it was not its size alone which was so terrifying. What chilled him was the impression of dormant power and indestructibility that the sleek gray body conveyed as he followed its remorseless and unhurried approach.

If only I had a knife, he thought, but at the back of

his mind he knew that even a knife would be of little use against such a fish. Their skins were unbelievably rough and thick, and he had seen a smaller shark than this one with an axe buried deep in its evil brain, thrashing and snapping as it bit and flailed and splintered the planking of a big *canot*.

He remembered the harpoon he had been hauling in, and which he had forgotten about when he first saw the shark. He knew it was not much, but it would be better than a pair of empty hands. The minute he started hauling in the line the shark accelerated toward the fish on the end of the harpoon. The lazy rhythm of its waving tail did not change, but he knew without a doubt that it was moving faster. He wondered fearfully how fast it could move in the water if it thrashed out the way that dying shark had done in the boat.

With a last furious heave on the line he got the harpoon into his hands. The hammerhead came on unhesitantly. He snatched a quick breath and dived to confront it. He was not brave: he did it without thinking, because he could think of nothing else to do.

The shark closed to within six feet of him and then veered off suddenly as he went down to meet it. It began to circle him in the water. He turned with it, so that he could keep it in sight. He saw the strange-looking eyes on either side of the grotesque hammer. They focused on him, one at a time, cold and strange and like something made from stone.

He began to feel dizzy as he turned endlessly round and round to keep the circling shark in sight. That wasn't too bad, but his chest began to feel as if it were going to explode. He thrashed out suddenly for the surface four feet above him and snatched a breath of air.

He dived instantly after that, choking on the water he had swallowed. It was not a second too soon. The shark was already closing in on him. It veered off the moment he faced it, and it began to circle him once more.

A minute later he ran out of air. He went up for a breath, and his stomach turned over as he lost sight of the shark. In that instant his terror was so great that he thought he felt a compression wave in the water and he imagined the shark arrowing in towards his naked belly.

He dived again. For a second he did not see the shark. He spun round wildly, half hoping that it had gone. But it hadn't gone, and his heart lurched violently as he saw it coming up through the water toward him. He drew his legs up into his body protectively, and then in a moment of sudden fury, without thinking of what he was doing or of the possible consequences, he lunged out at the shark with the harpoon, thrashing angrily after it. As he floundered awkwardly he realized it had been a futile and very foolish gesture. To his astonishment the shark darted away. It began its circling once again, but farther out than it had been before.

He felt a moment of unspeakable relief, and then he felt a little flutter of hope within his breast. He began to wonder if the shark might not also be afraid of him. He did not really believe it, but the possibility sent his hopes soaring. If he could keep it at bay by poking it with the harpoon and frightening it off, he might just be able to work his way back to the safety of the pirogue. It never occurred to him to get rid of the porgy on the harpoon which had attracted the shark in the first place.

He went up again and gulped another mouthful of air. Already he was beginning to feel tired. He did not think he would be able to go on much longer, not like this, snatching a little air and then having to hold it till his lungs were almost bursting. He dived quickly, and the momentary elation he had felt drained away.

The shark was again closing on him rapidly. He felt a sudden spurt of rage at its treacherous behavior. He stabbed out at it with the harpoon. The shark veered off instantly. It began to circle him again, but not as far out as it had been before.

The boy stayed down till his breath ran out. When he could hold it no longer he struck out for the surface. He took two quick breaths and then slipped under the water again.

The shark had closed the distance between them. It was right on him. He struck out at it desperately. The harpoon point glanced off its blunt head, and it shot off six feet and then began its endless circling once again.

The boy knew then that it *was* afraid of him, but he knew also that it was a thing which did not matter at all. The shark was tireless, and it could go on forever, and soon he would be too tired to move and frighten it away. He realized then with a numbing certainty that it was hopeless.

He felt the beat of his frantic heart begin to slow, and as he turned slowly in the water to keep the shark in sight he felt a spell of terrible dizziness. He began to think that he was going to lose his balance and fall, and he wondered if the shark was waiting for that. It was funny to think of falling when he was already under the water. It was a foolish thing to imagine, but any second now he knew it was going to happen just the same. He spread his arms wide in the water to steady himself as the silent green world round him began to spin wildly.

I have done this before, he thought, and he remembered turning round and round as a child till he had lost all equilibrium, and then laughing and screaming as the spinning world far below him came closer and closer till finally it came up close enough to knock the breath out of him, and then he knew it was he who had fallen as he lay giggling and gasping on the grass, waiting drunkenly for the earth and sky to separate.

He saw the shark sweeping in towards him. The shape of it was vague and blurred. He steadied his reeling senses with a great effort of will. He felt a sudden calmness then, and the dreadful knot in the pit of his stomach untied itself. He knew it was the end, and because he understood it so perfectly he no longer felt afraid. The fingers of his left hand clamped lovingly round the slim shaft of the harpoon.

I will hurt you also, *requin,* his mind screamed at the shark.

He tensed himself to strike, but he realized without any consternation that he would not hurt it at all.

Under the water his face twisted in a silent grimace. The shark was almost upon him when he saw the dark shape of another great fish. It swept in furiously from the murky water which stretched away to his right in deepening shades of blue. He thought it was a shark, and though he had never heard of such a thing before, for one wild moment he wondered whether it might have come to attack the hammerhead. If they fought over the right to eat him, he might be able to slip away while they tore each other to pieces.

He felt a spurt of hope which was so intense it sickened him. It entered him so suddenly and violently that he felt its entry as a physical assault on his body. He sagged limply in the water for a moment, and then a fresh current of fear shot through his nerves and electrified him.

The great fish closed the distance between them at an astonishing speed. He saw with another wild surge of hope that it was heading directly for the shark in front of him. The pointed snout of the great fish slammed into the gill-slits of the shark. The battering impact rocked the shark in the water. It turned over on its side and then righted itself slowly, and then in a state of shock and fright the big hammerhead voided a cloud of excrement and darted away. It vanished into the dark blue shadows on the other side of the reef.

The boy felt the return of a terrible despair. In the still silence of his mind he cursed the cowardly hammerhead with monotonous repetition. He used up all the terrible words he had ever heard, and they went through his mind and passed without leaving a trace of meaning or understanding. If only the hammerhead had stayed to fight, he thought.

He forced his arms and legs to start moving. He kicked himself wearily to the surface. He drew a sobbing breath and went under again, and he wondered what kind of a shark it was that could frighten a hammerhead off with a single blow from its pointed snout. He searched for it, twisting and turning frantically as he scanned the water. He did not see it anywhere, and he began to wonder if it might not have followed the hammerhead out to sea in pursuit. He began to hope again. Just then the great fish swam up from below him.

He recoiled in terror, but in that instant he saw clearly for the first time the protruding beak with the undershot jaw which seemed to set the mouth in a fixed smile of smug and secret satisfaction.

Marsouin, he thought, and his heart gave a great shout of exultation.

He had seen porpoises before, far out to sea, and once

when he had been fishing with his father he had seen a great school of them which looked a mile long and a mile wide in the blue sea. And as he watched the black shapes coming up out of the water to breathe and then sliding back into the sea together in a slow smooth roll he was glad for once that the school was far away, because it did not seem right to him that any of them should die. In all the times they had caught the black-backed fishes he had never really appreciated their swift grace and beauty till then, and it saddened him a little to think that such a beautiful fish should lose its freedom and then die with a harpoon in its heart.

The big fish swam past the boy just below the surface of the water and then it turned and swam back towards him. He had never heard any fisherman tell of a porpoise harming a man, but he eyed it warily just the same. It was a big fish, and the fear of the shark was still in him, and he feared it because of its great size which was equal to that of the shark.

He went up for a breath of air, and the fish went up with him. He saw a fine spray of water shoot from the crescent-shaped blowhole at the top of its head. The instant it stopped spouting he heard a noise which was like the sound of a quickly drawn breath and then the blowhole shut off with a soft plop.

The big fish swam in closer to the boy, and he was astonished to hear the faint whistles and squeaks which came from its blowhole as it swam past him in the water with its head held high and its swept-back dorsal fin sticking up in the air and looking like a piece of slippery wet rubber.

The black-colored back, which had a purplish tint, slipped past him two feet away. The boy paddled himself round so that he could keep an eye on it, because he was still unsure of the great fish. He saw it turn and start back towards him, and he saw the startling whiteness of its belly as it rolled over onto its side just before it turned.

It swam past him again, and he realized then that the big fish was not a *marsouin*. It did resemble the porpoises he had seen, but he saw that it was only a superficial resemblance. It had a definite beak, and the undershot jaw sticking out like a chin turned the mouth upwards and fixed it in a smile, whereas the mouth of the porpoise was simply an opening in a blunt-shaped head which no amount of imagination could transform into a beak. He thought the big fish must be a kind of porpoise, but he was not certain.

He knew it was not a fish in the true sense of the word. He had listened in the past to the man explain that a porpoise was a mammal and not a fish. But it came from the sea and it lived in the sea, and that was why he preferred to think of it as a fish.

He studied the big fish. It was longer and heavier than any porpoise he had ever seen. He knew then without a doubt that the fish swimming in the water beside him was certainly not a porpoise as he knew it.

It was a bottle-nosed dolphin, a close relative of the porpoise, but even if he had known this it would not have allayed his mounting apprehension: to him it was a fish he had never seen before, an unknown quantity, and because he was without any knowledge of it he felt afraid. He knew only that it had driven off a hammerhead shark with one blow from its powerful-looking beak.

As the dolphin slid past him in the water that was the thought which was uppermost in his mind, and he wondered whether it was going to attack him on its next pass. The great head of the fish half turned to keep him in view as it glided past: it actually turned, and to his astonishment he found himself looking straight into one enormous eye. In that instant all his fear vanished, because the eye that regarded him was like the eye of a man. It did not stare at him with a cold glassy malevolence as the eye of the shark had done. The eyeball itself was almost two inches in diameter, and in the huge black pupil he saw an expression of friendly curiosity that was almost human.

Ten feet away from him the dolphin made a wide sweeping turn and then it plunged its beak into the water and its glistening back seemed to roll forward slowly like a wheel as it followed the head below the surface of the sea in a continuation of the same fluid movement. The last thing he saw was the black tip of the raked-back dorsal fin and then that too slid smoothly under the water.

He saw the big fish come curving in towards him at a depth of five feet. It looked black and sinister, but he felt no fear because the memory of the big friendly eye was still fresh in his mind. He stopped treading water and allowed himself to sink till the faceplate of his mask was just below the refractive surface film which blurred his vision.

He did not see the fish. He was wondering whether it had already gone past him when he felt a sudden gentle jolt. His heart skipped a beat and he felt a moment of breathtaking terror. He felt the body of the great fish come pressing up between his legs and then he felt himself being lifted up on its back till his head and shoulders were right out of the water. The fish started to swim off with him, heading towards the open sea. He was facing backwards as they moved off, and it was a terrifying sensation.

He kicked out wildly, trying to get free of the fish. But he did not get free, and the fish only increased its speed. In desperation the boy threw his whole body to the right. He toppled off the back of the fish, with the harpoon and the speargun flailing wildly. He felt the smooth rubbery skin on the flank of the fish sliding and rubbing against the inside of his thigh and then finally all contact between them was broken as it swam on past him.

He came up to the surface choking and gasping. He transferred the harpoon to his right hand, holding it together with the speargun. He struck out for the pirogue. The hot panic left him and he felt a great bursting relief. But it lasted only a moment, because he had not taken three strokes when he felt the fish coming up beneath him once more.

It came up from behind him, and it lifted him up so quickly that he had no time to struggle and escape it. He felt himself come surging up through the water and then he slid along the wet back of the fish till the dorsal fin brought him up short. The fish accelerated suddenly, and he saw that they were heading directly towards the distant pirogue.

He threw his arms round the neck of the big fish to keep himself from falling off, at the same time gripping its body with his knees and his thighs. He bent his right wrist backwards, so that the harpoon and speargun did not touch the fish: he acted not out of consideration, but because he was still a little bit afraid of the fish and he did not like to think of what might happen if he prodded it accidentally with the sharp point of the harpoon.

He lay crouched forward over the back of the fish as they sped through the water and he felt the drag of the sea against his body as it tugged at him and tried to tear him from the slippery back of the fish. The water sprayed round his shoulders and face. In a moment of sudden wild exuberation he started to laugh and shout and cheer.

The fish began to rise even higher, and the top of its head broke the surface of the water. The boy fell quiet, and in the abrupt silence which followed he heard the startlingly loud *whoosh* as the fish spouted, and his nostrils twitched at the warm fishy smell of its breath which came straight up into his face. He heard the soft moan of air being drawn into the blowhole. It snapped shut with a wet plop an instant later and he felt the back of the great fish arching smoothly beneath him.

The boy began to cheer wildly again. His elated cries were cut short a second later as the dolphin dived. He barely had the time to snatch a hurried breath before the water closed over his head. Panic shot through him. What if the fish dived right to the bottom of the sea and stayed down there with him for longer than he could hold his breath? He felt a little foolish when he realized that all he had to do was let go and make his own way up to the surface whenever he wanted.

The dolphin leveled out at three fathoms. The boy felt his breath running out. He wondered whether he should abandon the fish and strike out for the surface or hang on in the hope that it would go up itself within the next few seconds. He decided to stay with the fish for as long as he could. If he jumped off now he knew he might never see it again, and for some reason or the other the thought of being parted from the great fish filled him with a deep sense of loss.

He stayed with it a while longer. He lay almost flat along its back and he rode it like a racehorse as it slipped noiselessly through the silent blue water. He glanced at the seabed which sped by two and a half fathoms below him. The coral pattern looked familiar. He was not quite sure about it though, but then he recognized the spreading antlers of a large elkhorn coral and he knew that they were not far from the deep channel which ran between the mainland and Île aux Cerf.

His head began to hurt and his chest felt on fire. He knew he did not have a moment to spare, but at the same time he could not bring himself to part company with the great fish that was carrying him through the water with such effortless ease.

He hung on a little longer, punishing his body heedlessly. With each second of suffocating agony that passed he prayed for the miracle that would start the fish swimming up towards the surface so that he would not have to leave it. But his prayer was not answered, and the miracle never came.

The big fish swam on tirelessly at the same depth. The boy felt a sudden dizziness sweep over him. He shook his head to clear it and hung on grimly. Black spots began to dance in front of his eyes. He knew it would be madness to stay down any longer. He threw himself sideways and off the back of the great fish.

He turned end over end through the water. When he got his bearings he struck out for the surface. The air inside his bursting lungs began to bubble from his mouth. Out of the corner of his eye he saw the big fish swimming away on its side with the bow-shaped flukes of its tail pointing straight up and down in the water.

The boy surfaced with a last frantic kick. He turned over onto his back and lay gasping and blowing. He barely managed to summon the strength to keep his legs moving and stay afloat. After a while his breathing returned to normal.

He flipped over onto his belly suddenly, remembering the big fish. He pushed his face down under the water and searched for it anxiously. He did not see it anywhere. He lifted his head and began to tread water. He felt a moment of utter desolation as he stared round the empty sea.

He started swimming towards the pirogue. His arms and legs felt heavy and tired as he splashed through the water, and his heart was full of despair.

When he got back to the pirogue he reached up over the gunwale and dropped the speargun and the harpoon into the boat. The striped porgy was still on the end of the harpoon. It was quite dead now, and its cold fish eyes looked like pebbles of colored glass.

He swam round to the stern of the boat and dragged himself aboard. The effort took the last of his remaining strength. He sat down on the planking and peeled the mask off his head. He stared out across the sea, but it was quite empty. He felt a hurting disappointment.

If only he would show himself to me again, he thought.

He did not know what he would do if he saw the big fish again, but he knew that it would make him very happy. He felt an aching emptiness as he thought about the dolphin.

It was a fine fish, he told himself reverently, and I think that it truly saved my life from that pig of a shark with his ugly flat face.

He searched the sea again, but there was nothing to be seen. He scuffed despondently at the planking of the boat with his bare toes. The porgy on the harpoon caught his attention. He stared at it. It was dead, and it looked dead, and the brilliant fires which had flamed in yellow and black beneath its scales had all gone out. He reached out listlessly for the harpoon, and just then the surface of the sea burst open fifteen feet away to his right. He saw it out of the corner of his eye, and he was so startled and surprised for an instant that he was unable to move.

It seemed to him that there was a big black hole in the water with a tunnel going down into the sea, and then as he straightened up and swung to face it he realized that it was not a tunnel or a hole but the body of some great fish coming up through the water.

He saw the blunt domed head of the dolphin break through the surface and then the rest of its body followed dripping and black and wet from the hole in the water. For a second it appeared to be standing on its tail, and then with a final lazy wriggle of its flukes it cleared the water completely. It went up with an agonizing slowness, but then suddenly it gained momentum and it lifted higher and higher till finally it seemed that it was hanging in the air ten feet above him. He saw the great white expanse of its belly, and then a second later it turned its head and he saw the friendliness in the big brown eye which watched him. It seemed to hang in the air a moment longer and then it rolled gracefully and plummeted down. It entered the sea with a splash that sent a burst of spray all over him and the boiling water which shot back to the surface made the pirogue rock and heave.

The boy stared at the place where it had disappeared. He was still staring at it when the dolphin surfaced quietly five feet away from the side of the boat. He sprang to his feet. He began to dance up and down with excitement. He did not want the fish to go away, but he could think of nothing which might hold its attention and so delay its inevitable departure.

He sat down suddenly in the pirogue and leaned far out over the side. He stretched his right arm out and snapped his fingers together coaxingly. The wallowing dolphin veered away and swam off with a flick of its tail.

The boy snatched his hand back as if he had been burned, but then his heart leaped with joy as he saw the big fish turn in the water and swim back towards him. Once again he stretched his arm out. He did it slowly, and he did not reach quite as far as he had done the last time. He forced himself to move without haste, lest any sudden movement on his part frighten the fish away.

The dolphin lifted its head right out of the water and examined the boy. He snapped his thumb against his fingers softly in what he thought was an enticing gesture. The dolphin watched all his movements warily, but it did not come any closer. It dropped back into the water suddenly, where it lay wallowing comfortably on the surface.

The boy made strange clucking noises with his mouth and continued to snap his fingers together. He wanted to touch the dolphin, but it was too far away. He saw the big fish eyeing him, but it remained exactly where it was, floating in the water a few feet beyond his reach.

"Ici, *marsouin*," he crooned softly. "Viens ici, mon garçon."

It never occurred to him that the fish might be a female. It had saved his life, and that made it a friend, and therefore it could only be a boy like himself. He clucked and crooned and called softly to it but the big fish did not move. He wanted desperately to have it

80

come closer, because he wanted to reach out and touch it and stroke it with his fingers and thank it for having saved his life.

The dolphin stayed where it was. He called out again, pleading with it to come closer. It had suddenly become very important to him that he touch it: he could think of no other way of expressing the gratitude and admiration he felt for the big fish.

In desperation he reached for it, leaning far out over the side of the pirogue as he tried to touch it.

The dolphin moved its right flipper against its body and then with an almost imperceptible flick of its tail it swung away from him. The boy drew back quickly, but the damage had been done already. The dolphin continued to move away from the boat.

The boy leaped to his feet in consternation as the big fish increased the distance between them. He clucked at it till his throat ached, but it took no notice of him at all. He wished suddenly that he could speak to the big fish and have it understand the words he spoke before it swam down into the sea. There were so many things that he wanted to say. He wanted to thank it for saving his life, and he wanted to thank it for the breathless underwater ride, but most of all he wanted to tell the fish how fine and strong and beautiful he thought it was.

He danced up and down in the boat in a little jig of helpless frustration. For a second he thought of diving overboard and racing after the dolphin, but the memory of the hammerhead was still too fresh in his mind. He did not doubt that the big fish could deal with it again, but it was not a chance that he was eager to take.

He glanced round wildly, and his eyes fell on the *bourjois* which was the fish he had speared before all the others. He darted forward and snatched it up, cursing himself for not having thought of it already. He pursed his lips and whistled piercingly, and at the same time he took the fish by the head and waved it slowly in the air.

Attracted by the trilling whistle the dolphin came about suddenly. It swam back towards the pirogue, its head held high in the water. The boy shivered with excitement. He sat down quickly, so that he would be in a position to give the fish to the dolphin the moment it swam up alongside the pirogue.

"Ici, *marsouin*," he called softly. "Ici, garçon, ici."

Twenty feet from the boat the dolphin turned suddenly and dived under the water. The boy cried out involuntarily. He felt a sickening emptiness in his stomach. It took his breath away for a moment, but then after that he felt a burst of anger at the insufferable effrontery of the dolphin.

"Aye yo!" he cried out. "You big, stupid fish-pig!"

He jerked the snapper backwards and forwards in frustration and then in a sudden spurt of rage he leaned out over the side of the pirogue and brought it smacking down flat against the surface of the sea. An instant later he was astonished to see the dark shadow of the dolphin coming up towards him, wagging its head from side to side as it swam up through the dark blue water.

The big fish swam right up to him, and before he had time to recover from his surprise and snatch his hand from the water it took hold of the snapper and with a gentle tug pulled it from his fingers. Staring down into the water he saw the dolphin turn the snapper crosswise and work it a little farther back inside its mouth. He saw the beaked jaws close tightly, and he heard the crackling sound of crisp flesh and scales being crushed and the crunching sound of little bones being broken and then he saw the big fish turn the snapper once again in its mouth with a quick movement of its beak and swallow it down headfirst.

The dolphin lifted its head from the water. It seemed to the boy that there was a look of inquiry in its expressive eyes. He snatched up the striped angelfish and held it out to the dolphin. The big fish watched his movements warily, but it displayed no interest in the *papillon*. He thrust the angelfish a little closer towards the dolphin and waved it entreatingly in front of the pointed beak. The dolphin eyed him a moment longer and then slipped back into the water so that only its curved back and dorsal fin protruded above the surface.

The boy stopped waving the fish. His face wrinkled with vexation and bewilderment. He called to the dolphin, and he began to wave the fish again tentatively when it occurred to him that perhaps the dolphin did not associate the object in his hand with food. He remembered what had happened the first time he waved the *bourjois* in the air, and how the big fish had shown no interest in it until he had smacked it down loudly into the water.

Thinking of what had happened he was baffled for a moment, but then there came into his mind the memory of mackerel jumping in the sea and the noise of their smacking down on the water as the big *carangue* and striped *thon* drove hungrily into them, coming up from far below in the dark water to feed. He remembered the man working the pirogue in among the leaping school to catch the big tuna which fed on the mackerel, and then in a sudden burst of comprehension he understood why the dolphin came back when it heard the smacking sound of the snapper being slapped against the water.

The dolphin was starting to move away from the boat when the boy lifted the little striped *papillon*. He smacked it down smartly against the water and then held the fish a little way below the surface. The dolphin turned immediately and swam straight for the fish he was holding.

The boy quivered with excitement. He noticed the strange way in which the dolphin wagged its head from side to side as it approached. To him it was a comical diversion: he did not know that it was sending out bursts of ultrasonic sound which enabled it to locate the exact position of the fish. Its blowhole came out of the water and he heard strange whistling and squeaking noises, but now they were louder and pitched high with frenzied enthusiasm.

He flinched a little as the dolphin opened its mouth. He saw the sharp conical teeth and he saw that they were unlike the spade-shaped teeth of the other porpoises he had seen, and it took all of his courage to hold his hand steadily in the water when what he wanted to do was snatch it away from the long jaws which were opening wider and wider and which had long rows of teeth which seemed to extend right into the very throat of the big fish. In blind terror he watched it closing in on his hand.

The dolphin took the fish from him without touching his hand. It drew the angelfish from his fingers with such gentleness that he barely felt the withdrawal. He woke from his trance, and he felt a sudden rush of affection for the big fish which had the strength and courage to tackle a hammerhead shark and yet could be so gentle with a boy who had nothing to offer it but a fish.

He fed it the blue-green *cacatois,* smacking it down into the water first, and he heard the crunchy noise of its horny bill breaking as the dolphin crushed the parrot wrasse between its powerful jaws. He had nothing left now to offer the dolphin except the fat porgy. He eyed it with indecision. He wanted to give the porgy to the dolphin, but at the same time he was a little unwilling to part with the sweet-fleshed fish. It was a meal for two, and it was the last one left, and he was tired and he did not want to have to go into the sea and start hunting for their food all over again. He reached out reluctantly for the harpoon on which the fish was impaled, still undecided.

He glanced at the dolphin wallowing in the water beside the boat. It seemed to him that it was beginning to get restless and impatient. He did not want it to go away, and so he made up his mind about the porgy without any further hesitation.

He snatched up the harpoon, unscrewed the head and then ran the fish off the end of the shaft. He picked it up and leaned out over the side of the pirogue and smacked it down into the water. The dolphin made its head-wagging approach. He felt a renewed affection for it because of the gentle and considerate manner in which it took the fish from his fingers.

I wish you could be my friend, he thought. I would like to ride on your back again, and I would shoot many more fish for you.

He picked up the harpoon head and began to screw it back on the shaft. He worked automatically, doing it without looking, and his eyes were on the big fish in the sea. He saw it crush the fat porgy between its jaws and then swallow it headfirst, and he saw the sun reflecting brightly on the little waves which broke wetly over its glossy back.

He gave a final twist to the harpoon head and then tightened it up with all the pressure he could apply. He compressed the barbs, and then holding them down with his thumb and forefinger he secured them with the locking ring. He laid the harpoon down beside the speargun and then returned his attention to the dolphin. It was then that the idea first occurred to him.

He ran his eye over the great length of the big fish in the water. At a rough guess it would scale at well over three hundred pounds. If it dressed out at less than half that weight there would be more than one hundred and fifty pounds of prime meat. At fifty cents a pound that would be a lot of money. His forehead wrinkled and his lips moved silently as he worked the sum out laboriously in his head. The answer he got made his breath catch. Seventy-five rupees was a lot of money. They would be able to pay the rent for the house and there would even be enough left over to buy a pair of flipper feet in one of the big stores in Victoria. Fish was scarce, and it was even possible that the meat of the *marsouin* would sell for more than fifty cents a pound.

He picked up the harpoon and hefted it thoughtfully in his hands. He glanced at the dolphin, and in his mind he saw himself standing up and stretching to his full height and then driving the spear deep into the heart of the big fish. The picture shocked and horrified him.

He threw the harpoon down with a sudden oath, appalled at the monstrous treachery of his thoughts. He did not know how he could have even contemplated such a dreadful thing. For a few moments he hated himself with an intensity that made him feel sick.

It is only a fish, he thought angrily, trying to quiet his

accusing conscience, but at the bottom of his heart he knew that he could never again think of the big fish as anything but a loved and trusted friend.

He was glad then that he thought of it as a fish, and not as a mammal, which was the same thing as a man. It was not that he did not think a dolphin worthy enough to be compared to a man: it was just that he felt a greater sense of importance by thinking of it as a fish. Anyone could have a man for a friend, but it was not everyone who could boast of being friends with a fish. He wondered if he would ever see it again some other day, and he wondered if the big fish knew how happy he was to be near it.

He reached out over the side of the boat and smacked the palm of his hand into the water. When the dolphin swam in close he lifted his hand quickly from the sea and ran his fingers lightly over the bulging dome of its head. The skin felt smooth and slick like the rubber on his mask when it was under water and wet.

I have touched it, he thought triumphantly.

The dolphin jerked its head aside and darted away in alarm. The boy felt a sudden stab of remorse and apprehension. The big fish was already twenty feet from the pirogue and still moving away fast. He did not think it was going to come back now, and he began to wish that he had not acted so impetuously as he watched the shadowy shape of the dolphin scudding away below the surface of the sea.

He stood up quickly, so that he could keep it in sight for as long as possible. The shadow disappeared for a while, and then suddenly the dolphin rose bursting from the sea.

It lifted high into the air, with transparent drops of water spraying from its dark purple back, showing all its great beauty and all its great strength. It crashed back into the sea, still moving away from him, and then a second later he knew it must have made a turn deep down in the dark water where he could not see it because he saw the dark shape of its great body arrowing straight back towards him. It did not look like a fish, but like a flickering shadow that flew swiftly just beneath the surface of the sea. The boy held his breath.

The dolphin sped straight for the bow of the little boat, and then it slowed suddenly and turned onto its side and swam slowly on its side till it was lying motionless in the water right alongside the boat. The boy saw the pale whiteness of its belly, and then he started in alarm as the big fish rolled and twisted in the water and rubbed its belly against the planking of the pirogue.

The boat rocked violently, and he thought at first that the fish was trying to capsize it. Panic clawed at him as he fought to keep his balance, but then a second later it dawned on him that the dolphin was only scratching its belly. The tension left him and he laughed with relief. He sat down quickly, and now he wanted to touch the dolphin again and prove to it that he meant it no harm.

He reached out cautiously, not wanting to frighten it, remembering what had happened the last time he touched it. Hardly daring to breathe he placed the tips of his fingers against its belly. The big fish became suddenly still, but it did not swim away. The boy began to hope that he might be able to make a friend of it at last. He started to stroke his fingers very gently up and down over the smooth white skin of its belly.

The dolphin lay on its side for a while, permitting the boy to caress it, but then it righted itself abruptly and darted off. Twenty yards out the dolphin turned and came straight back towards the pirogue.

He waited for it eagerly, and then as the dolphin came alongside and began to rub its belly up and down against the smooth planking he reached out and tickled it. He was very gentle, and once again the dolphin grew quite still and allowed him to caress it. He felt the vulnerable softness of its belly, and in that moment there was born in him a great love for the big fish which trusted him so implicitly.

He felt a great thrill of pride and satisfaction at his conquest, but at the same time he felt a little bit subdued. He must think that I am his brother, the boy thought with sudden amusement, because it is certain that when he first saw me I looked more like a frightened fish than a fisherman.

He continued to stroke his fingers up and down over the belly of the dolphin. He did not know that the skin he caressed so lovingly was extremely sensitive to continuous friction. The dolphin turned suddenly and streaked off under the water. It surfaced fifty yards away, and he saw the smooth roll of its back in the water as it came up to breathe and then it vanished below the surface once more.

The boy sat up quickly, staring at the place where the fish had disappeared. He was not particularly anxious, because the dolphin had done it before and he thought it was going to come back. He waited patiently, expecting it to reappear at any moment. A minute passed, and then another minute, and when there was still no sign of it he became apprehensive.

He jumped up, sweeping his glance anxiously over the surface of the sea, and twice he turned back to stare dully at the spot in the water where he thought he had last seen the big fish. The minutes dragged by, but the fish did not return. He began to feel hurt and a little bit resentful at the way it had deserted him.

He began to wonder where the big fish could be, and he wondered why it did not come up to breathe. It occurred to him then that it might have surfaced behind him while his head was turned. He thought about it, but he did not really believe it. He had been alert and very watchful, and he felt certain that he would have seen the dolphin if it had come up anywhere in the vicinity. He did not know how long it could stay down in the water without breathing. Many minutes had passed already, and he began to think that it must have surfaced far out to sea on the other side of Île aux Cerf. He stared accusingly at the island for a while, and then turned away despondently. He felt a little sad, because the big fish had deserted him so abruptly. He did not think he would ever see it again.

He moved up into the bow of the pirogue and he bent over and started hauling in the anchor. He worked mechanically, his thoughts still on the dolphin, and he pulled the dripping wet rope in hand over hand and coiled it down with a flick of his wrist. With a final heave he lifted the anchor over the point of the bow and lowered it into the boat.

He sat down and put the oars out, and he used the left-hand oar to turn the bow of the boat a little and then he leaned forward a bit and splashed both oars into the water. He pulled for the shore with a slow, easy stroke. He threw a last reproachful glance at the rocky island which he thought had prevented him from seeing the dolphin for the last time and then he bowed his head and stared unseeingly at the planking of the boat. He was certain now that he would not see the dolphin again.

He felt a burst of overwhelming loneliness. He lifted his head suddenly and threw it back, and there were tears in his eyes as he stared up at the sky. It had cleared a little more, and it was brighter now than it had been earlier. He saw two dark clouds with the wind in their sails racing each other towards the sun. The one on the right got there first, and as it passed over the face of the sun and swallowed it up, the color of the sea changed from a dark blue to a darkness that had no color.

He did not actually notice the change: it registered only as a gloomy oppressiveness. He thought of the big fish again. A little moan of pain burst from his mouth. He felt a moment of unreasonable anger then, and all of it was directed at the dolphin. It swelled him up, and it filled his chest to bursting, and he felt that he would burst if he did not do something to stop the swelling in his chest.

He wondered suddenly whether the big fish might not hear him if he whistled. He remembered how it had turned back before.

He took a deep, measured breath, filling his lungs to capacity, and then he shut his mouth and held it. He took another quick breath which made the muscles of his stomach stretch in pain, and then in a sudden explosive outburst he blew all the pain and anger from his heart in a high-pitched, drawn-out whistle. The shrill sound of it pierced his own ears, and the effort left him limp. He did not think he had ever whistled as loudly before. He began to feel better. He grinned to himself and pulled a little harder on the oars, holding to the same measured stroke which had not faltered once even while he had been exorcising the devils in his heart. He flicked his gaze across the water perfunctorily: he did not really think that the fish would come.

An instant later he froze suddenly and the grin died on his face. The pirogue swung sharply to the left and the port oar was almost torn from his right hand as the forgotten blade dragged through the water. He saw the big fish bursting through the surface of the sea about ten feet to his left. It seemed to him as he stared in apprehensive astonishment that its whole body shook and undulated as it fought to free itself from the clutching grip of the sea. A second later it rose right out of the water in a burst of spray. He saw the great length of its body coming straight towards him with the dark sea shining wetly on its smooth skin. He cowered down in the boat and watched it out of the corner of his eye, his arms clasped protectively across the back of his head, tensing himself for the moment of impact.

He thought the fish was going to land right in the boat. The big white belly seemed to fill the whole sky, but then it began to lift, and he saw the whole great length of the fish lifting higher and higher into the air till it was so high he had to raise his head to watch it and then it was hanging like an arch in the air high above him and he saw the single slit on the underside of its tail just before it curved through the sky and splashed into the water fifteen feet away on the other side of the boat. If he had understood the significance of that single slit he would have been a little dismayed: his boy friend was a girl.

The boy slumped with relief. He felt quite weak for a moment, but then a sudden exultation swept through him. He stood up in the boat and started cheering and shouting and waving his arms.

"Marsouin! Marsouin!" he called. "Come back, *marsouin."*

He knew now that the big fish had not forgotten him. He thought of its magnificent leap, higher then he had ever seen a fish jump, and he felt a warm glow of pride, for the big fish and what it had done, and also because he was the friend of the fish.

Eighty yards away, and far out in the deep channel, the dolphin surfaced. It came halfway out of the water, standing straight up in the air on its tail, and it turned its head and watched him for a moment before sinking slowly back into the water and disappearing out of sight.

The boy waited expectantly, but it did not come up again. After a few minutes he sat down and pushed the oars out and started rowing again. He felt no despondency as he had before. The fish had not deserted him: it had returned, and it had leaped high in the air to show him that it still remembered, and he knew then with a quiet and unshakable conviction that he would see it again. He did not understand his feeling of certainty, but it was so strong within him that it left no room for inquiry or doubt.

A little farther in the boy shipped the oars and stood up. As he reached for the bamboo pole he wondered whether the appearance of the big fish had been an accident, or whether it had heard and actually come in response to his whistle. He thought about it hopefully for a while, and then suddenly he remembered once again the last time he had whistled at it, and how it had come about immediately after that.

He decided that the dolphin must have heard his whistle, and he was ecstatic to think that he could call it. He was almost tempted to whistle again, but the fear that he might fail to summon the big fish stopped him. He evaded the test and excused his defection neatly by telling himself that the fish was probably much too far away to hear him by now in any case.

THE boy limped up the steep side of the mountain towards his home. He was always more conscious of his limp just after he had been swimming. Once again he felt a dull antipathy towards the land which made him limp and hurt him when he walked, and at the same time his love for the sea increased proportionately. It was always the same when he stepped onto the unyielding earth after having been in the water for a while.

He climbed on up the hill, his wet shorts stuck down hard against his lean-fleshed buttocks. In his right hand he carried his speargun and mask, and clutched in his left hand were half a dozen tightly rolled leaves of choice tobacco. The ends of the leaves stuck out on either side of his fist.

He lifted his hand and sniffed in the raw pungent aroma of the dry, golden-brown leaves. He held his breath for a while, savoring the rich sweetness of the smell. It was a good, clean smell, and he liked it, and he did not understand how anyone could prefer to burn the leaves and smoke the acrid fumes which only stung the nose and throat. He decided that it would be better to take snuff, but he had seen some of the fishermen who did. He had watched them sneeze till the snot spurted from their nostrils and their eyes filled with tears. The idea did not appeal to him, especially the snot.

He sniffed at the leaves again, his nose pinching in as he inhaled. He glanced back across his shoulder suddenly, but no one was in sight. He smiled, thinking about the leaves in his hand. He had broken one of his rules to get them, because he had stolen them from the property of Jean Morel. He consoled himself with the knowledge that though they had been grown on his land they were not for his personal use: he smoked only the fat white cigarettes which he bought in the shops of Victoria, and which the Chinaman sometimes stocked. Pierre Vigot had grown and dried the tobacco for himself.

The boy paused for a moment to catch his breath, leaning his back against the thick bole of a takamaka. He took most of the weight of his body on his left leg, resting the right, which was feeling tired and trembly.

My left leg is the bad one, he thought, and yet it never hurts as much as the right. He knew it was because of the way he had to walk.

He glanced at the leaves in his hands, remembering that he had almost been caught. If it had not been for the thick bushes at the edge of the stream he would certainly have been seen. He wondered if Pierre Vigot would miss the leaves he had taken. He did not think so, but he hoped that he would.

He pushed himself away from the tree and started up again. He walked more slowly now, with his body bent far forward against the steep slope of the mountain. He wondered what would have happened if Pierre Vigot had seen him with the leaves clutched in his hand. He pushed the thought from his mind quickly, because it was not a pleasant thing to think about. He told himself that he would have to remember to ask his father about how he could almost kill a man with one blow from his hand. He thought of the great size of Pierre Vigot, and he doubted that such a thing was possible. He *would* ask his father about it though, because he knew that one day he might have to face the big Creole without the speargun in his hands.

He thought of the big fish, and he wished that he had its speed and all its great strength.

The boy lifted his head and stared up the hill. He saw the edge of the flat terrace, and beyond it the top of the thatched roof of his home. He lengthened his stride and began to walk a little faster, shutting his mind to the hot pain in the muscles of his legs. He was suddenly impatient to tell the man about the big fish that had become his friend.

He reached the end of the stony path and stepped up onto the flat land of the terrace. It was a relief to stop climbing. He saw the man sitting exactly where he had left him. He wondered if he had sat there all the time he had been gone, without ever getting up to make a move. The thought saddened and dismayed him, but then he saw that he was seated on the middle step, and he knew he must have moved. It made him feel better. He hurried forward, his body rolling as he limped.

The man looked up as the boy approached, and a smile lit his dark face which had been a lighter brown before the sun darkened it.

"You did not have any luck," he said.

It was a statement, not a question, and though he spoke of the fishing, his eyes were on the leaves of tobacco in the boy's hand. But he did not mention them, because he had his pride, even now.

"Papa!" the boy exclaimed, panting from the exertion of the climb. "I was working just inside the reef —"

He broke off suddenly, because he saw that the man was not really paying attention. He followed the direction of his gaze, and he found himself staring at the rolled leaves in his own left hand. He glanced up at the man, and he saw the eagerness and longing on his face. He held out the tobacco.

"I have your leaves," he said.

The man nodded. He wanted to reach out quickly and take the beautiful tobacco, but he restrained himself. There was first the matter of a little ritual which had to be observed, and though he knew in his heart that all of it was just an elaborate pretense, it helped him retain the remnants of his dignity.

"So I see," he said softly, and then measuring his words and putting only a hint of inquiry into them: "They gave you credit at the store?"

The boy felt a stab of irritation. It was a foolish game which the man played, and he did not understand why they should have to play at it so often. He wanted to shout out at the man and tell him that he had stolen the tobacco, but the trusting confidence he saw in his dark eyes made him swallow his vexation.

"Yes," he said quickly. "They gave us credit."

"Thank you," the man said simply, and he stretched out without haste and took the tobacco.

The boy knew that the man was thanking him for more than the tobacco. It made him feel mean about having been angry a moment ago.

"The proprietor of the store has faith in you," he said, embellishing his tale to ease the pricking of his conscience. "He knows you are the greatest fisherman in these parts, and he is not afraid of allowing you credit until you are able to fish again."

"We will pay him when I am well again," the man said, speaking with an expressionless gravity which matched that of the boy.

Not if I can help it, the boy said under his breath.

"Can I get you some paper and the matches?" he asked.

The man held his hand up quickly, and then he laughed. "I took the liberty of being prepared," he said. "I have the paper and the matches with me."

He put the tobacco down carefully beside him and then stretched his right leg out so that he could get at his pocket. He reached inside it and took out a box of matches and a small fold of scuffed brown paper. He tore off a piece about three inches long and an inch and a quarter wide and then returned the paper to his pocket. He put the box of matches down and then he lifted the bit of paper to his mouth and gripped one corner of it between his lips.

He separated the outermost leaf from the loose roll of leaves and broke the rib two inches from the top and then tore the leaf straight across. He put the larger bit down on top of the other leaves and then after stripping the rib from the piece in his hand he shredded the leaf as finely as he could, tearing it straight up and down and then tearing the strips across.

He brushed all the little pieces of tobacco into the center of the palm of his left hand, and then he covered them with the palm of his right hand and kneaded them till they were stuck together. He sniffed at the tobacco and breathed out with a loud sigh of satisfaction. He took the piece of paper from between his lips and put it over the little mound of leaf on the palm of his hand.

He turned his wrists over with a quick flick and transferred the tobacco to the piece of wrinkled paper. He spread the tobacco and then rolled the paper round it. He gummed the edge down with a liberal application of spit and then after smoothing out the kinks stuck the cigarette between his lips.

He struck a match with a little flourish. He lifted it towards the cigarette, and then halted the flame when it was an inch away from the tip. He paused, deliberately prolonging the moment in order to heighten his forthcoming enjoyment. When he could stand the agony of it no longer he touched the flame to the tip of his cigarette. He drew on it hungrily, and his cheeks grew hollow with the force of the suction he applied. The loose paper on the end of the cigarette flamed momentarily and went out.

The man sucked the smoke deep down into his lungs and held it there. He drew on the cigarette again and inhaled a second time without releasing his breath. He felt the warmth of the smoke right inside his stomach. He turned the cigarette around in his hand and studied the freshly formed ashes with satisfaction. When he could hold his breath no longer he opened his mouth and exhaled. He blew the smoke out slowly, savoring to the full the ecstasy of that moment.

Good, he thought, though it is not as excellent and strong as a *carot* of tobacco in which the leaves are first smeared with molasses and coffee essence and then aged inside a fiber rope made from the fronds of a *coco maron*. He drew on his cigarette again and then looked up at the boy. It is better than nothing though, he thought.

"You were telling me about the reef," he said, coming back to it as if there had been no interruption at all.

The boy had been bursting with impatience all the while the man had been busy with his cigarette. He had wanted to tell him about the big fish and the shark, but he had been unwilling to start his recital because he knew the man's attention would be divided. He started forward eagerly when the man spoke, the words bubbling in his throat.

"I shot a small *bourjois* first, and after that a *papillon* and a *cacatois*," he said.

He saw the man's eyebrows lift in questioning astonishment. He felt a bit guilty, remembering that he had fed all the fish to the big *marsouin*. He waited for the man to comment, but he remained silent. His remorse vanished in a spurt of defensive indignation.

What if he had given the fish away? The big porpoise fish had saved his life. It had also become his friend, and it was the duty of a man to repay his debts, even to a friend. It was a simple code, and he had come to value it when he was still a young boy, because the life of a fisherman was hard enough even when they helped each other.

"I swam out across the channel after that and worked towards the reef," the boy went on. "I saw this fat porgy sitting in the water at four or five fathoms and I went down and put the harpoon into him. I brought him up to the surface, and I tell you my wind was already gone when I got there."

The man saw a sudden flicker in the boy's eyes. It came and passed so quickly that he did not have the chance to recognize it for what it was. He knew that there was some meaning to it though, and he sat forward suddenly, intent and very alert.

The boy drew a deep breath. Remembering the big hammerhead made him shiver deep inside. He hid his fear, because he did not want to show such a thing, but he could not hide it from himself. He breathed out and in again and then he began to speak. His voice rose, and the words tumbled from his mouth one over the other.

He told his father about the shark, and how it circled him endlesssly in the water and only came in to the attack the instant he went up to breathe. He spoke about his fear, because it was an easy thing to talk about when the mark of it was not there on your face, and he told the man about turning round and round in the water to keep the shark in sight till he became dizzy and exhausted. He told of that final moment when he faced the shark, with all of his strength gone and all his hope gone, and nothing in his hands but a small harpoon and in his mind the knowledge that he was going to die. But he did not die, because that was when the big fish that did not look quite like a porpoise came out of the deep blue water beyond the reef and drove the shark off with one blow from its pointed snout.

He told the man of the big fish coming up between his legs and of how he had ridden it under the water with his legs astride it and his back pressed up against the smooth dorsal fin.

He went on more slowly then, telling the man about how he had touched the *marsouin* and rubbed his fingers up and down over its white belly. He told about giving it the four fishes he had speared, and he explained it as a repayment of a debt. He did not mention the fact that in the beginning he had given the fishes to the porpoise because he had not wanted it to go away. He thought the man would think him foolish, and so he kept the knowledge of it to himself.

He came to the end of his story, and he told the man about the great loneliness he felt when he thought that the fish had deserted him. It had saved his life, and he had come to think of it as a friend, and he felt saddened because it had left him without any farewell. It was stupid to think like this about a fish, he said, but it was something which had grown in his heart and which he could not help.

He had been feeling angry and very sad, and it was then that he remembered how the fish had come about and swum back towards him when he whistled at it once before. He did it again, whistling as loud as he could. He did it more out of hope and frustration than any-thing else, and he did not really expect the fish to answer him, but then suddenly it came bursting from the water and it jumped like no other fish he had ever seen. It leaped clear out of the water and high into the air, and he saw the white of its belly as it passed high over the pirogue and crashed into the sea on the other side of the boat.

The boy paused to catch his breath. He stared blindly out to sea. Once again in his mind he saw the great leap of the big fish. He remembered that it had jumped in answer to his whistle, and the thought of it lit a fire in his heart. He turned suddenly to the man, his eyes shining with excitement. He was glad then that no one else had seen the dolphin leaping: the memory of it would belong to him alone.

"What manner of fish was it, Papa?" he asked. "It could not have been a *marsouin*, because it was unlike any porpoise I have seen."

"It is a fish of the same family," the man answered. "And though some people call it a dolphin, it is truly the same thing as a porpoise. I have seen them often before, but seldom in these waters, and certainly never have I seen them working in so close towards the shore."

He drew reflectively on his cigarette. The butt was so small that it burned his lips. He held it between the broken nails of his thumb and forefinger and sucked on it once again before tossing the mashed-up end away. He reached out suddenly and touched the boy.

"You must be more careful, Paul," he said. "If it was not for the lucky happening of that porpoise I do not think you would be here now."

He spoke quietly and very matter-of-factly. He was a fisherman, and he himself had survived many near-disasters, and he knew he would survive many more before he finally died. A man was always in danger when he clawed a living from the sea, and it was one of the things which had to be faced. He did not think he would die in a bed when his time came. Thinking about it he hoped that he would not.

It would be better to die out at sea, he thought, tied to a great fish and doing what he had to do, or caught in a storm and fighting it till he had no boat left to fight it with.

He did not think the boy would die in his bed either, because already he loved the sea too much.

But he is so young, he thought, and the vision of the shark put a cold emptiness in his belly.

"What I cannot understand," the man went on, "is how that shark came to cross the reef. They will come in at night, yes, but in the day they do not like the reef behind them. The only thing I can think is that he was very hungry, and he was attracted by the struggles of the fish you had speared."

"It is possible," the boy agreed.

"Did you not think to throw the fish to the shark and get away while he was busy with it?" the man asked roughly.

The boy shook his head and looked away from the accusation in the man's eyes. "I did not think of it," he said with humility.

"No matter," the man said, and he spoke gruffly to hide the remorse he felt for having shamed the boy. "There are times when there are too many things to be thought of all at once, and the little things are forgotten. It happens to all of us, and perhaps it would not have made any difference even if you had thrown the fish from your harpoon."

He did not believe it: he knew it would have made all the difference, but a little lie was a small price to pay for the feelings of his son.

"Do you think so, Papa?" the boy exclaimed, brightening at once.

"Yes, I think so," the man said. "Who can tell what a shark will do?"

"That is true," the boy said thoughtfully. "They are the most stupid and unpredictable of all the fishes in the sea. They are cowards too, which is what I have learned today."

He felt a moment of righteous superiority, but then he remembered the tiger shark he had seen off the Amirantes when he had gone there with his father on the schooner. It had been after a big shellback, and he watched in a panic of excitement and excruciating anxiety as the turtle made it to the shore just in front of the shark and began to waddle up the coral beach. He breathed out in relief, glad that the shark had been foiled, but the next second the enormous body of the tiger shark burst through the water and followed the turtle up the beach, writhing and twisting and clicking its jaws together as it strained to reach the shellback. He stared in horror as it thrashed after the slow-moving turtle, and then the snapping jaws closed on the left rear flipper of the giant shellback.

The shark turned away after that and floundered back into the sea, and the turtle limped on up the beach with red blood from the stump of its severed flipper staining a path along the white sand.

"But they are also the greatest and fiercest of all the killers in the sea," he admitted with awe. "Is that not so, Papa?"

The man nodded silently. He scratched at his thigh under the plaster and then leaned back on his arms, the palms of his hands down flat and his fingers spread wide. He stared out to sea pensively for a moment. He turned suddenly to the boy, thinking of the porpoise which had come so close that the boy had been able to touch it with his hands.

"It is a pity you did not have the harpoon with you," he said a little wistfully.

"But I cannot swim under the water with that heavy harpoon," the boy protested. "Besides, I need both my hands to load the speargun. Would I drop the harpoon to the bottom of the sea every time I had to reload?" He shook his head decisively and went on without waiting for an answer. "In any case, even with the big harpoon I do not think I would be any match for a big *requin*. From a pirogue, yes, but under the water, never, not even with a harpoon. My God, Papa, you should have seen his size from close, and his strange cold eyes that watch without letting you know what is in his mind."

"I was not thinking of the shark," the man said. "The meat of a dolphin is like the flesh of a porpoise. It is excellent to eat, and as you know, it is always in great demand. We could have sold the meat of such a great fish for much money. Certainly we would have made enough to pay all of the rent which we owe on this house."

The boy stared at the man in mute astonishment. For a second he could not believe that he had heard correctly. He went over the words once again in his mind, and when the meaning of them penetrated finally he gasped in horrified disbelief.

"But, Papa!" he exclaimed. "The big fish saved my life. How could I do such a thing to a friend?"

The man smiled indulgently. "I do not believe that the dolphin saved your life intentionally. Sharks have always been their enemies. I have never heard of a lone porpoise attacking a shark before, but I have seen schools of them kill a shark more than once, especially when they are afraid for their young."

The boy thought about it for a while, but then he shook his head. "No," he said stubbornly. "I do not think it was that way. The *marsouin* had no fight with the shark. It came only because it saw my danger, and it drove the shark away to save my life."

"What foolishness is this?" the man exclaimed testily. "Do you think that a man can be the friend of a fish?"

The boy stared back levelly. "I had never thought such a thing possible before," he said gravely. "I do not know whether a man can be the friend of a fish, but I do know that the big *marsouin* is *my* friend."

"You talk like a child," the man said, anger stirring within him. "No man can be the friend of a fish, and no fish can be the friend of a man."

"If there is no feeling between us, why did he take me for a ride on his back?" the boy cried angrily. "And why did he save my life and allow me to scratch the smooth white skin of his belly?"

"I do not know about the ride," the man answered

dryly. "Because I do not think like a fish. As for allowing you to scratch his belly, have you never seen a porpoise rubbing himself against the bow of a schooner, and then coming back to do it again and again because there was pleasure in it?"

The boy fell silent. He had seen it, and remembering what he had seen he began to doubt. For a moment he wondered whether he might not have misconstrued the behavior of the big fish and attached to it more significance than was justified. But then he remembered how it had answered him when he whistled, and all the uncertainty which had been sickening him went away and left him with his faith unshaken.

"That may be so," the boy said. "But how do you account for the fact that it answered my whistle?"

The man heard the triumph in his voice and he laughed. "I swear you are as jealous of this fish of yours as a young man with his first love. Are you sure it was not a *sirène* which allowed you to ride on her?"

The boy was puzzled for a few moments by the little leer on the man's face, but then he understood. He blushed, and he felt the blood clotting in his cheeks. He knew what the man was getting at.

"*Papa!*" he remonstrated. "It was a fish, and I asked you to explain the fact that it came to me when I whistled."

The man laughed again and then he became serious. "I do not think that it actually answered your whistle," he said. "I think its appearance at that moment was quite accidental, and since you were longing greatly to see it again, you came to think in your mind that it had come in answer to your call. Question what has happened with an open mind, my Paul, and ask yourself if there is not some truth in what I am telling you."

"But even if you are right," the boy persisted doggedly. "It does not explain why it *did* come."

"Who knows?" the man said, and he shrugged his shoulders eloquently. "They are playful fishes, and they will often jump clear over a boat just for the fun of it. It might have been playing, or it might even have come back in the hope that you would feed it once more."

The boy began to doubt again, and the man saw the look of it on his face. He has no girlfriend, he thought, and he has fallen in love with a fish. He felt a sudden rough compassion for the boy.

"I do not speak to discourage you, my Paul," he said gently. "But it is better to face the truth of a thing, even if it is unpleasant, because in the end it is less painful than hoping for the impossible."

The boy stared disconsolately at his father. He did not doubt the sincerity of his words, and he was beginning to accept the logic of them. A dark despair was blanketing his mind when he remembered the way the dolphin had come up in the water after its great leap over the boat and turned its head to look at him while it stood straight up on its tail. He straightened up suddenly, and his belief in the big fish and its friendship came back even more strongly. He wondered how he could ever have doubted it.

He felt like running straight down to the beach and whistling it up. But he was superstitious about his luck, and he did not want to put it to the test twice in the day. It was then that he decided never to search for the dolphin more than once in each day. It was not a conscious ruling he made at that moment. The directive was still only a vague idea at the back of his mind, but he was aware of it just the same. He glanced down at the man, and the expression on his face was almost pitying.

"You do not discourage me, Papa," he said quietly. "I have a strong feeling in me that I will see my friend again, and I have an even stronger feeling that he will come to me when I call."

Anger burned momentarily in the man's eyes, but then it died and was replaced by an amused contempt. "You are very foolish to consider that a dolphin can be your friend. You are a fisherman, and it is no different from any other fish which swims in the sea." He looked away suddenly, and his voice grew very gentle. "It is there to be caught, my son, and remember if you can that there is not another fisherman who would value the friendship of a dolphin more than its meat."

The boy gasped with shock. He stooped quickly and snatched up the speargun which he had put down on the bottom step. His mouth twisted in a snarl of hate and fury.

"I will put this harpoon through the first man who harms the big fish which saved my life," he said, and he spat the words out past his clenched teeth.

"Even me?" the man inquired mildly, amusement in his eyes.

"Papa!" the boy exclaimed, and the color drained from his cheeks, leaving them pale and white.

The man laughed and leaned forward. "I do not think it will ever come to that, because I am sure you will never see your fish again." He tapped the plaster on his thigh significantly. "Besides, I am not in a position to be of any danger to your fish."

"And if I do see it again?" the boy challenged him.

The man stared thoughtfully at the boy. He knew what the question implied, but what the boy was asking of him made a mockery of the right he had to think of himself as a fisherman, and he had fished the seas for a great number of years.

"You wish me to be honest, Paul?" he asked.

"Of course."

"Then I will be honest with you," the man said quietly. "With your permission, I would put my harpoon into the heart of your fish."

A look of pain and disbelief passed across the boy's face. "And if I did not give my permission?" he asked.

"Then I would do it without your permission," the man said bluntly. "If we did not need the money so badly, I would be tolerant, and I would humor you in this foolish whim of yours." He saw the effect of his words, and he knew that he had hurt the boy very badly. His own heart cried out for the pain of his son, but he did not show it as he tapped the plaster on his left leg again. "But as I have already said," he went on, "I think you are worrying yourself over nothing. In the first place you will never see the fish again, and in the second place I am the least able of anyone to harm your fish."

The boy felt a little of the tension leave him. "I will see him again, Papa," he said softly, and there was absolute conviction in his voice.

"And *if* you do," the man said, "will you act like a fisherman or will you behave like a fool?"

The boy was torn between his desire to please the man and the loyalty he felt he owed the big fish. He stared wildly at his father for a moment, and then a moan of anguish burst from between his tightly compressed lips.

"I don't know!" he cried in torment.

"Be honest with me, Paul, and be honest with yourself," the man said.

The boy stared at the man a while longer, and his

eyes were frantic. "I won't do it!" he shouted suddenly, desperately. "The fish is my friend."

The man bowed his head: it was an admission of defeat. He felt a great hurt, thinking that the life of the fish meant more to the boy than his own need for its flesh and the money it would fetch. He thought of the rent which he owed, and of the ultimatum he had been given, and his humiliation deepened. At the height of his dejection he remembered that the whole question of the fish was purely theoretical, since he was certain it would never make another appearance. The knowledge cheered him a little. He looked up, and he felt a sudden warmth for the boy, because he knew it had taken courage to answer as he had done.

"My head tells me that you are thinking like an idiot," the man said. "But I cannot find it in my heart to agree with what my head says."

The boy remained mistrustfully alert.

"Come, my Paul," the man went on, and he reached out and pressed the boy's leg with his calloused fingers. "Let us never again speak of your fish and the harpoon in the same breath."

"Truly, Papa?" the boy asked.

"Upon my honor," the man replied.

He saw the smile which lit the boy's face, and he felt a great happiness himself, because it was he who had put it there. He nursed the glow of warmth inside him, but then suddenly it all went flat. He felt guilty, because there was no true worth to the little sacrifice he had made, and he did not think he would have made such a promise if there was the remotest possibility of the fish returning.

"Tell me, Papa," the boy said abruptly. "Have you

spoken so only because you feel certain my fish will **not** come back?"

The man started, and for a moment he wondered whether his thoughts had shown so plainly on his face that the boy had been able to read them. He dismissed the idea before it could take root.

"Perhaps I have," he said. "I am not sure of it myself, but what concerns you is that I *have* said it, and what I have said will remain good —" he paused for emphasis, staring coldly at the boy — "even if your fish comes back."

If it did, the man thought suddenly, I would regret my rashness for a very long time. He consoled himself with the knowledge that with his leg as it was it would be virtually impossible for him to do anything about it, and he could never *order* the boy to do such a thing against his will.

The boy saw the sudden flicker of apprehension in the man's eyes. It lasted only a moment, and then it was replaced by a dull resignation. He looked away, because the sight of it made him uncomfortable. It was beyond his grasp, but he knew that it had something to do with his fish. He fidgeted for a while, running his thumb aimlessly up and down over the shaft of the harpoon. Toying with the speargun made him recall what had taken place earlier on in the morning before he went fishing.

He felt a sudden contraction in his stomach as he thought of Pierre Vigot, and of how he had almost been caught stealing his tobacco. He knew then that there was something important he had wanted to ask his father about, but he could not remember what it was.

THE boy woke late the next morning. It was still early, but it was late for a fisherman, because the sun had already been up for more than half an hour. He was glad then that the man had broken his leg, because more than anything else he hated rising early in the morning when it was dark and damp.

He was not really glad about the leg. What he enjoyed was the respite which the unfortunate accident had provided, but in his mind cause and effect were so closely associated that he was unable to differentiate between them. He knew he should not be glad that the man had broken his leg, and he was not, but no matter how hard he tried he could not help feeling pleased.

He began to feel ashamed of himself. He remembered the big fish then, and he forgot his shame in a sudden surge of excitement.

He swung his legs to the floor and sat up. He stretched and yawned and scratched sleepily at his matted hair, and then after that he yawned once again and stood up. He was naked. He glanced at the man in the other bed, and he saw that he was awake and watching him. He reached out and took his shorts from the foot of the bed where he had laid them before going to sleep. He flicked them up and down snappily, just in case a centipede had crawled into the folds during the night, and then he stepped into them. They were stiff with salt, and he began to wish that he had rinsed them in the stream yesterday instead of being so lazy. He sat down on the bed again and looked across at the man.

"You have been awake a long time?"

"Have you ever known me to sleep late?" the man countered.

"No," the boy replied. "But if I were you, I would make up for all the mornings I'd had to wake up early."

The man pushed himself up on one elbow. "What!" he exclaimed. "And forego the enjoyment of being able to lie here and watch you having to get up before me?" He lay back with a contented sigh and yawned with deliberate exaggeration.

The boy grinned and stood up quickly. "If you weren't an old man with a broken leg I would roll your bed like a pirogue in a cross sea and tip you right out."

"Even if I have a broken leg," the man said slyly. "It does seem to have its advantages."

"Mon Dieu!" the boy exclaimed, and he struck his forehead against the heel of his palm, in mock exasperation. "I walked right into that one with my eyes closed."

He stretched out and scooped the box of matches from the table, and then he turned and limped out of the room. He shot the bolt on the front door and swung it open. He picked up the large breadfruit lying against the wall and skipped down the front steps. He hefted it in his hands, rubbing his thumb against the congealed trickle of sticky white milk which had run from the broken stem and dried on the dark green skin.

He thought about the fruit as he walked round to the back of the house. He had taken it from one of the trees which grew a little higher up on the mountain. Technically it was the property of Jean Morel, since the tree from which it came grew on his land. But breadfruit were abundant, and no stealth had been called for, because no one would consider it stealing in any case. He began to wish that breadfruit were as highly prized as bananas, because then they would be more worthy of his attention. But he liked them, and so did his father, and he thought it was perhaps better after all that they were so easy to come by.

He made a fire in the ashes of the last one. He started it with dry grass and palm leaves, and then when it was going he broke and split the dry stem of a palm frond over his thigh and added the fibrous wood to the fire. When the first embers began to collect he laid the breadfruit on top of them and then put more fuel on the fire. He pocketed the box of matches and brushed his hands off against the seat of his pants. He walked off a little way and urinated against a tree and then started out for the stream. The bucket on the veranda was full, and he could have carried it outside and used some of the water to wash, but he preferred washing in the stream where the water was running and fresh.

He thought about the big fish as he walked towards the stream. He wondered where it had spent the night. He knew it did not breathe under the water like other fishes, and he began to wonder how it managed to sleep, if indeed it slept at all.

But it has to sleep and rest, he thought, like every other living creature.

What if it slept on the surface all night, naked and exposed? He could not imagine any other way in which it might sleep, and the thought alarmed and appalled him. There was many a fisherman who went out at night with a kerosene pressure lamp flaring in the bow of his pirogue. It was an easy way to spear mullet if the moon and the tide were right. What if one of them saw his fish sleeping on the surface of the sea?

He felt a moment of panic, but then he wondered if he was not being foolish. The big fish would probably have slept far out to sea in the deep water, and no fisherman ever went out past the reef at night. He would have felt much happier if he had known that a dolphin did not sleep continuously throughout the night. It slept two to three feet below the surface of the sea, and then only for short intervals, and every minute or so a few flicks of its dangling tail brought it up to breathe. He would have been even happier if he had known that it usually opened its eyes once or twice during the intervals between breathing when it was under the water, but of course he did not know this.

He reached the stream, still thinking about the fish. He pushed his way past the dew-wet ferns which grew in wild profusion on both banks and stepped into the icy water. He was so preoccupied with thoughts of his fish that the cold did not make him wince as it usually did.

He wondered what the fish was doing now, and whether it was very far away. He thought it might be hunting other fishes for its breakfast, but he had the feeling that it would be quite close. It had to be, because in a while he was going to go down to the sea and take the pirogue out and whistle till the fish came to him.

The boy bent down and scooped water up in his cupped hands. He sucked it into his mouth. He puffed his cheeks in and out, squelched the water around and then spat it out. He did it three or four times, and in between he rubbed the forefinger of his right hand briskly across his teeth and over his gums till the friction made his whole mouth tingle. When he had finished with his teeth he splashed water over his face. He washed the sleep grit out of the corners of his eyes, and after that he dampened his hair. He straightened up, running his fingers through it, and as he slicked his hair back he began to think of the girl he had spoken to in the morning yesterday.

When he got back to the house he walked round to the back and stopped in front of the smoldering fire. The outside of the breadfruit was charred and blackened, and it bore no resemblance to its original state. It looked almost repulsive, but he knew that beneath the blistered hide the white flesh would be cooking to a pale honey color. He inspected it carefully for a few moments, and then he bent forward over the fire and sniffed critically at the rising smoke. The hot fumes made his nose wrinkle, but through the pungency he detected the subtle nuances of odor. He sniffed cautiously at the smoke again, and then shook his head: there was a delicate richness in the smell of the smoke when the meat of the breadfruit was properly cooked, and it was not discernible now.

He squatted suddenly beside the fire, and then he reached out and rolled the breadfruit over. He jerked his hand back quickly, shaking it and sucking his breath in painfully, and then he stuck the tips of his blackened fingers into his mouth and licked away the sting of the heat. He thought of the steaming meat of the breadfruit which was cooking inside the burnt shell, and he wished that he had some coconut milk and sugar to sprinkle it with when it was ready to be eaten.

He thought about it for a while longer as he squatted on his heels and stared into the smoking fire, but then he shrugged abruptly and stood up. There was no money to buy sugar, and to get the milk from a coconut was a long and tedious process. First the flesh had to be grated on a *râpe,* and then after adding a little hot water the juices in the meat had to be squeezed out through a thin cloth. He had done it once or twice, when there had been nothing else to do, but he had not been enthusiastic about the task. It was work more suited to the wife of a fisherman, and it was foolishness for a man to waste his time on such trifles. He wished for a moment that the man had a wife, because then she would be his mother and she would grate a coconut and squeeze the milk for the man and for himself.

The boy turned away from the fire and limped into the house. He went into the room where they slept, and he saw that the man was up and sitting on the edge of his bed.

"Will you wash now, Papa?" he asked.

"Merci, mon Paul," the man said, and he leaned forward suddenly and pushed himself up off the bed, taking the weight of his body on his good leg.

The boy turned and walked out on to the veranda. He picked up the brimming bucket. He carried it down the steps, his body leaning slightly to the right and his left arm extended and lifted up straight from his shoulder to give him balance and counter the weight of the bucket. Some of the water slopped over the edge, and it splashed cold and wet against his leg and ran down across his foot. When he got to the bottom of the steps he set the bucket down on the ground beside them. He skimmed the water off the side of his leg with the edge of his hand and then straightened up.

"It is ready, Papa," he called.

He heard the man grunt an acknowledgment, and then he went round to the back of the house where the breadfruit was cooking in the coals of the fire. He rolled it out of the coals, using the sole of his left foot. It would be ready to eat now, and even if it was not, it did not matter. He could waste no more time in being overly particular: the big fish might already be getting impatient.

He picked up the curved stem of an old palm frond. He broke off a piece about a foot long. It was four inches wide and slightly concave along one surface, and he scooped the smoking breadfruit up and carried it round to the front of the house. He rolled it off onto the ground near the steps, on the opposite side to where the man was washing. He went into the house and returned a few moments later with a broad-bladed machete. He split the breadfruit right down the middle, and then when the man had finished rinsing his face and had seated himself on the steps he handed him one of the steaming halves, joggling it up and down in the palm of his hand to prevent any accumulation of heat. The man took the breadfruit gingerly and put it down on the step beside him.

The boy laid his own half on the bottom step. He sat down beside it and dug out some of the steaming meat with the point of the machete. He blew on it for a while, and then he picked it off with the fingers of his left hand and popped it into his mouth. He chewed, sucking air in through his mouth to cool the scalding hot flesh of the fruit. He cut and loosened the remainder of the meat in the shell and then offered the machete to his father.

The man laughed and shook his head. "I have a little more patience than you," he said. "The taste of the steel seems to get into the meat, and it has a sharp bitterness which does not please my tongue."

The boy shrugged and laid the machete on the steps.

"You always say that, but I have never found any difference myself, either way."

"You eat to fill your stomach," the man said. "I am old enough to disregard my stomach and think a little more of my palate."

The boy shrugged again and continued to eat. He scooped the soft meat of the breadfruit from the shell and then pushed it into his mouth, licking his fingers clean with each mouthful he took. When he had finished the flesh he picked up the roasted *coque*, and then with the machete he scraped and flaked the burned crust from the outside of the shell till it was smooth and brown. He broke off a piece of the shell and munched at it.

"Will you eat your *coque* this morning?" he asked.

"I would save it for later on," the man replied, "if I thought I might have a fine fat fish to eat with it. But of course, small fish for the coals of the fire are difficult to come by, since in this season there are many big fishes preying on them."

The boy had been about to agree, but there was something in the man's voice which made him pause. He stared curiously at his father, and he saw the suppressed smile which made the corners of his mouth turn down and link up with the two deep lines which ran from the side of each nostril and down a little way past his mouth. He grinned slyly.

"You are right," he said innocently. "It is just so at this time of the year, and I must remember all these things you tell me, because they will help me become a more able fisherman."

The boy scrambled out of the way as the man aimed a good hard kick at him with his right leg. He picked up the machete, and the piece of *coque*, and then he lifted the bucket up by the handle and carried it inside. He put it down against the wall and then walked into the room on the left-hand side of the veranda. He dropped the shell on the table and laid the machete down beside the coiled lines in the corner of the room.

He walked out and into the adjacent room. He went down on his hands and knees beside his bed and drew out his speargun and the mask. He stood up and limped out. He crossed the narrow veranda in three strides and went down the steps. He stared out to sea for a moment, and then he turned to face the man.

It is a good day to be in the sea, he thought, because the water is calm and the sun is shining. My big fish will like this weather.

"I will go now, Papa," the boy said.

The man chewed a little longer and then swallowed what was in his mouth. "I think you should take the harpoon, Paul."

"But, Papa!" the boy exclaimed, and shock bruised his face.

The man stiffened, but then he forced himself to relax, and it seemed that a veil came down over his dark eyes. It hid the anger and the sudden pain that had come into them.

"I was thinking of the sharks, my Paul," he said softly.

"Oh . . . oh, I thought — " The boy faltered, too ashamed to go on: the man had been concerned only with his safety, and he had thought otherwise.

"I know what you thought," the man said. "But it is only a little mistake which anyone could make quite easily."

The boy nodded eagerly, feeling relieved. "It is too heavy to swim with, though," he protested.

"You have told me that before," the man said. "And I agree with you. But what if you should be in the boat and a shark or another great fish swims in close? You will have nothing with which to kill it. Even the flesh of a shark has value, mon garçon," the man concluded.

Indignation crept into the guilt the boy was still feeling. The man had not been concerned about his safety, after all: he had been thinking about his missing an opportunity to kill a fish. He began to feel less ashamed about his thoughtless accusation.

"And once again," the man went on, "let me remind you not to swim out past the reef or swim too close to it. You may not be so fortunate the next time you face a shark in the water."

The boy bowed his head, and his shame came back to him. "I will take the harpoon," he said, and he started up the steps.

"It is also a good day for fishing," the man reminded him quietly.

The boy paused on the steps. He stared down at the man, and then he nodded humbly. "You are right again," he said.

He went into the house and he collected the big killing harpoon and the short twenty-fathom handline with the three hooks on it and the strip lead twisted around the line five feet above the first leader. He took the handline, mostly to please the man, but he felt bad about taking it, because he knew he had no intention of using it. He wanted to shoot with his speargun, and he wanted to ride on the back of his friend the big fish. He walked out of the house and down the steps.

"If I took the sail and the mast and worked out towards the banks I might get something worthwhile for my trouble," he told the man.

"And if a storm blows up and you are blown far out to where the land falls below the horizon?" the man asked. "Would you be able to find your way back across the sea with only the smell of the breeze and the stars to guide you?"

The boy shook his head wordlessly.

"Then enough has been said about the sail and the mast," the man said.

The boy nodded and turned away disconsolately. He wanted to sail the boat on his own far out to the distant fishing banks where the bonito and the big bluefin tuna ran in great schools. He wanted to fight the big fish alone and without any help, but the man had never permitted it.

"Your time will come, mon Paul," the man said, seeing the dejection on his face. "And when you are ready, I will know it, and even when you are ready, I can tell you that you will not like it the first time you find yourself alone and without the sight of any land."

"But give me the mast and the sail and I will not go far out," the boy pleaded.

He was thinking of sailing far out to sea, but not so far out that the land fell off below the horizon. In his mind he saw the big fish swimming beside him in the water as he sailed the pirogue across the sea, following him as a faithful dog will follow its master.

The man laughed. "With a good wind in your sail you will forget all about the land. In the great happiness of your freedom you will trap yourself, because when you do look back again, you will find that the land is no longer there."

"Hah!" the boy grunted. "You are afraid that I might catch more fish than you have ever been able to bring in from the banks."

123

The man grinned back at the boy, but then suddenly he grew thoughtful and his face became a little melancholy. "I wish that you could," he said.

"I wish that I could too," the boy replied quickly, and then he turned away. "I will go now," he said again. "I think the big fish will be waiting for me."

"I hope you see him," the man called out after the boy. "And I hope he brings the shark or another fish to you while you are in the boat."

He did not believe it, but he thought about the possibility just the same. You are becoming like a boy again, he told himself. Full of dreams.

"Perhaps I will be lucky like that," the boy called over his shoulder. "But in any case I will certainly bring you a fish to eat with your *coque.*"

The man raised a hand in acknowledgment, and the boy turned and went on down the hill. He half ran as he hurried down the side of the mountain. His feet slipped and skidded dangerously on the stones and loose earth. He did not slacken his pace, though, because there was no room in him for caution. He was bursting with an expectant excitement. It was like a living thing, but separate and distinct from himself and his own awareness. A little bit of it was his eagerness to be reunited with the sea, but most of it came from the anticipation he felt at the thought of seeing the big fish again. And all of it urged him on in reckless haste.

He came to the bottom of the hill, and then he crossed the road and ran limping through the grove of coconut trees. He reached the seawall, and he climbed up on top of it and jumped down onto the wet sand. He was breathing fast, in and out through his open mouth. He glanced to his right, and far away where the bay curved out to sea he saw a group of dark-skinned children playing in the water of a shallow tidal pool. They looked like black puppets against the shining whiteness of the sand, and intermittently he saw the gem-bright sparkle of the sun on splashing water.

He turned and looked to his left. He ran his gaze the length of the seawall, and over as much of the elevated terrace as he could see. His heart began to beat a little faster as he searched for the daughter of Jean Morel. But she was nowhere to be seen, and he felt a sharp disappointment.

He climbed back on top of the seawall, so that he could see a little further in along the terrace. He saw the house, and he waited a while, watching it, hoping that she might come out from inside or walk into view from around the back which was out of sight from where he stood.

If I see her, he told himself, I will walk along the wall and wave to her.

But she will laugh at me and call me limpleg, he thought.

He felt a sudden stab of humiliation. He jumped off the wall and walked down the beach. He thought of the sea, and the big fish in it. He felt a surge of throat-tightening gratitude, because in the water he was no different from any other man, and also because a great strong fish had saved his life and singled him out to be its friend, and he had never before heard of anyone being able to boast of such a thing. It was a vindication, and he began to feel less unhappy as he limped along. By the time he reached the edge of the sea he had forgotten all about the girl. He was thinking only about the fish, and it filled all of his mind.

He splashed into the water. He wondered whether he should whistle out straight away and try and call the fish to him. What if it did not hear him, or what if it was too far away to hear his whistle? The idea filled him with panic as he waded into the sea. The water rose past his knees and climbed slowly up his legs as he went out farther and farther, out towards where the pirogue was anchored on the edge of the deep channel.

And what if it is not even out there, he thought suddenly. What if it has gone away?

He halted suddenly, and his shock was so great that for a moment he was unable to breathe. The possibility lingered in his mind, and he felt an aching, hungering desolation. If the big fish had gone, it meant that it did not love him enough to stay.

For some reason he found himself thinking of the girl, and her mocking voice rang loudly in his ears. A deep resentment filled him. He begin to hate the girl, and the big fish, but especially the fish, because it was supposed to be his friend and it had no right to desert him.

The boy shook his head unconsciously in a vigorous denial. The big fish *was* his friend, and it could not have deserted him. The awful empty feeling in him went away. He walked on, but for the first time he felt the nibbling agony of doubt.

The water was up around his waist when he reached the pirogue. He put the mask and the speargun carefully into the boat, and then the handline and the big harpoon. He went aboard over the stern. He moved into the bow of the boat and hauled in the anchor, coiling the short rope down as it came in. He moved back into the stern and lifted the bamboo pole.

He used the pole to drive the boat till the water in the channel was too deep, and after that he trailed it astern and used it to steer the boat a little way. He steered toward a dark blue patch of water. It looked almost black from where he stood, against the rest of the turquoise-colored sea which encircled it. He knew it would be a good place to spear fish, among the coral and the brown bladder kelp and the red Irish moss. But the thought of going under the water did not excite him as it usually did: he was preoccupied with his hopes and doubts about the big dolphin.

He moved forward into the bow of the boat and squatted on his haunches. He untied the anchor rope from the cleat and lengthened it before making it fast again. He stood up after that and threw the anchor over the side. When the pirogue started to swing he moved aft and sat down astride the thwart.

He scanned the sea all around him, but the surface was empty. He went over it again, excitement and anxiety making his heart hammer wildly, but there was nothing to be seen. He began to nibble at his lower lip. He bit with his teeth and methodically peeled off little strips of skin, unaware that he was doing it, and not conscious of any discomfort.

He stopped chewing his lip abruptly. He sat up straight, flattening his lower lip the way he always did just before he whistled. He began to fill his lungs. They were three-quarters full when he breathed out suddenly and sagged limply. He wanted to whistle and call the big fish to him, but at the same time he was afraid to do it.

What if the *marsouin* did not answer him? He did not consciously consider the possibility, but the thought was there at the back of his mind and it made his heart skip a beat. He fought the consternation which began to swell inside him.

It would be stupid to whistle now, he told himself, before you have caught any fish to give your friend.

He seized on the idea at once. It was logical, and it excused his vacillation. He felt a sweeping sense of relief that the moment had been postponed.

It *was* inconsiderate of me, he thought, to think of calling my friend when I had nothing to offer him. I must shoot some fish for his breakfast first.

He stood up, and he tried to tell himself that he was quite correct in not whistling for the fish until he had some food for it, but he could not silence the little voice inside his head which told him mockingly that the big dolphin had probably caught and eaten its own breakfast by now.

He rinsed his mask over the side, drawing it swiftly through the water. He pulled it on and adjusted it, and then he picked up his speargun. He moved forward into the bow of the boat. He sat down on the gunwale and swung his legs over the side. He balanced there briefly, and then holding the mask pressed to his face he wriggled forward till he felt himself begin to slide. He straightened his back with a quick movement that flicked him forward, dropping feet first into the water with hardly a splash. He allowed himself to sink, and when the downward momentum of his plunge had died he kicked out lazily. He turned his head from side to side, searching the water as he went up, half hoping that he might see the big fish. He surfaced a few seconds later, without having seen it.

He took a fresh breath of air and loaded the speargun under water. As he pulled back on the rubbers he told himself it was foolish to expect that the fish should come swimming up to him, especially when he had not whistled. That was what he told himself, but even as he jackknifed and swam down through the sea towards the patch of weed and coral he searched the dark water at the outermost limits of his vision, still half hoping that the big fish would suddenly swim into view. He did not see it.

In the next fifteen minutes the boy speared three green-and-white *lascars* and a black *maconde*. He climbed back into the boat after harpooning the *maconde*, and then he peeled the mask off his face. He knocked the fish off the spear and then ran the harpoon back into the gun.

He blew his nose over the side, and after that he rinsed his face, scooping water up in the palm of his hand. He knuckled the wetness off his eyelashes and then began to search the surface of the sea. He turned right round on the thwart as he went over it, drawing his glance inward from the horizon. He did not see the big fish. He knew then that he would never see it unless he whistled, and he knew that the moment was now at hand. He felt excited and apprehensive.

He stood up slowly, and he looked around once more, even probing the depths where the angle of vision was not too oblique to prevent it. He saw nothing, and the empty feeling inside his stomach became more intense.

For a moment he stared blindly at the granite boulders which littered the far line of the shore where the shallow bay commenced its wide sweep into the land. He allowed his glance to linger, and the color of the sea and the white line of the shore and the green slope of the mountains which came down to meet it etched themselves on the motionless canvas of his mind. He blinked suddenly, and then he blinked again, and he woke from his trance. He studied it with the eye of a fisherman, and he wondered how it could have looked so different a moment before.

He drew a quick breath, and he lifted his tongue up towards the roof of his mouth and blasted the breath out between his tongue and his teeth and out past his lips in a shrieking, high-pitched whistle. He did it again, and then again and once again, sending the call out to his fish. He whistled four times in all, in a different direction each time, and when he had finished he was breathing heavily from the effort.

He stood frozen with suspense, the side of his leg braced against the forward edge of the thwart. His glance flickered hesitantly across the water, and he had to force himself to search it methodically. He stood there in the gently rocking pirogue, expecting at any moment to see the big fish come bursting from the water in answer to his summons.

But the seconds passed, and the fish did not come. The seconds lengthened into a minute, and then another and another, and still the dolphin did not appear. The bright hope in his eyes died, and it was replaced by a look of pained disbelief. He waited a little while longer, and when he did not see the fish he knew then that it definitely was not going to come. It had all been a dream.

He felt a moment of utter despair, and then he felt angry. Once again he began to hate the fish which had saved his life, and then he began to hate the girl, but he hated the fish even more than the girl. If it had not let him down he could have forgotten that the girl had called him limpleg.

In sudden fury he drew another deep breath and sent his call out across the mockingly empty sea. He whistled again and again, till his lips hurt and his chest ached, and then when he was too exhausted to whistle any more he sat down on the thwart and buried his face in his hands. For a long time he did not move.

He stirred after a while, and his hands slid from his face and dropped into his lap and he lifted his head with a great weariness inside him and stared out along the length of the deep channel.

My father was right, he told himself.

He thought he saw the place in the sea where he had first come face to face with the big fish. He threw a glance towards the land, checking its position in relation to the line of the shore. He looked back at the place in the water, and he knew it was there, or somewhere very near to there.

He stared at the bright reflections of the sun on the water in that one particular spot. He remembered the shark, and he remembered the big fish, and then after a while he could not see the place in the water any more because his eyes were filled with tears. His shoulders heaved once as the pain inside him tried to fight its way out.

He straightened up suddenly. A low growl burst from his mouth: it was an inarticulate exclamation, without any meaning, but it conveyed all of the anger and disgust he felt at his sentimentality.

"Mon Dieu!" he rebuked himself aloud. "Are you a fisherman or what?"

He dug the blindness out of his eyes with the heel of his hand. Once again he blew his nose over the side of the pirogue and rinsed his face, scooping the water up in his cupped palms. He stared out across the sea to the place in the deep channel where he had first seen the dolphin.

I will go there, he thought, even though my father is right.

He stood up, and he moved into the bows, and he felt a little flutter of hope and excitement stir in him as he hauled in the anchor. He told himself that he was being foolish, but the fever in him mounted.

Perhaps he has been waiting for me there, he thought. It is quite far, he went on in his mind, and it may be that my whistle did not reach him, especially if he is deep down under the water.

He tried to ignore the fact that the dolphin had to come up to breathe. He told himself indignantly that even if it had to surface now and again it was quite possible that it had come up while his back had been turned.

He fitted the oars and then pulled on them till the bow came round in the water and the length of the pirogue was lying parallel to the line of the shore. He began to row, but then in a sudden burst of anger he splashed the flat of the blades into the water before lifting his wrists and pulling. He did it for the first four strokes, and the blades struck with a sharp report each time. It was a childish exhibition of temper and frustration, but it helped to soften the pain and humiliation that was still in his heart. The tempo of his short, frenzied strokes slowed, and he began to pull with a long rhythmic sweep of the oars.

He leaned a little to his right and glanced over the side of the pirogue to see how fast he was going. He saw the water which rippled and bubbled as it slid past the hull and he heard the gurgling chinkle of the bubbles as they formed and broke and flowed into the wake which streamed smoothly astern. He gave a grunt of satisfaction.

You have always been good with the oars, he thought. He admitted it to himself with an innocent and unaffected modesty. He began to row a bit harder. He was leaning over the side to gauge the effects of his increased effort when the dolphin jumped.

It came out of the water twenty feet to his left on the seaward side, and it made its leap parallel with the boat. It cleared the water with a flurry of its tail, and as he watched it seemed to him that it rose straight up out of the water and into the air, and then when it was at the height of its leap he saw the big domed head turn towards him. The large brown eyes regarded him for a moment with the same friendly curiosity they had shown before, and then the whole great length of its body did a graceful half-roll in the air before the fish plummeted back into the sea.

The boy backed water and then quickly shipped his oars. He stood up in the rocking pirogue and stared at the spot where the dolphin had vanished. He peered into the depths all around it, tense and shivering with excitement. To his right he saw what looked like a dark shadow about two fathoms below the surface, and as he turned towards it the shadow flashed upward and the dolphin surfaced ten feet from the side of the pirogue and lay quietly in the water.

"You came back, *marsouin*," he crooned breathlessly. "You came back to me."

He wondered then whether it had come in response to his whistles, or whether it had answered the flat reports of the striking oar blades which made a noise something like a big mackerel or a mullet jumping in the water. He decided it must have been a combination of both, because he refused to believe that the big fish came to him only for the food he gave it.

He felt a sudden urge to be close to the dolphin, and to touch the big fish gently with his hands and with his body. But the big fish did not come closer.

He danced a little jig of impatience, never once thinking of the fish he had speared for the dolphin or remembering how he had called it to him before. All he could think of was that he had to touch the fish before it swam away once again. An idea came to him suddenly. It was so simple that he did not know why he had not thought of it before. If the fish would not come to him, he would have to go to the fish.

He turned in a flash and picked up the anchor. He lowered it over the bow and into the water without making a splash, so as not to frighten the fish, and only when the anchor was a full fathom below the surface did he let go of the rope. He turned back quickly to see whether the fish was still swimming close to the boat where it had been before.

But the fish had gone, and the sea was empty. His belly turned over and the nerves knotted. He searched the depths frantically. At last he saw the dark length of the dolphin's body arrowing down through the water after the sinking anchor. He was wondering whether it would come back when it abruptly lost interest in the stone and rolled over in a sharp turn. He saw the white flash of its belly, and then it came streaking back towards the surface. It came up a few feet from the side of the boat, and the turned-up mouth made it look as if it were smiling at him.

The boy snatched up his mask and pulled it over his face. He moved right into the bow of the pirogue. He crouched down, and holding onto the gunwale with both hands he swung his legs over the side and lowered himself into the water. He kept his eye on the dolphin, and when it did not swim away he lowered himself to the full extent of his arms. He hung like that for a moment, and then he let go and sank silently into the water.

Before he had time to orient himself he felt the broad body of the big fish come nudging up tentatively between his legs. It came from behind him, and the smooth wet-rubber kind of skin brushed coldly against the inside of his thighs. He felt a moment of fear as the big back of the fish pressed up into his crotch. It slid forward smoothly between his legs and then he felt the dorsal fin hard up against his buttocks and the awful slippery sliding movement between his legs came to a sudden end. He felt himself begin to move off through the water.

He leaned forward quickly, and he tightened the grip of his legs without making them too tight and wrapped his arms around the big neck of the dolphin. They gathered speed, and he lay low across its back, with his face low down and close up against the shut-off blowhole. His arms only reached halfway round the neck of the dolphin.

They were two fathoms below the surface, and moving at about six knots. It was slow for a dolphin, but it seemed to the boy that he had never traveled faster in his life. He glanced down, suddenly apprehensive, afraid that the fish might be taking him out to sea. But he saw from the slope of the seabed four fathoms below and the familiar coral outcrops that they were not moving seaward, but toward the shore.

He became conscious abruptly of the strangling pressure in his lungs. He knew he would have to let go of the fish and go up to breathe. He was beginning to relax the grip of his thighs and arms and getting ready to fall off the back of the fish when he felt the first minute alteration in the angle at which it was swimming. He paused uncertainly. The pressure of the dorsal fin against his back increased with a rude abruptness and then the whole length of the great fish canted suddenly and he realized with astonished delight that they were rising quickly towards the surface. He did not let go.

He heard the blowhole of the big fish open and snap shut, and he barely had the time to breathe out and take in one hasty breath before the splashing water closed noisily over his head once again. He became conscious instantly of the sudden startling silence which followed. It contrasted shockingly with the sound of rushing water that had been in his ears a moment before, and as they slipped smoothly and silently through the water he remembered the feel of the small wave which had slapped against his mouth and the faceplate of his mask in that instant before they submerged.

He wondered why the fish had gone up, and he wondered whether it was possible that it had known he needed air. He thought about it, and then he remembered how the fish had come up from *behind* him and carried him off in a forward direction, and he wondered if it was because it knew that he did not like to ride on it with his back facing forward as it had made him do yesterday, when he had become frightened and thrown himself off.

He began to think then that it might have surfaced just now because it remembered how he had been forced to abandon it yesterday when it stayed down swimming while he hung on with his lungs bursting.

Perhaps it is beginning to understand that I am not its brother, he thought.

He felt the need for air again, and he began to loose

the grip of his arms and legs on the neck and on the back of the dolphin. Once again he felt that minute alteration, and then as the big fish rose and bored smoothly through the blue water towards the surface his heart gave a silent shout of exultation.

It knows, his mind cried ecstatically, it knows that I am not its brother, and that is why it gives me air when it has no need itself. It must love me, he thought, even though I am a man.

As they went in towards the shore the boy lost the last of his apprehension. It seemed to him that the big fish truly understood. He experimented, relaxing his grip on it even when he had no need to breathe, and to his increasing awe and delight, every time he did it the great fish responded unfailingly and began its drive towards the shimmering milk-white film of the surface.

They passed the beginning of the deep channel, the dolphin and the boy who rode on its back. They were in four feet of shallow tidal water when the dolphin rolled suddenly onto its side. The boy fell off its back, and he floundered helplessly for a moment before gaining his feet. He peered anxiously into the water which had become clouded with sand, thinking that the dolphin had gone. A moment later his anxiety vanished as he felt the wash of the big body and the touch of the smooth wet-rubber skin against his legs. The head of the dolphin came up in the water beside him.

The boy moved against it. He slid his left arm under the lower jaw of its beak directly below the beetling forehead. He did it because he thought it might be tiring for the big fish to keep its head lifted out of the water, and then he put his right arm over its back. He held the dolphin like that, pressing gently up against its body, and then he began to rub the tips of his fingers up and down over its flank. In that moment he truly loved the big fish. He saw one big brown eye watching him, and in a burst of sudden tenderness and affection he bent and laid his cheek against the sleek head of the fish just in front of the blowhole.

"What a fine fish you are," he murmured softly, in the lilting musical patois of his Creole. "I wish that I could change into a fish like you, because then I could leave the land and swim by your side through all the great seas and all the great oceans."

I wish I could change into a fish and be your brother, he thought. He remembered his leg, and the idea filled him with a passionate and desperate longing.

He heard a sudden shrieking cry. It came from the direction of the beach, and it was shrill with half-hysterical excitement. He lifted his head quickly and glanced across his shoulder, irritated by the intrusion, and more, alarmed that the big fish might take fright and swim away. It trusted *him* now, but it was a wild thing, and he did not know how it would react in the presence of other people who were strangers.

He was concerned only for its safety and well-being, but at the same time he could not help the sudden stab of possessive jealousy he felt when he saw the girl. It was his fish, and he did not want to share it with anyone, nor did he want another to have its trust.

"Limpleg!" she screamed frantically, dancing up and down on the beach at the water's edge forty yards away. "Is it a shark you have caught?"

She had been throwing stones at a wagtail on the beach when she first noticed the big fish as it surfaced to breathe. She saw the masked face close against its back, and she stared in astonishment, unwilling to believe her eyes. She blinked them rapidly, convinced that they were playing tricks on her, but then when the fish surfaced again closer in towards the shore she knew that she had not been imagining things. She stared incredulously, and the first thought which crossed her mind was that a man was fighting with a shark. She turned and ran, and she ran down the steps which led to the beach, and before she reached the edge of the water she saw the man stand up dripping from the sea. She recognized him at once, and she knew then that it was not a man but a boy only a little older than herself who had been gripping tightly to the back of some great fish.

The boy pushed the mask up onto his forehead and then hastily resumed his gentle caressing of the dolphin's flank. He waved at her angrily, motioning her away. He did not want to shout out, because he was afraid he might frighten the fish.

"But what is it?" the girl shouted at him. "Is it a shark? Have you killed it?"

He saw that she had no intention of leaving. "Can't you see that it is not a shark?" he called back furiously, pitching his voice low and just loud enough to reach her.

Just then the undershot lower jaw of the dolphin bore down heavily on his left arm. The weight was tremendous, and it broke the cradling support of his arm. He saw the fish sink into the water, and then with a sudden flick of its tail it darted away. It moved fast, and with the water still heavily clouded he was unable to follow its flight. He thought the big fish had gone and left him. He turned towards the beach and the girl, and he felt a burning anger rise chokingly inside him. It was all her fault.

He lifted a clenched fist and shook it at her, and there was no mistaking the meaning of the gesture. He was on the point of starting an abusive tirade when the dolphin sliced silently through the water and knocked his legs out from under him. The boy let out a half-strangled gasp of fright as he crashed face first into the sea. He thought it was a shark, and as he thrashed around trying to regain his feet he searched the water frantically for it.

He got his legs under him and stood up, and that was when the big fish surfaced quietly about ten feet away. Its right eye stared at him unwinkingly. He thought he saw amusement in it, and the set smile of its mouth seemed to have a smugly mischievous tilt.

The nervous tension ran out of the boy. It drained him completely, and his relief was so great that his legs felt weak and trembly for a moment. After that he started laughing softly, partly out of reaction, but mostly because of the realization that the fish had only disappeared to play a trick on him. It added another dimension to the bond that was between them already. He did not have the words to define it, but the knowledge was in his mind, and he knew it was a good thing.

He smacked his hand down lightly into the water, whistling softly at the same time. He watched the big fish in a fever of anxiety. For a moment it did not move. He was disappointed, but a second later it flicked its tail lazily and came gliding up to him. He could not believe at first that it had happened but then he cried out joyously. The dolphin had *actually* answered to his call.

He tickled it just behind the left flipper, along the smooth white belly and the flank. The dolphin swam past him and then it began to circle him slowly in the water, making those strange creaking whistles he was getting to know so well.

He heard the girl calling out again, and he turned

patronizingly towards her. "What do you want?" he asked.

He squared his shoulders and straightened up. He felt smug and complacent, and he felt that it was more than justified. Was he not a boy who could call the very fishes of the sea to him? He felt elated and proud, but at the same time he did not forget that it was a wild creature, and that it came of its own free will. The realization humbled him a little.

"What *is* it, Limpleg?" the girl called.

"Can you not see?" he asked. "It is a *marsouin.*"

He heard her shrill exclamation of delight and surprise, and he straightened his shoulders again and stood up a little taller. He saw her come dancing a little way into the sea and then she paused, hesitant and wary.

"Is it dangerous?" she asked.

He smiled at her with a tolerant superiority. He shook his head, beginning to enjoy himself. "He does not harm *me,*" he said.

"But will it bite me?" she called anxiously.

"I do not think it will bite you while I am here," he replied airily.

She thought it over for a while and then came on cautiously. "I saw you riding on its back when you came in from the sea," she said incredulously. "Were you fighting with it?"

"I *was* riding on his back," he called back. "And not fighting with him."

"But how can a great fish allow you to ride on its back?"

"Because he is my friend," the boy replied smugly, and then he became conscious for the first time that he had used the word *he* instead of *it* when speaking about the fish. He was startled for a moment, but then he came to accept it as quite natural and even more fitting.

He saw with alarm that she had approached already to within fifteen yards. He held up his hand. "Do not come closer," he warned her peremptorily.

She froze, instantly apprehensive. "But why?" she asked.

"Because he's my fish!" he cried suddenly, harshly.

For a second he was startled and dismayed at the words which had burst from him so involuntarily. He saw the look of hurt on her face, and he wished he had not spoken. He looked away from her pain, and he told himself he didn't care. It *was* his fish, after all.

"Oh Limpleg," she said softly, with an understanding and compassion that, coming from her, shocked him and made him feel even more mean. "I know it's your fish."

She spoke to him, not in the classical French she had been using before, but in the slurred, bastard French of his Creole patois. It was her first move towards identification with him and the world in which he lived. The significance did not escape him, and he felt worse than ever.

"Then if you know it is my fish what do you want with it?" he asked sullenly.

"Oh Limpleg!" she rebuked him quietly. "I only want to see it from close." She also wanted to touch it and ride on its back as the boy had done, but she knew it was neither the time nor the place to mention these matters.

"My name is not Limpleg!" he cried angrily, and to soothe himself he reached out and caressed the fish as it swam by him in the water. He looked up at her suddenly, and when he spoke again there was a simple dignity in his voice. "My name is Paul Mistral," he said.

"Won't you let me come a little bit closer and see your fish, Paul?" she asked.

"Well —" He eyed her suspiciously, warily, but the look on her face made him weaken. "All right," he said grudgingly, "you can come."

She started forward eagerly, and as she waded in deeper the water swirled up around her waist and lifted her dress. It floated in a circle, and as she moved he caught glimpses of the curved white sweetness of her thighs. He looked up quickly, almost ashamed of himself, and his attention was caught by the swelling roundness of her breasts which showed quite clearly underneath her dress where the water had splashed and made it wet. His eyes shied off nervously. He had never seen so much of a girl before, and the shape and promise of her body which was contoured so very differently from his own excited and frightened him at the same time. He took refuge in belligerence.

"Don't splash and make so much noise," he whispered harshly. "You might frighten him away."

She nodded breathlessly and came on. Her eyes were fixed on the dolphin which was swimming lazily in the water now, circling in front of the boy and watching her approach. She was two yards from his side when the big fish turned suddenly on the outward sweep of its circle and sped in towards her with its belly scraping up clouds of sand.

She screamed in terror. She felt the body of the dolphin sliding past her legs and the next instant a flick of the powerful tail knocked her feet right out from under her. She came up spluttering and gasping, and she flung herself against the boy and held to him frantically, using his body as a shield between herself and the big fish which was now circling placidly fifteen feet away on the other side of the boy. She stared at it in horror, choking and sobbing.

"It tried to bite me," she whimpered.

Instinctively he put his arms round her. "No, no!" he said quickly, defending his noble fish. "He was only playing. Did you not see him doing the same thing to me a little while ago?"

"When you dived into the water?" she asked.

The boy laughed. He felt the girl stir within his arms, and it accentuated the contact between them. He felt a quickening in his body, and it was a pleasurable sensation. He began to feel embarrassed that he was holding her, but neither did he want to let go.

"Yes, when I dived into the water," he said, laughing about it again. "Only I did not dive. It was Marsouin who knocked my feet out from under me just as he did it to you." For the first time he thought of the word *marsouin* as being the *name* of the dolphin: listening to the echo of it in his mind he decided it was a fine name for his great fish.

"Oh!" the girl exclaimed. "Is that what happened?"

"Oui."

"I thought you were diving after it to catch it," the girl said.

The boy shook his head. He felt her body moving restlessly against him and then suddenly she twisted out of his arms and turned towards the fish.

"Why do you call it *he* all the time?" she asked. "It is a fish, not a person."

"It is a boy fish," he said profoundly.

"Oh —" She stared at him doubtfully. "Are you sure?"

"I am sure."

She was silent for a while. "Could I touch the fish as you did?" she asked suddenly.

The boy became instantly wary. It showed plainly on his face, and the girl saw it. She reached out quickly and touched his arm.

"Please, Paul," she pleaded with him.

He began to weaken. He hesitated a moment, not at all happy about the idea. He glanced at the circling dolphin, and then back at her. The look in her eyes was becoming increasingly difficult to resist.

He wanted to let her touch the fish, but he was dreadfully afraid that if he allowed her to play with it the big fish might develop a preference for her. The girl saw his indecision, and with the wisdom of a woman she understood it for what it was.

"I'll only touch him a little, Paul," she said.

"All right," the boy said, suddenly making up his mind. "Go and see if you can touch him then."

It would be a true testing of the love that was between him and the fish, he thought, and by refusing to permit the trial he himself was admitting to a lack of faith and trust. It had to be, he knew, and if he did not allow it he would wonder about it and be fearful every day of his life.

We will see, he thought, we will see.

"How will I touch him?" the girl asked.

The boy shrugged. "Just touch him."

"But he is far out of my reach," she protested.

"Walk over to where he is swimming," the boy said unhelpfully.

"He might knock me into the water again," the girl said. "And this time he might bite me."

The boy grunted in exasperation and disgust.

145

"Would you like me to call him to you?" he asked sarcastically.

The girl was too preoccupied to notice it. "Can you call him?" she asked, and her eyes rounded on him in wonder and awe.

He was not prepared for it. "I think —" He saw her lip curl in derision, and his stammering uncertainty was replaced by anger and resentment. He remembered that he *had* called the big fish to him a little while ago, and he wondered if he could do it again. He had to try though. He hoped he could do it, because it would be a terrible thing to fail now, in front of her.

"Yes," he said firmly. "I can call him."

"Go on, then," she said, and her voice was tinged with amusement.

The boy drew a deep breath. He felt the quivering inside him die. He whistled softly, the trilling note he had used right from the beginning, and then he slapped the palm of his hand lightly against the water. Spraying drops splashed into his eyes, but he did not blink or flinch. He watched the dolphin with a fixed stare, and his heart raced painfully.

Come on, fish, he said inside his mind. Come on, Marsouin, my beautiful fish.

Before he had finished his invocation the dolphin was turning in the water. It turned head on to him and then a single flick of the tail sent its body gliding effortlessly through the water straight towards him.

The boy felt the muscles of his stomach begin to unknot. He glanced surreptitiously at the girl, bursting with conceit. She was staring at him in astonishment, and the look in her eyes was something very close to reverence. He glanced away hastily, pretending he hadn't seen it. He reached out with a studied nonchalance and scratched the flank of the dolphin as it swam up close against him. It remained motionless while he caressed it, and only its flippers moved lazily as it held its balance in the water. The boy felt very proud of the big fish then, and his heart was warm because of what it had done for him.

"You had better touch him now," he said. "He will not stay forever."

The girl stretched out eagerly, and the moment she laid her hand on the back of the dolphin it shied away from her sharply. Its tail flicked up and down once and it shot off under the water and came up thirty feet away.

"Oh no!" she cried, and her face crumpled with disappointment. She stared after the dolphin. She watched it circling and cavorting in the water and then she turned suddenly to the boy. "Why did it not allow me to touch it?" she asked.

"But you did touch him," he said calmly.

He felt a fierce exultation sweep through him, but he kept it hidden and did not let it show. In that moment he loved the big fish more than he had ever loved it before. It had answered his call without hesitation, and more, it had rejected the advances of the girl. That, as far as he was concerned, was positive proof that its affection and loyalty were reserved for no one but himself.

He began to wonder why the big fish *had* darted away, and then he wondered whether some sixth sense had not perhaps made it aware of the test to which it was being subjected. He thought it quite possible, and since he could think of no other explanation which might account for its behavior, he convinced himself finally that it was so.

"But not the way you did," the girl complained. "He swam off the moment I touched him."

The boy began to feel a little sorry for her. "Perhaps it is because you are strange to him," he said, trying to console her, but he knew in his rejoicing heart that there was another reason for it.

"Do you think," the girl said hesitantly, "do you think if you called him again I might be able to touch him?" Unconsciously she had begun to emulate the boy, speaking of the dolphin as a person and not as a fish.

"I do not think he will allow it," the boy said gravely.

"How can you know?" the girl cried, and there was anger and irritation in her voice.

"I know my fish," the boy replied simply. His eyes looked inward on the secrets in his mind, and his mouth curved softly in an enigmatic smile.

The girl did not understand it: she thought he was mocking her, and she became infuriated. "I will call your fish myself!" she cried angrily.

She whistled, and then she slapped the palm of her hand down on the water as she had seen the boy do it. The dolphin surfaced instantly. It stared at her for a moment, and she thought she saw a look of indignant reproach in the large brown eyes just before it sank out of sight and swam off again. She bowed her head, and her face burned red with humiliation.

"I will call him for you," the boy said gently. "But I do not think he will let you touch him."

He called the fish to his side once more, but somehow its obedient response did not thrill him as it had done the last time. He saw the girl reach out, but before she had even touched the dolphin it veered off abruptly. It circled round her and came up on the other side of him against his leg. He saw the look of despair and resignation on her face.

"I am sorry," he said, and though he felt truly sorry for her he could not help the feeling of complacence that was also in his breast.

"Do not feel sorry for me," she said with haughty indifference.

The boy's eyes took on a green tinge. "Then I will not," he said stiffly.

She realized instantly that she had gone too far. She glanced covetously at the big dolphin wallowing in the water beside him and then she smiled brightly.

"In any case," she said, changing the subject quickly, "I think your fish is a girl."

"Why do you think that?"

"It is a fact that one woman is always jealous of another when there is a man to be thought about."

The boy shook his head and smiled at her with an amused tolerance. "No," he said with quiet conviction. "He is a boy fish."

"How do you know?" she retorted.

"I just know," he answered, and the calm assertion in his voice defeated her for a moment.

"But wouldn't you prefer it to be a girl?" she persisted.

"No," he said, thinking it over carefully. "Then it could not be — " He caught himself abruptly. He had been about to say that it could not be his brother. But such a thing was not to be spoken about: it was, with all it implied, a closely guarded secret of his mind.

He glanced at her furtively. She was waiting patiently for him to go on, and she appeared not to have noticed his confusion. With his secret safe, his distress went away.

"Then it would not be strong enough to carry me on its back," he improvised quickly. "Girls are never as strong as boys."

"They are stronger in some ways," she countered obliquely. She tossed her head, and her long wet hair swung back across her shoulders. "In any case," she went on, "I think that a big girl fish could carry you just as well as any boy fish."

"Never!" he stated, scornful and indignant. "I told you before, girls are not as strong as boys."

He looked her up and down contemptuously. Her small thrusting breasts arrested his attention. His eyes started, and the patronizing contempt in them turned to painful confusion. He looked away quickly.

The girl did not miss it. She laughed triumphantly. "I think you say your fish is a boy only because you are afraid of girls," she said.

He blushed with confusion. He shook his head in frantic denial, but he could not bring himself to meet her eyes.

"You are!" she crowed, mockingly, hurtfully. "Aren't you, Paul?"

He snatched the mask down over his burning face and adjusted it hastily. He wanted to get away from her as soon as he could, from the knowing mockery in her eyes. He began to wade through the water, moving straight out to sea. He did not think he had ever felt so humiliated or inadequate in all his life.

He looked for the big fish, and he saw that it was five yards away. Its head was halfway out of the water, and it was watching him attentively. He was on the point of whistling to it and plunging into the sea for the long swim out to the pirogue when another idea occurred to him. It was truly audacious, and he felt a thrill of excitement shoot through him. If he did not bring it off, he would never be able to face her again. But if he was successful, his departure would be so spectacular it would compensate him for all the pain and humiliation he had suffered at her hands.

He paused for a moment, alarmed by the magnitude of the decision and the extent of his aspirations. Just then the girl called out anxiously.

"Where are you going, Paul?" she cried.

I will show her, he thought, suddenly defiant, I will show her where I am going. I will ride out to the pirogue on my fish.

He whistled at the dolphin. It swam up beside him, and when he realized that it had answered even though he had not slapped his hand down into the water he felt an incredulous delight. His confidence soared. He turned so that he was facing it, positioning himself opposite its left flipper. He reached an arm over its back, and he began to tickle it on the flank. He bent towards it, crouching a little in the water.

"You are a fine fish," he crooned softly. "You are the most beautiful fish in all the sea, and of all the fishes you are the strongest and the noblest. Do you hear me, Marsouin? The strongest and the noblest . . . the finest and the most beautiful."

In a state of suspense and agitation the boy began to lift his right leg up so that he could get it across the back of the dolphin. He did not rush the movement, and he continued to caress the dolphin and whisper to it. He lifted his leg higher, and then a bit higher, and then when it was high enough he began to slide it across the back of the dolphin.

His heart began to pound like a jackhammer. He slid his right leg right over the back of the fish, but he let the water take the weight of it. He paused for an instant, balancing on his left leg, his right leg poised over the back of the dolphin. The next second, he knew, was going to be the most difficult and crucial moment of all. If the big fish swam off as he was settling onto its back he would slip and fall ignominiously into the water. The thought appalled him, and for a second he wished he had never thought of trying to mount the dolphin. But he knew it was too late now for wishes.

He brought the weight of his right leg down on the back of the dolphin, and he felt the big fish sink a little lower into the water.

"Wait for me, Marsouin," he whispered.

Now, he told himself, and he stood up on the toes of his left foot and slid across the back of the dolphin. He felt the big fish go right down in the water, and he fell forward across its back and wrapped his arms around its neck.

For one terrible moment nothing happened, and in his mind he began to imagine all the dreadful and humiliating things which could happen. What if the big fish refused to move, or what if it threw him off its back? And supposing it swam farther in towards the shore instead of taking him out to the pirogue? It had, after all, made straight for the shallow water when it lifted him onto its back in the deep channel, and he certainly did not have any way of steering it.

My God, he thought, I did not think of that. A fish cannot be steered like a pirogue, even if it is my brother.

He was beginning to make himself feel quite sick when the dolphin moved off. It headed straight out to sea, and through the intoxicating relief which numbed his senses he heard the girl's frantic cry.

"Paul!" she screamed. "Wait, Paul!"

His head and shoulders were above the water. He twisted round to look at her, still crouched down low across the back of the dolphin. He felt the increasing resistance of the water against his body, and the sea which streamed past him began to hiss more loudly. It was a song he had heard ever since he could remember, and it was the same song that the sea sang when a pirogue moved swiftly across its surface.

He felt the bulge and contraction of the great tail muscles of the dolphin as a liquid shiver which ran up and down its back and flanks. The fluttering tempo grew faster and faster, and the rushing song of the sea filled his ears. He knew the big fish had never carried him so swiftly through the water before.

He saw the girl splashing after him desperately. He wondered if she thought she could catch up with him. It was comical and futile. No one could ever hope to match him in the water, not when he was riding on the back of his mighty fish. A sudden laughing cry burst from his mouth, but it was not aimed at her in mockery. It was a simple and spontaneous expression of all the great happiness that was in his heart.

What a fish, he thought to himself, what a great fish I have.

"Wait for me, Paul!" the girl screamed out again.

The boy shook his head furiously. Even if he had wanted to wait for her, it was not possible. There was no way to stop a big fish when once he had started his run, not unless you had him on a strong line with a sharp hook driven deep and fast into the flesh and bone of his throat. He certainly was not going to admit such a thing to her.

"Paul!" the girl called again. "Let me come with you tomorrow then."

He was about to shout a reply when the dolphin went down into the deepening water. It went down to six feet and held that level, and the boy on its back turned and faced forward, still choking on the water he had swallowed. He eased the pressure of his arms and legs, and when the dolphin surfaced he cleared his lungs and breathed in quickly. It dived again instantly, and behind the mask the boy's face cracked in a delighted grin.

They crossed into the deep channel, still heading straight out to sea. The boy began to think of the girl. It would be a fine thing if she could sit in front of him on the back of his big fish, where he could hold her with his arms and have all those strange and fascinating curves and swellings close to him. It was a pleasant thought, but he did not know whether the fish would permit such a thing, and he doubted whether even a fish as strong as his own great fish could carry such a burden through the water.

Sixty yards out in the deep channel the dolphin once again responded to the slackening of his grip. He blew the air out from his lungs an instant before they surfaced, and when his head broke through the water he was ready to breathe in and he lost no time in first having to exhale. He managed to take two breaths before the dolphin slipped below the surface again, and he saw at the same time that the heading of their course would take him out to sea fifty yards to the left of the pirogue. He was not perturbed about the fish taking him out to sea, because he knew that he could always abandon it if he had to. But he had been hoping that the dolphin would take him right up to the pirogue, and though he knew it was foolish to expect even an intelligent fish like his to be able to read his mind, he felt a little disappointed, because he had been expecting it. He began to wonder if there was any way in which he could communicate with his friend and get it to understand his thoughts and wishes.

He tried increasing the pressure on his right knee, but it made no difference. He tried it with his left knee, but that too made no difference. The big fish swam on tirelessly. The bed of the sea and the world below him unreeled like an endless carpet that was marked with beautiful colors, and he saw the shapes of the many fishes which moved in and out among the different colors of the carpet.

He began to think of the way a man could sail a pirogue and steer it with one oar trailing in the water over the stern. He did not think of it as a rudder, because he had no knowledge of the word and its application. To him it was a steering oar, and it was used on either the left or the right-hand side of the boat, depending on the direction in which the boat was being sailed, and when you wanted to change to the other tack you pulled hard on the oar so that it was sticking out at right angles to the side of the boat and then when her head swung up into the wind and she fell away from it on the other tack the steering oar had to be used on the other side of the boat.

It passed through his mind in a flash. In an instant of sudden hope and inspiration he settled himself more firmly on the back of the fish. He let go his right hand and pushed his arm out in the water with the palm of his hand facing in the direction they were moving and his fingers pressed tight together so that it offered the maximum amount of resistance.

The dolphin lurched in the water and swung a little to the right. He felt the great drag on his arm, and his body slewed sideways a little. He flattened himself as much as he could and gripped more tightly with his legs. His balance steadied, and he glanced down at the seabed. They were moving over it at a slightly oblique angle to the direction in which they had been traveling before. The boy felt a sudden surge of triumph.

It is working, he thought exultantly, it is working.

Just then the big fish swung back to the left and resumed the course along which it had been swimming before. He almost fell off, and he grabbed for its neck quickly with the arm he had been using as a steering oar. He felt a deep disappointment, and he got angry with himself for having been such an idiot as to imagine prematurely that he had succeeded in making a fish swim where he wanted it to swim in the water. It was as bad as selling fish before they had been caught. He was on the point of abandoning the whole idea when it occurred to him that it *had* worked after a fashion.

I will try it once more, he thought, in defiance of his common sense.

He pushed his right arm out in the water once more, determined but not very hopeful. He felt the big fish lurch again and swing off course. He waited tensely, expecting it to change its heading at any moment. He waited a little longer, but still the fish did not turn. He glanced down and checked his direction with the seabed, and to his absolute delight and astonishment he saw that the big fish was swimming under the water in a sweeping arc.

It must understand me, the boy thought in awe, and it learns even faster than some men.

He withdrew the drag of his arm, expecting the

dolphin to turn and swim back in the direction it had been taking before he turned it. But the big fish merely halted its swing and settled down to swim steadily on its new course. He felt a moment of alarm, and with his mind frozen on a preconcieved idea he was unable to think for a few seconds. But then he remembered the steering oar, and he realized that when once the heading of a pirogue had been altered with the oar it did not return of its own accord to its previous course.

He wanted to shout out and laugh in his happiness, but he was under the water and he could not do it. He stuck his left arm out instead, and as the big fish veered to the left he felt a drunken ecstasy which made his senses reel.

He went up for a breath of air, searching for the pirogue. He did not see it. He glanced back across his shoulder quickly. It was already fifty yards behind him. He felt a heart-squeezing rush of panic, but then he remembered that he could turn the fish in the water.

The dolphin dived again, and he saw that he was almost on the edge of the reef. He pushed his right arm out, and he held it there against the fierce drag of the water. The big fish began to turn in a wide circle, and when it had turned through a hundred and eighty degrees and was swimming straight back towards the shore he withdrew his arm and took the dolphin up to the surface.

He spotted the pirogue as he snatched a breath. It was quite a way over to his right. He put his arm out in the water as he went under and he turned the big fish a little more. When he thought he had turned it enough he pulled his right arm in again and took the dolphin up to the surface.

The pirogue was twenty yards in front of him, and he

saw that they were heading straight for it. He took a quick breath just before the fish dived. Almost immediately he relaxed the grip of his arms and legs again. The dolphin streaked back towards the surface. He did not instantly renew the pressure of his grip as he had always done before. The dolphin surfaced, and to his delight it did not dive again but continued towards the pirogue, swimming half-submerged along the surface of the sea.

I did not think he would do that, the boy thought with wonder.

Five yards from the pirogue he allowed himself to slip easily off the back of the dolphin. It turned immediately in the water and came up beside him. He thought he saw a look of interrogation in the large brown eyes before it slipped below the surface and came up between his legs from behind.

"Non, non, Marsouin!" the boy cried softly, laughingly.

He slipped off its back again and struck out quickly for the pirogue. He reached the stern and hauled himself aboard. He pushed the mask up on his face and turned to the dolphin that was swimming slowly up and down in the water beside the boat.

He fed the big fish. He fed it all of the four fishes he had speared, without ever remembering that he had promised to take his father a fat fish to eat with his breadfruit *coque*.

When he had no more fish to give it the dolphin swam off a little way. It leaped high out of the water beside the pirogue and he saw its head turn as it looked down into the boat. He wondered if it was looking to see if there were any more fish.

It crashed back into the water, and it entered the sea so close to the pirogue that the boat rocked violently and he felt the sting of splashing spray across his chest and face.

It vanished after that, and though he waited a while he did not see it again. He whistled for it, and he called out loudly, but it did not reappear. He remembered the oars, and how earlier it had come soon after he had smacked them loudly into the water. He bent and lifted one of the oars, and he whacked it down flat-bladed as hard as he could, straight down into the water. He did it again and again. In a while he became too tired to lift the oar, but still the big fish did not show itself.

He laid the oar down in the boat. He began to wish that he had played with his friend a little longer before giving it the fish, because he was beginning to think that it was the way of the dolphin to leave him and go about its own business after he had fed it. He did not feel any resentment as he had done before, nor did he think that the fish was being ungrateful to leave him so soon after it had been fed. He had played with it and ridden on its back, and he had fed it, not as a reward, but simply because he loved it. He was certain the fish had not allowed him to ride on its back only because it was thinking of the food it was going to get from him. The big fish loved him too, but he had to remember that it had many other things to attend to in the sea.

He wondered how the fish was going to spend the rest of the day. It was a big fish, and it would need to catch and eat many more fish to keep the great strength full in its body. He began to wish that he had speared more fish for his friend, because four little fishes would certainly not provide much strength for the great muscles of its tail which drove the mighty flukes tirelessly up and down through the water. He remembered the feel of the great pulsing muscles against his thighs and against his buttocks, and the shivery vibrations of power as they stretched and pulled along the entire length of the fish's back.

My God, he thought, but how they can work.

He thought again regretfully about the four little fishes he had given the dolphin. He felt a stab of remorse, and then he remembered suddenly that he had no fish for his father to eat with his *coque*.

Mon Dieu, he thought again, and he started guiltily.

He snatched up the speargun and rammed the mask down over his face. He moved up into the bow and then jumped into the sea, holding the mask tightly. In half an hour he speared three parrot wrasse and a large mottled grouper. He was very pleased about the *vieille babone*. It was about six pounds, and all Chinamen seemed to consider its flesh a delicacy.

He wondered how much the old robber at the store would give him for it. Perhaps three rupees, he thought, knocking the grouper off the harpoon and into the bottom of the boat. Thinking about it he began to shake his head.

I do not think he will give me more than two rupees, he thought, and if he is not in a good mood it might quite easily be as little as one-seventy-five or one-fifty. He decided that he would take nothing less than one-fifty for it.

But what if the Chinaman offered him only one rupee?

He bridled at the idea, but calmed down quickly. It would still be enough to buy some real tobacco for his father and a little coffee and sugar. But then thinking about the rupee he began to get angry again. He shook his head stubbornly. It would be better to eat it than give it away.

He hauled in the anchor, coiling the rope down as it came in dripping wet and cold to his touch, and he continued with his dream about the money he was going to get for the grouper from the Chinaman at the store. If he did get one-fifty for it he could buy extra sugar and coffee and there would still be enough left over after buying them to get himself a handful of those large sticky sweets that were so stuck together they had to be dug out of the glass jar with a long knife.

He pressed his tongue up against his palate, and he could almost remember what it was like to suck the honeyed sweets. The memory of them was so real and vivid that he felt saliva collecting in his mouth. He smacked his tongue up and down once or twice, and through the bitter saltiness he imagined he tasted the sweetness of the big sugary balls.

He licked his lips, and that was when he remembered they had no rice, and that it would be better to spend the last of the money on something which both the man and himself could enjoy.

He heaved the anchor inboard, and as he lowered it into the boat he swore to himself about the rice. But there was no heat in the words under his breath, because it was a way of life and living which he understood, and he had long ago become resigned to it, even though it was difficult at times.

He rowed the pirogue shoreward till the water was shallow enough to use the pole. He shipped the oars after that and drove the boat straight for the line of the shore till it ran aground in the tidal water beyond the deep channel where he had been fishing. He shortened the rope on the anchor and then threw it out over the side.

He grubbed about in the bow of the boat, and he

lifted out an old strip of palm fiber. He examined it with idle curiosity. *Vacua,* he thought, and he pictured the tree that looked like a sisal plant when it was still young and then changed out of all recognition when it matured. He tugged at the strip to test its soundness, and he nodded with satisfaction. It was far better than rope from the fiber of the coconut palm, which did not last long. He wondered how long it had lain there, this *vacua* in the bow of the pirogue.

He threaded the three wrasse together, passing the strip of fiber through the gill of each fish and then out through its mouth. He threaded the grouper to the string last of all. He picked up his speargun and the mask, and then the handline and the big killing harpoon. He jumped out of the boat and down onto the sand. He waded through the ankle-deep water, and he began to wonder again how much money he would get for the grouper.

If I do get more than one-fifty, he thought, then there will be sufficient to buy the rice and I will still have enough left over for some candy. He began to get the taste of them in his mouth once more.

He limped up the gently sloping beach. He kicked idly at a red starfish which the tide had left behind. It slid along the sand and came to rest with its yellowish-white underside facing up. He saw the blunt arms stretch, and then the tips, which had grown pointed, writhed and curled aimlessly in the air. He knew it would die there on the sand, and the next tide would wash it farther up along the beach.

He glanced up suddenly, wondering if the girl was anywhere in sight. He did not see her, and his mind busied itself once more with the delightful thought of the money he was going to get.

He reached the seawall. He jumped up on top of it, and then down on the other side. He walked through the grove of coconut palms, through the sunlight and the shade that lay spread below the dark green fronds. He turned to his left, heading in a direction that would take him out of the trees and onto the road right alongside the Chinaman's shop.

He began to think of the candy again, and he wondered suddenly whether the dolphin might not also like them. He did not think so, because he had never heard of a fish eating candy. It was a pity, he thought, because he would have liked to have shared them. It was then that another idea fired his imagination.

I will save some candy for the girl, he told himself, and he began to hope that she would really come out in the pirogue with him tomorrow.

He walked on, thinking about the girl and the candy and the big fish who was his friend. His eyes were bright with the magic of his dreams. A flash of movement to the right caught his attention. He swung round quickly. He froze in his tracks as he saw Pierre Vigot step out from behind the trunk of a breadfruit tree fifteen yards away. He wanted to run, but his muscles had turned to mush, and he knew at the back of his mind that running would be a waste of time, because he could never outstrip the giant Creole, not with his leg the way it was.

Fear made a hard knot deep down inside his belly as the Creole advanced towards him. He wondered whether he had found out somehow about the tobacco, or whether he had been waiting for an opportunity to get his revenge and carry out the threat he had made yesterday, there on the side of the mountain. He felt terribly afraid, and in the blindness of his fear he mistook the expression of awe on the Creole's face for one of cruel anticipation. He was on the point of turning and trying to make a run for it when he remembered the big killing harpoon he was carrying. It posed more of a threat than even the speargun.

He dropped the handline and the necklace of fish, and then he snatched the harpoon from his left hand and gripping it in his freed right hand three-quarters of the way down the shaft he drew his arm back and tensed himself to hurl it with all his might. He focused on a mark he made quickly with his eyes. Pierre Vigot was seven yards away, and the mark was in the middle of his chest.

"Stop!" the boy cried shrilly. "Stop or I will kill you!"

Pierre Vigot halted, but the expression on his face did not change. He gazed at the boy with the same trance-like stare, unmindful of the quivering harpoon that was aimed at him. He shook his head fretfully.

"No, Paul," he said thickly. "I do not seek to do you harm."

The boy lifted his eyes from the mark on which he had been concentrating and stared at the blunt-featured face. He scrutinized it objectively, and he realized with a sudden start of disbelief that the big Creole was himself dreadfully afraid. For a moment he thought it was the menace of the harpoon in his hand, but the fear he saw in the dark eyes was of more than the terror of death. He stared a while longer, not understanding it, and the harpoon wavered uncertainly. He lowered his arm hesitantly, but he remained on guard, alert and mistrustful.

Thinking about what he had been ready to do he felt a sudden blind panic. He knew without a doubt that, if it had been necessary, he would have killed Pierre Vigot. And if he had killed him, what then?

He pursued the inevitable sequence of events in his mind, and the conclusion he reached appalled him. Even the mountain forests would not hide him, and when the police hunted him down and caught him they would take him to Victoria and lock him up in the jail just outside the town and he would never again feel the movement of a pirogue beneath his feet or hear the singing sound of the sea slipping past its hull.

But then he remembered the big fish, and how he had ridden it through the water, and he knew they would never catch him, because he would mount his beautiful fish and ride it right across the oceans and the sea to some other land far away. He felt the coldness leave his heart, but he was glad just the same that he had not killed the big Creole.

"What is it, Pierre Vigot?" he asked, and his voice was guttural with the choking relief that clogged his throat.

"I — I saw you," Pierre Vigot began in a whispering stammer, and his eyes rolled fearfully with the memory of what was in his mind. "In the beginning I could not believe what I had seen, and I thought that I was in a dream. But the dream did not go away, and that was when I realized that the truth of the matter lay in one of two directions. Either I am going mad, which is not what I think, or — " he crossed himself quickly, and his dark eyes rounded with awe — "or you are the greatest *sorcier* I have heard of in all my life."

His agitation and his words puzzled the boy, but he kept his face impassive. He knew now that Pierre Vigot was afraid of him for some reason or other, but he couldn't even begin to guess what was behind his fear. He was alert enough to appreciate the advantage it gave him, though, and he did not intend to lose it through any inadvertent admission which might reveal his own ignorance and arouse the other's suspicions.

"It was nothing," he said calmly, infusing the words with what he hoped was just the right amount of arrogance.

Pierre Vigot nodded with a ready servility. "It was a shark, was it not, Paul?" he asked reverently.

The boy had no idea what he was talking about. His mind raced frantically as he tried in vain to fit the pieces of the puzzle together. But none of it made sense, and he knew it would be dangerous to hesitate much longer.

"Yes!" he declared firmly. "It was a shark."

"I thought it was," Pierre Vigot said quickly. "I did not believe what my eyes told me at first, but when I gave it my attention I recognized you, and I knew it was a shark upon whose back you were riding."

In a sudden burst of comprehension the boy understood exactly what the big Creole was talking about. He wanted to laugh, but he kept his face grave.

So my fish is now a shark, he thought. Very well, he told himself, if it is to be a shark, then it will be a shark.

"What kind of *requin* was it, Paul?" Pierre Vigot went on deferentially.

"A tiger shark!" the boy replied without hesitation, naming the most ferocious of the species with which he was acquainted.

"Mon Dieu!" Pierre Vigot breathed fearfully. "How is it that anyone can tame such a whore of the sea?"

"I did not tame it," the boy replied smoothly, and then with the sudden inspiration that had come to him he went on and embroidered the tale. "I put my spirit into the *requin,* and at the same time I made the demon within the shark enter my own body." He lifted his head haughtily. "It is easy to ride on the back of a shark when such an exchange has been made."

He watched the big Creole covertly, trying to assess the effect of his fabrication. He saw him start nervously, and it was only with a great effort of will that he prevented himself from bursting into laughter.

Pierre Vigot blanched. He felt a violent trembling take hold of his great body and shake it as if there were no substance or strength to his flesh and bones. Over two hundred years ago his ancestors had first landed on the island, fettered with the chains of slavery. They were a black-skinned people, and they came from a land he had heard about but never seen, and the name of the land was Africa. They had brought with them their own beliefs and superstitions, and even now, two centuries later, with a thousand miles of water separating them from the dark forests and great plains of their native land, the children of those long-dead slaves believed and feared.

Pierre Vigot shuddered again. He recalled the tales of his childhood, and then he remembered the old *sorcier* who lived up in the mountains near Cascade, and how he could kill a man or cause him to vanish from the face of the earth by taking the sand on which a single foot had printed its mark and mixing it with the magic of his evil heart. He had heard of this, and many other things, but he had never in all his life heard of one who could enter into the body of the fiercest of all the creatures in the sea. He stared fearfully at the boy, and he believed him and every word of the story he had told. He glanced at the crippled leg and shivered. That too was a part of the spell: the devil worked hand in hand with the maimed and deformed.

"I — I beg of you, Paul," he cried in anguish. "I beg that you forget the words I spoke in fear and anger yesterday."

The boy stared contemplatively at Pierre Vigot for a moment, and then he swung his gaze away and assumed what he thought was an expression of thoughtful deliberation. He felt the anxious eyes of the Creole on him. He held the suspense a little longer, and then he turned suddenly to face him once again. He remained silent for a while, watching the other's mounting agitation.

"I will think about it," he said at length.

"Merci, mon Paul, merci," Pierre Vigot whimpered ingratiatingly.

The boy scowled. It was the only way he could ease the aching tension of the muscles which were threatening to rip his face apart in laughter. He stooped quickly, and transferring the harpoon to his left hand he reached for the handline and the necklace of fish.

Pierre Vigot hurried forward. "Let me carry the fish and the line for you," he said.

The boy looked up at him, from where he was, half-bent towards the ground. He saw the other's desperate anxiety to please. The idea appealed to him for a moment, to take his revenge and sanction this final abasement, but the cringing subservience in the dark eyes only made him sick at heart. He shook his head quickly and scooped up the coiled handline and the fish that were strung together on the strip of *vacua*.

"No thank you," he said stiffly. "I will carry them myself."

"Is there nothing I can do for you?" Pierre Vigot went on shamelessly.

His obsequiousness embarrassed and discomforted the

boy. "Perhaps some *tabac* now and then for my father," he said brusquely, inviting it only out of compassion.

Immediately the words were out of his mouth he began to wish that he had not spoken. It was not only an admission of their poverty, but more, if Pierre Vigot *gave* him tobacco, it meant that he would never again have the pleasure and satisfaction of knowing that he had managed to steal it without being apprehended.

"I will go for it now," Pierre Vigot said quickly. "I have some fine leaves which are ripe enough and dry enough to smoke, and I will bring you the best of them."

"No!" the boy said sharply, and he felt a deep distress at the Creole's overt obsequiousness, because in a way he was responsible for his debasement. "I bought some yesterday, and there is enough tobacco in the house."

It shattered Pierre Vigot, but then he brightened a little. "Some other day then?" he offered. "When he has finished the *tabac* he has now."

"I will let you know," the boy said, and he turned and began to limp towards the road.

"Adieu, M'sieur Paul," Pierre Vigot called after him.

"Adieu, Pierre Vigot," the boy said.

He walked on without looking back, and he began to feel ashamed of himself, for what he had done to the big stupid Creole. He shook his head suddenly, angrily, and he pushed the thought right out of his mind. It had nothing to do with him, and it was certainly not his fault that Pierre Vigot was a superstitious fool. But his melancholy lingered, because it was always a saddening thing to see the strength and the pride of another man diminished. Only when he saw the Chinaman's store did he forget about the big Creole and his depreciating behavior.

The boy lengthened his stride, and he began to think about the sweets again. A chicken squawked and fled from his path in a quick beating flurry of wings, and a fat sow snorted in alarm and bolted into the trees with her squealing brood jostling each other behind her. He reached the road and turned left, and as he walked onto the beaten earth under the porch of the small store he wondered whether he would find the Chinaman in a generous mood.

A LIGHT rain fell steadily throughout the night, and then a little while before dawn the skies cleared suddenly. Though the boy had not witnessed it, he knew it must have been so. He limped down the side of the mountain, and he felt the dampness of the earth under his bare feet and in between his toes. He glanced away to the southeast, searching the blue horizon for a sign of the dark clouds which usually swept in with the monsoon wind. But the sky was clear, and he thought that the sun might shine for him all day.

The rain had cleared the air, and he breathed in deeply. He liked the smell of it, especially after it had rained, because each time he breathed in he could taste the wet richness of the earth and the sweet green strength of the trees.

In his right hand he carried the speargun and his mask, in his left hand the heavy killing harpoon. He had not wanted to bring it, but his father had told him to take it just in case the need for it arose. He knew it could serve no useful purpose, not the way he was fishing: there was another reason for it, and though the man had said nothing, he could guess what had been in his mind.

In the right-hand pocket of his shorts there was a brown paper bag with four large pieces of candy inside it, and as he walked he was conscious of the bulge against his thigh. But he drew no comfort from it, and this morning as he made his way down the side of the mountain there was a heaviness in his heart which neither the bright freshness of the new day nor the sight of the calm blue sea which stretched away below him to the far horizon could dispel.

He had spoken to his father yesterday. He had told him about the big fish, and how it had come in answer to his call, and then he told him of how he had ridden on its back and turned it in the water. He told him about the girl with the beautiful long hair that was a little darker than the color of the sand. He left her behind, and he rode his big fish out to sea where the pirogue was anchored in the channel. She called out to him before he had gone very far though, and she asked him to take her fishing the next day. He knew it was the *marsouin*, really, that made her want to come with him. But it was his fish, and if she liked the fish she might get to like him also. He was shy about telling it, but it was important to him, and he wanted his father to understand and share the happiness that was in his heart.

The man had laughed about the girl, but the boy saw that he was also pleased. The fish had been a different matter. At first he had been incredulous. He came to accept it finally, and when the full import of it reached him his apathetic resignation vanished. Hope lit a fire in his eyes. Instantly and unconsciously they sought the big killing harpoon. They swung back to the boy, with the fever in them burning brighter, and then suddenly, as quickly as they had kindled, the fires burned out and left them dull and hopeless once again.

True to his word, the man made no mention of the thoughts which had been in his head. But the boy had read them, and he knew that the harpoon he was carrying now was his father's prayer that his son would change his mind and think of himself once more as a fisherman.

The boy crossed the road, and he walked swiftly through the grove of coconut palms. He remembered the meeting with Pierre Vigot yesterday, and the degrading servility of the big Creole. It angered him, and at the same time it saddened him, and he did not think he could face it all over again. He looked about warily, but nothing moved in the sunlight and in the shade, and the oppressive sadness in his heart became a little more tolerable.

He reached the seawall and climbed over it. He saw the anchored pirogue, and the smooth stretch of the blue sea beyond it. He thought of the big fish who was his friend, and of how he would soon be riding on its back, and it jolted him from his mood of melancholy. He glanced furtively to his left, hoping to see the girl, wondering whether or not she still wanted to go fishing with him. He saw no sign of her. He climbed back onto the wall, and he stood up on the tips of his toes and tried to see over the crest of the sloping land which flattened out into the terrace which fronted her house.

He was a little low down though, and he could see nothing. For a moment he was tempted to walk along the wall till he was far enough along it to be able to see over the rise, but he discarded the idea angrily and almost immediately. If she did not want to go fishing, it was all right with him. He certainly was not going to run after her and beg her to come. It would be a kind of victory for her, and she would know it, if she saw him walking along the wall towards her house.

He stifled his disappointment and jumped down onto the beach. He pulled the small bag of candy out of his pocket. He opened the mouth of the bag and studied the candy undecidedly. After a moment he reached into the bag and picked out one of the sticky candies. He put it into his mouth, almost regretfully, and then he closed the bag up and stuffed it back into his pocket. He started forward, his cheek bulging. He sucked greedily, and he told himself, not without a little spite, that he was eating one of the pieces he had saved for her.

The girl saw him when he was a little way down the beach. She had been waiting half an hour for him, pacing fretfully up and down the lawn between the wall and the front of the house, telling herself that really she did not care whether he came or not. She paused briefly at the wall each time to scan the beach and the line of palms from which she knew he must emerge. She was furtive about it, and she did not stand for long beside the wall because she did not want him to see her standing there. He would know that she had been waiting, and she did not want him to have the satisfaction of knowing such a thing.

She was wearing a bathing suit of black crepe nylon. It was a severe one-piece, but its very simplicity only served to emphasize the young body it was meant to conceal. It fitted her snugly, even more so when it was wet, and she was not unaware of the fact.

She felt a surge of excitement the instant she saw him, and all her doubt and apprehension vanished. He had come, after all, and he would take her to that wonderful fish which allowed him to ride on its back. She cupped her hands to her mouth.

"Paul!" she cried, shouting out across the distance between them.

She saw him pause, and then he turned slowly. He raised his arm and waved it briefly, and then he went on down the beach, moving with that funny limping walk of his. She snatched her mask off the wall angrily, and then she turned and ran for the steps which led down to the beach. She took them two at a time and sprinted after him.

She had planned how it would be while she paced up and down the lawn. She would call out to him, and when he saw her she would wave with decorum and restraint. He would hurry to meet her then, and she would walk to the bottom of the steps and wait for him. At the very outside, if he merely stood and waited for her, it would be permissible for her to make the initial advance. She would walk down the steps, taking her time, and then she would saunter indifferently across the beach towards where he was standing, holding her mask by its strap and giving it a casual twirl now and again. That was the way she had thought it would be.

It had never occurred to her that he might not even wait, and his actions had thrown her into confusion. She was furious with him for having left her no alternative but to pursue him, and the fact that she *was* complying with such shameless abandon mortified her.

She caught up with him when he was knee-deep in the water and twenty yards from the pirogue. She splashed through the sea, wading strongly, and then she fell into step beside him.

"Why did you not wait for me, Paul?" she said angrily, her breath coming in quick gasps.

Her rebuke was unexpected, and it took him by surprise. He faltered but then he resumed his steady wading. He had wanted to run to her when she called out, but some obscure and nameless obstinacy in him precluded it. He thought about it now, trying to rationalize his actions. He gave up after a while, because he could not find the words to define the awareness that was in him. He knew he had done the right thing though, because if he had gone to her he would have felt the way Pierre Vigot must have felt when he offered to carry the handline and the fish. He did not think it could be a good way to feel.

The boy shrugged his sinewy shoulders abruptly. He glanced at the girl pacing beside him, and his eyes strayed from her face to the bumps of her young breasts which appeared almost naked to his eye beneath the wet film of her clinging suit. He saw the thrusting outline of each pointed nipple, and the sight fascinated and intrigued him. He looked away quickly when she turned her head and saw him watching, but the memory of what he had seen was burned into his mind.

"It does not make a difference," he said curtly. "You are here as it is, and we are nearer to the pirogue than we would have been if I had waited for you."

His assertion was logical, and it mollified her somewhat. "Why have you brought the big harpoon?" she asked, indicating it with a nod of her head.

A shadow passed across the boy's face. "I might meet a shark," he said gruffly. "Or perhaps a big fish might come close enough for me to kill it. I am a fisherman, and I have to be ready."

"You would kill the *marsouin?*" she asked in alarm.

"Are you mad?" the boy growled. "I am speaking of other fishes."

"I'm glad," the girl said quickly. "When you spoke of killing a big fish, I thought you meant the *marsouin.*"

The boy turned on her savagely, his own vulnerability driving him. "Do not think of things you know nothing about," he snarled. "It is my fish in any case, and if I wanted to spear it I would."

She recoiled from his furious attack, staring at him in astonishment, bewildered and shocked by the outburst she had provoked. She knew that her words had in some way been responsible, but that was all she knew.

"I did not mean anything, Paul," she whispered.

"It is nothing," he said shortly, and then because he could see that she was still upset he became at once apologetic. "I am sorry that I spoke sharply, but the fish saved my life two days ago, and even to hear someone speak of killing him is more than I can bear."

An involuntary shudder passed through his body and made his shoulders heave. He put on a sudden burst of speed and covered the last few yards to the pirogue. He felt the increased resistance of the water against his pistoning thighs. He took it as a personal affront, and he drove himself harder. He reached the boat well ahead of her.

He laid his mask and speargun down carefully on the planking of the pirogue. He was reaching in to drop the harpoon when the sight of it suddenly incensed him. He took it in both hands, and he gripped the shaft of red takamaka wood so fiercely that he felt his arms begin to tremble. He lifted it up, and the unformed thought in his mind was that he should lift it higher and higher and then smash the harpoon down and break the shaft across the gunwale of the boat.

The harpoon in his hands was chest high when he realized what he was doing. He started violently, and then the tension ran out of him. He was a fisherman, before anything else, and no fisherman could afford to break a harpoon shaft in childish anger. It was a good shaft, one of the best he had seen, and his father had made it and fitted it to the head of the harpoon. He stroked the seasoned wood with his fingers and then put the harpoon down in the boat.

I think it must be truly the best I have handled, he told himself, and he knew his judgment was professional and unclouded by sentiment.

He turned to the girl who had come up beside him. "I will hold the boat while you get in."

"You do not have to do that," she said indignantly. "I have been in and out of a boat before."

"Get in," he said, simply and without rancor. "It is my boat, and my father's boat, and you must do as I say."

A pirogue capsized easily, and it was not a chance he was prepared to take, no matter how many times she had climbed in and out of one. Another boat, perhaps, but not this one which was the blood of their life.

"But, Paul — " she began.

"Get in," he said again, cutting off her protest bluntly.

His eyes were hard, and there was a look in them that she had not seen before. "All right, Paul," she said meekly.

She clambered into the pirogue while he held it steady, and then when she had settled herself on the forward thwart he lifted the anchor into the boat and jumped aboard nimbly.

It was then that he remembered he had forgotten to take the bag of candy out of his pocket before wading into the water. It had been in his mind to do it just before she called, but when he heard her voice it drove everything from his head. His mouth dropped open, and a look of stunned disbelief spread slowly across his face. When the shock passed he let out a startled yelp and plunged his right hand into his pocket.

"What is it?" the girl cried in alarm.

"My candy!" the boy groaned.

In that instant before his fingers made contact he was hoping that by some miracle or the other his fears would prove to be groundless. When he touched the sodden bag he knew positively that there had been no miracle. He worked his fingers around the bag and drew it gingerly out of his pocket. He stared at it ruefully, and then with great care he untwisted the mouth of the bag and peered into it. He brightened immediately. The candies were wet, certainly, but otherwise they seemed to have suffered no damage. They would dry out quickly, even inside the bag, and though they might taste a little salty at first, the sweetness would soon come up from underneath. The thing was, he wanted to offer her one, and he was afraid she might refuse, because the bag had been in the water and the candies were all wet and salty.

He thought about it for a while, weighing his misgivings against his desire to share something with her that was of his own. He made up his mind abruptly. He moved forward, and the pirogue rocked gently as the weight of his body shifted from one foot to the other. He squatted in front of her, holding out the open bag.

"Will you have one?" he asked. "They are a bit wet, but I do not think they will taste too bad."

The girl peered suspiciously at the cheap, sticky candies inside the sodden brown paper bag. A delicate flicker of distaste passed briefly across her face. She glanced up at the boy.

"Where did you buy *these?*" she asked.

"At the Chinaman's," the boy replied enthusiastically, completely missing the disdain in her voice. "He has many different candies there, but I did not have enough money to buy the chocolate-covered ones that are wrapped in paper."

He stated it as a fact, without any sort of apology, but he felt certain that she would have preferred the sweets that were wrapped in the colored silver papers.

For a moment she wanted to scorn his offering contemptuously, to humiliate him for having made her chase after him there on the beach. But then she remembered the big dolphin, and she knew that if she did such a thing he might not allow her to ride on its back. It never occurred to her that she did not *need* his permission: she had come to think of it as his dolphin, obedient to the commands of no one but the boy. She looked down at the bag again, her mind in a turmoil.

"Take one," the boy prompted her. "They are very good just the same."

She met his eyes, and she saw the dreadful alertness which flickered in them, and in that instant she realized with a start of surprise that she could never do such a thing to him, even if he did not have a dolphin.

"Thank you, Paul," she said.

She dipped into the bag and dug out one of the candies. She put it into her mouth, and she flinched involuntarily as she thought of the Chinaman's store.

She had passed it often, and each time she saw the dark, squalid interior with the flies buzzing in it she was glad that her mother did all of her shopping in the big stores of Victoria. She rolled the candy in her mouth and sucked at it, pretending an enthusiasm she did not feel.

The boy watched her happily. He smiled shyly and stood up. He helped himself to a piece of candy and then wedged the bag between the planking and the hull. He got the pole out and jabbed it into the water and turned the bow of the pirogue with one quick thrust and then drove it straight out to sea.

"The candy is not bad, is it?" he asked. "Even though it has been salted in the water."

"It is good," the girl replied, and she was sincere in her praise.

In the beginning, with the saltiness still on it, she had not liked the taste of the sweet in her mouth. But the bitterness went away after a few moments, and she found it to be quite palatable, even though it had come from the store of the Chinaman.

Her approval made the boy smile with pleasure. He rolled the candy in his mouth and nodded happily. "You did not bring your speargun?" he inquired.

The girl shook her head. "I want to play with your fish and ride on its back," she said boldly. "I do not want to spear fish today."

The boy's eyes widened momentarily, but he kept his thoughts to himself. "I would have liked to have seen it," he said. "This gun that works with air."

"I will show it to you another day."

"You will?" the boy asked eagerly.

"Yes."

"And will you show me how to use it and let me shoot with it?" he asked shyly.

"Mais oui!"

"I would like that," the boy said.

He turned the pirogue a little, taking his bearings from the island a little way off to his right, and then he looked down at the girl again.

"You have the flippers that you wear on your feet?" he asked cautiously.

"I have them, yes."

"You did not bring them?" he inquired politely.

"But why?" she asked innocently, knowing very well what he was leading up to.

"Well, it — it is easier to swim with them, is it not?" the boy improvised hastily.

"Oh yes," the girl replied brightly. "Then must I use them to help the fish swim when he is carrying me on his back?"

"Oh no!" the boy exclaimed indignantly. "He is a great fish, and if he needs no help in carrying *me* on his back, why should he require you, who are much lighter than I, to help him when he is swimming with a burden on his back?" He laughed, and then he became serious. "In any case, it is not possible to kick your legs when you are riding on his back. You must hold on to him, with your arms and with your legs, and if you did such a stupid thing as to try and swim for the fish you would be torn from his back by the drag of the water."

"Alors!" the girl exclaimed, and there was sly triumph in her voice. "To what use should I put the flipper feet? I have already told you that I do not wish to swim after fish and spear them."

He saw the mischievous grin on her face, and he knew at once that she had been baiting him. His cheeks grew scarlet with embarrassment. He looked away in confusion.

"And so, Paul," the girl prompted him smoothly.

He faced her suddenly, resentment flaring in him, but he saw that there was no mockery or cruelty in her amusement. She was only joking with him, and the revelation surprised him. The hot words died on his lips.

"I wanted to try them," he blurted out, his face blushing red again. "I have seen the flipper feet in the stores, but I have never used them."

The girl stared at him meditatively. He is a strange one, she thought, staring into his beautifully colored eyes. In some ways he is more like a man than any of the boys I have known, and in other ways he is like a little child. She decided that she liked him the way he was.

"But why did you not ask to borrow them?" she asked gently. "I would lend them to you with the good wishes of my heart."

"I do not like to ask," the boy growled stiffly.

"But you asked to borrow my gun," she pointed out.

"Yes, but to ask too often is another thing," he said harshly. "It is the same as begging."

He snapped the bamboo pole out of the water and swung it into the boat. He sat down on the stern thwart and unshipped the oars, and then with his back to her he splashed them into the water and began to row.

She stared blindly at the long, unkempt hair at the back of his neck. It was the first time in her life that she had been confronted with such pride and unabashed honesty. It was simple and basic, without affectation, and coming from someone who had so very little made it even more difficult to understand. She was not acquainted with it, and she began to think of him not as a poor Creole, but as a person who had some indefinable wealth that not even the money of her father could match. She thought about it, trying to define it in her mind. She knew it was a good thing, of true value, but she did not succeed in really understanding it. She gave up trying after a while, and the back of his head swam into sharp focus.

She studied his hair. It was a light blond, almost white with the bleaching it had taken from the sun and the sea, the ends curling upward a little where it spilled across the nape of his neck. It suited him, she thought dreamily and irrelevantly, her mind and body lulled by the easy motion of the pirogue and the soft, monotonous chinkle of the oars splashing into the water. She wondered idly whether the curling ends which fell untidily across his neck might not curl a little more if she wound them round her finger. The desire to reach out and do it obsessed her. She sat up suddenly and plunged her itching fingers over the side and into the water, bewildered by the immodesty of her thoughts and the intensity of her emotions.

The boy turned his head slightly, checking his position in relation to the island which was now almost abeam on the left-hand side. He heaved once more on the oars and then shipped them quickly. He turned around and stood up, moving past her and into the bow. He knelt down and undid the anchor rope. He gave it another six fathoms and then wrapped it over and around the cleat in a figure-eight and secured it with two half hitches. He tugged at the rope perfunctorily and then he lifted the anchor in both hands and heaved it over the side. He stood up, and he remained motionless for a moment, watching the flight of the stone as it tumbled down through the clear water.

"Have you seen the *marsouin?*" the girl cried out.

In her excitement she rose suddenly, and the pirogue listed to the right precariously. The boy quickly shifted the weight of his body to his left foot and brought the boat back on an even keel. He turned round slowly, keeping the weight on his foot.

"No, I haven't seen it," he said, and then he indicated the thwart with a nod of his head. "You had better sit down, before you turn the boat over or fall into the water."

She saw the same look of incontestable authority that had been in his eyes before, and she sat down obediently, the cutting rebuke dying on her lips. She glanced up at him as he shifted his weight once more, surprised at her own docile submission.

"Will we find the *marsouin* here?" she asked, her voice eager with anticipation.

"*We* do not find Marsouin," the boy corrected her. "It is *he* who will find us."

He stepped over the bow thwart and moved aft. He sat down on the planking, facing her. He picked up his mask and rinsed it in the sea. He shook the water from it and slipped it over his head.

"You are going to look for the *marsouin* now?" the girl cried excitedly.

"I told you," the boy said patiently. "He will come to me."

"But how will he know where to find you?"

"I will call him when I am ready for him," the boy answered simply.

The girl's eyes widened respectfully. "You talk with the *marsouin?*" she asked in awe.

The boy shook his head, smiling diffidently. "I cannot

184

do that, but I have a special way of whistling which brings him to me."

He picked up his speargun and got to his feet. He watched the girl covertly, gauging the effect of his words. She was staring at him with a heightened regard. He felt a little bit dishonest, because he still had his doubts about whether it was the whistle or the splashing of the oars which summoned the big fish from the deep water. Still, it was a small price to pay for the look of admiration he saw in her eyes.

"But where are you going now?" the girl asked, mystified.

"I am going to shoot a few fish for him."

"He only comes when you have fish to feed him?" the girl asked curiously.

"How can he know that I have fish for him?" the boy rebuked her impatiently. "The fish is for later, after I have played with him and ridden on his back."

"It is not you whom he truly likes then," the girl crowed triumphantly. "It is only because of the payment in fish that he allows you to ride on his back."

The boy looked at her, and the pity and disappointment on his face was not hidden by the mask. "Perhaps it is," he said quietly, his voice nasal and distorted. "But I would give him fish even if he did not allow me to ride on his back. You see, the big fish is also my friend."

She flushed angrily. "He will also be my friend when I have fed him," she declared vindictively.

"It will be a good thing for him then," the boy said.

He spoke without thinking of himself, and when he realized what he had said he felt a sudden stab of alarm. He did not want to share the big fish with anyone else. Animosity flared in him. He glared truculently at the girl. Even in his anger he could not help but notice that she was very lovely. He thought of the dolphin who was his friend, and he thought that the big fish might perhaps also like to have a girl such as this one for a friend. The jealous possessiveness in his heart died.

"If I am his friend?" the girl asked.

"Yes."

"You do not mind?" she went on, incredulous and suspicious.

"Perhaps it will hurt me a little in the beginning," the boy said simply. "But it will be better for him to have *two* good friends, will it not?"

The girl held his eyes for a moment. They were very steady and very calm, and even through the speckled faceplate of the mask she saw the mild reproof in them. She turned away, humiliated and confused.

"I will not be too long," the boy said, moving into the bow of the boat.

"Can I come with you, Paul?" the girl asked.

She reached out impetuously and touched him on the thigh, and then just as quickly she withdrew her hand, the color coming into her cheeks and staining them red.

"You did not bring your gun," the boy said. "How are you going to spear fish?"

"I don't want to spear fish. I only want to watch you."

The boy shrugged. "If you wish."

The girl began to tug on her mask. He stopped her, and then he took it from her hands and, crouching down, he wet it in the water of the sea. He straightened up and passed it back to her.

"It will stick better to your face when it is wet," he explained. "And also, the glass will not become clouded."

The girl studied him with renewed interest. "I did not know that," she said.

"It is something to remember," the boy said. "A little thing, but it is useful."

He remembered feeling smug about it before, wondering whether she knew about the little trick of wetting a mask before putting it on. He felt no elation now, and it puzzled him. He shrugged inside his head.

It is as I told her, he thought, only a little thing.

The girl nodded respectfully. She fitted the mask to her face. She stood up carefully, making sure that her weight was evenly distributed. The pirogue rocked, but it did not list violently as it had done the last time she got to her feet. She stole a glance at the boy, hoping that he had noticed it.

"You are learning," the boy said.

He turned away quickly, embarrassed, but at the same time secretly delighted that she should want his approval. He sat down on the gunwale and swung his legs over the side.

"Hold tightly to your mask when you go in," he said, looking back at her across his shoulder. "You will get it full of water if you do not."

He pressed the mask to his face and slipped into the water. He allowed himself to sink, making no attempt to arrest his downward movement. He twisted round in a circle, but the sea was clear and safe. He sank a little further, and then the pressure of the water arrested his momentum and began to lift him back towards the surface.

He struck out lazily, the girl completely forgotten. He felt the old familiar elation and contentment growing inside him. He kicked out with a sudden exuberance. He was free once more.

He was four feet from the surface when the milky film above him shattered like a splintering sheet of glass.

The taut body of the girl plummeted past him. He jackknifed and went after her. He swam down swiftly, wanting to catch her up and then swim back to the surface beside her. To his dismay he shot past her. She was on the way up already, and he glimpsed the laughter behind the plate of her mask just before she lifted her head and struck out for the surface.

The boy turned slowly under the water. He knew it was too late now to try to chase her. He drew his legs up, tensing them for that first scissoring kick which would start him moving. He threw his head back and stared after her. His breath caught at what he saw, and he hung unmoving in the water.

She was swimming upward at a slight angle to the surface almost directly above him. She was kicking her feet like a frog, and every time she drew her legs in her thighs moved apart and the tightening muscle hollowed the flesh on the inside of each thigh right up against the line of the black bathing suit. His eyes moved up, across the smooth lifting curvature of her stomach. He saw the indentation of her navel beneath the stretched costume. It looked like a flower, and as his gaze moved higher he saw the soft swellings of her beautiful young breasts. He looked at her face, searching for her eyes, but the mask obscured them. Her long hair streamed out behind her, and it reflected the light like gold.

He felt a leaping hunger come alive inside of him. It did not touch his body, but he felt the pain of it in his mind and in his heart. He thought she was the most beautiful thing he had ever seen. He wanted to reach out and touch her, and hold all of her close against him and let the strange hurting run out of his body and into her. He felt a sudden constriction in his chest, and he woke and came alive and kicked out frantically for the surface.

He came up right beside her in the water. He got his breath back, and then he turned away from her and loaded the speargun. He lifted his head from the water, clearing his lungs and filling them again, and then he drew his legs up under his belly and rolled forward in the water. He dived immediately, without looking at her, and he went down kicking with the speargun held straight out in his extended right arm.

The girl watched him for a moment, head down and treading water, and then she took a quick breath and dived after him. But the boy went deep, and he stayed down long after all of her air had gone, chasing after a snapper, and she broke away suddenly and kicked out for the surface.

She watched him from there, swimming along above him, and in the next twenty minutes she saw him shoot three snapper, two wrasse, and a porgy which he was lucky to get because he shot wide and the fish itself darted forward straight into the path of the flying harpoon.

She saw all of it from where she was, looking down on him from above, but it was the sight of the boy himself as he stalked remorselessly through the silent world below that thrilled and fascinated her. Here there was none of the halting awkwardness which marred and punctuated his movements when he walked. In the water below her he was free, as free and as graceful as the fishes upon which he preyed. As she watched him she felt a murmuring excitement and wonder stir within her.

His long ragged hair no longer looked unkempt: each hair was separate and distinct, and it floated free in the water, moving and waving with each movement of his head. There was something flawed about the whole picture though, some little thing which struck a violent discord in her mind. She puzzled over it for a moment, and then in a sudden burst of perception she realized just what was wrong.

It was his patched shorts which destroyed the purity of what she had visualized. It was not the fact that they were patched, but just that he had no business wearing shorts of any kind in the blue silences through which he swam. He should have been naked, like the fishes, with his body bare and nothing of him hidden, so that he could be seen in all his beauty, with none of it diminished.

In her mind she saw him naked, and there was no shame in her heart because of the picture, only a whispering sadness and a dark sense of loss that she should not see him in the one way she was sure he was meant to be seen. She thought then, in a half-understood moment of comprehension and fantasy, that he had been born, not to live and move on the land like other human beings, but to live and rejoice in the quiet world that existed below the sea.

He would be like a fish, she thought, staring down at him dreamily, and he would be the most beautiful boy fish in all the sea.

The sun was warm on her back, and she saw him going after the porgy. She turned her face lazily to one side and drew a breath, and then she looked down at him once more. She began to dream again, and in her mind she saw herself as a *sirène*. She did not have a tail like a mermaid, but her feet were webbed and her hands were webbed, and she swam beside the boy naked through the silent water.

She saw the sudden contraction of the rubbers on the speargun. The harpoon arrowed through the water, and she woke from her dream. She perceived instantly that it was going wide. She was beginning to feel an acute disappointment because he had missed, when the porgy darted forward and swam straight into the harpoon.

The boy surfaced, blowing and gasping, and he motioned the girl towards the pirogue. She reached it and climbed aboard nimbly, and then when he swam up beside it she took the gun from his hands and hauled in the line and the harpoon while he dragged himself over the stern and into the boat. He pushed the mask up on his face and then moved to her side. He took the gun and the harpoon from her, and he knocked the porgy off the harpoon and then screwed the head back on again.

The girl took off her mask and shook her head from side to side. Drops of water sprayed from her long hair, and it was dark with the wetness of the water in it.

"And now, Paul," she said, her voice catching with excitement. "Is it now that you call the *marsouin?*"

The boy nodded silently, and once again he felt an acute uncertainty about his ability to summon the fish with nothing but his whistle. He remembered the last time he had been in the pirogue, and how it had only come after he splashed the oars into the water. He did not want to have to do that, not in front of her. He wanted the big fish to answer his *whistle,* because there could be no ambiguity about such a thing. He swept his glance across the sea. The unbroken surface seemed to mock him. The enormity, and the impossibility of what he had to do began to weigh heavily on him, but then he remembered how he had called the fish to him in the shallow water with only his whistle, without even smacking his hand down in the water.

He lifted his head suddenly, before the rising confidence in him could begin to spoil with doubt, and he sent his whistle soaring and lifting and rolling out across the sea.

He waited awhile, not daring to look at the girl, but the dolphin did not appear. He searched the sea, his anxiety increasing. He stole a glance at the girl. She was staring at him with a mixture of accusation and disappointment on her face. He turned away quickly, crushed with humiliation and shame. He became conscious of the way he was standing, of the one leg of his which was shorter than the other and which always made him stand with his body leaning a little to one side. He wanted to dive over the side of the pirogue and hide himself under the water. Down there he was no different from the fish. He could swim, and he did not have to stand or walk.

He thought of the place in the sea where he had first seen the dolphin. He turned towards it, hope mounting in him again, and that was when the girl screamed and set the pirogue rocking dangerously with her wild cavorting.

"Paul!" she cried, stabbing her finger into the air again and again.

"The boat!" he said sharply. "Be careful or — "

"There, Paul!" the girl cried, and she took him by the arm and shook him wildly.

He turned in the narrow confines of the boat, and he followed the direction of her pointing arm. A great bursting relief swept through him suddenly. The dolphin was fifty yards away, its body half out of the water. It was standing straight up on its tail, watching him. Once again he felt a great love for the big fish, especially this time, because its coming had been more important to him than his life.

He wanted to shout and yell with all the happiness and joy that was bursting to get out of him when he remembered just in time that such a demonstration would be an admission of the doubt which had been in him.

The girl shook him again. "Do you not see it?" she cried. "It is there, looking straight at us."

"Of course it is there," he replied, making his voice indignant. "He heard my whistle and it is only natural that he should answer."

He saw her eyes widen with awe. He kept his face stiff and impassive. It was not from any exaggerated idea of his own importance: if he had allowed the muscles in his face to relax, he knew he would not have been able to stop himself from grinning. He did not want to do that, because it would give everything away.

"Paul!" the girl shrieked in sudden alarm. "It is going!"

The boy did not share her dismay as the dolphin sank out of sight. It went straight down, and he drew his glance in along the surface towards the pirogue from the place where it had gone down in the water. He picked up the shimmering shadow that speared towards them a fathom and a half below the surface.

"He is not going," he stated calmly. "Marsouin is coming to me."

The dolphin came up beside the pirogue. Its head lifted out of the water. It watched him for a moment, and then the eyes which looked so unlike the eyes of a fish rolled in their sockets and focused on the girl. He thought he saw a flicker of apprehension in the brown eyes, but before he could make up his mind about it the dolphin dived and shot off under the water. It came up twenty-five feet away, and it rolled over once and then came up again and lay motionless with only its head above the surface of the water.

The boy whistled, and he called to it, but the dolphin did not respond. He sat down on the planking of the boat, and he leaned out over the side and smacked his hand down into the water. The dolphin did not move. He did it again, but still the dolphin took no notice. He tried it a third time, and he called and whistled again. The big fish swam in a little distance, but it veered off suddenly and darted away.

The boy got to his feet slowly. There was a puzzled expression on his face. "It is strange," he murmured thoughtfully. "He has never done such a thing before."

"What shall we do?" the girl cried anxiously. She watched the wallowing dolphin, and she began to doubt that she would ever get the chance to ride upon its back.

"He has never done such a thing before," the boy said again, and there was a note of complaint and mystification in his voice. "I really do not understand it."

"It is as I told you," the girl said, disappointment making her resentful. "The *marsouin* is a girl, and she is angry with you because of her jealousy."

The boy stared at her thoughtfully for a moment, deliberating over what she had said. There was neither truth nor reality in her words, but he knew that in some obscure way they held the answer to the riddle of the strange behavior of the big fish. He stared at the dolphin, studying it, struggling with the elusive idea. It seemed to him that the eyes of the fish were focused intently on the girl. He began to wonder whether it was only his imagination. He concentrated on its eyes, and he thought he saw a look of wariness and mistrust in them. The glimmer of understanding in his brain burst into sudden comprehension. He swung back to the girl, quickly pulling the mask down over his face.

"It is not a girl fish," he said emphatically. "It is a boy fish, and he is not angry with me." His eyes became accusing. "It is the first time I have come to meet him with another in the boat, and I do not think he understands it, and so he is wary."

He moved into the bow of the pirogue, and he sat down on the gunwale and swung his legs over the side.

"Where are you going?" the girl asked immediately.

"Since he will not come to me for now," the boy replied. "I must go to him and show him that there is no cause for his uneasiness."

"But, Paul!" the girl protested. "When will I be able to ride on his back?"

"I do not know," the boy said. "We will have to wait and see what happens."

He turned himself, so that for one moment he was facing the boat with the weight of his body on his arms, and then he lowered himself quickly. He let go and sank into the water with hardly a splash. He came up and pushed off against the side of the pirogue, swimming out towards where the dolphin lay wallowing on the surface. He had covered half the distance when the big fish dived suddenly. He felt the familiar touch of its body between his legs, and then the gentle bump of its dorsal fin against his back.

He lay down flat along the dolphin as it dived. A tremendous sense of elation filled him, and at the back of his mind was the knowledge that the girl would be watching him.

For several minutes the boy rode on the back of the big fish. In the beginning he took it straight out to sea and over the reef into the deep water. After a while he began to think about the sharks, and he turned the dolphin and came back. He guided the fish straight towards the pirogue, and then when he was close enough to see the excitement in the girl's eyes he turned the dolphin and rode off away from the boat. He did it again and then again, going in closer each time before turning the fish, letting her think that he was coming in to give her a turn. He was beginning to enjoy himself, especially the look of anticipation on her face which turned to sudden despair each time he turned away. He did it for the fourth time. Her face seemed to crumple and break, and he felt so terrible and mean that he turned the dolphin back straight away and brought it right up beside the boat. He slipped off its back and caught hold of the gunwale. He hung there, and when the big fish came up to him squeaking and blowing he reached out and tickled it along the flank.

"See if he will allow you to touch him," the boy called.

The girl reached out over the side of the boat. The dolphin darted away. It went out twenty feet, and then it stood up on its tail and looked at her for a moment before sinking slowly and swimming back to the side of the boy.

"Oh Paul," she lamented. "He does not like me."

He heard the humiliation in her voice, and the brokenhearted sound of it. He felt very ashamed, for tantalizing her the way he had. He wondered what there was to be done. He remembered the fish in the boat. He thought it might work, even though he did not really like the idea of her feeding his dolphin. He forced himself to speak.

"Take one of the fishes in the boat," he said. "Smack

it down in the water so that he can know it is a fish, and then hold it under the water and let him take it from your hand. It may be that it will help him to get to know you and like you."

The girl picked up the porgy. She leaned over the side of the boat and struck it down hard and flat into the water. The dolphin came gliding up, and it took the fish from her fingers with the same gentleness that had amazed and delighted the boy. She reached out and touched the dolphin while it was crushing and swallowing the fish. It submitted to her caress for a moment, and then it swam off lazily. It turned fifteen yards out and then swam back to the side of the boy. The girl was delighted with her small success.

"I touched it, Paul, and he let me touch him!" she cried excitedly. "Did you see it? Did you see it happen?"

"Yes, I saw it."

"Can I give him another fish?" the girl asked. She saw the flicker of alarm and uncertainty which passed across his face. "Please, Paul," she implored him quickly.

Once again the boy fought the unwillingness that was in him. "All right," he said eventually. "Give him one of the *cacatois*."

"Can't I give him the *bourjois*?" the girl asked. "It is a much better fish."

He knew it was a better fish, and that was why he had told her to give one of the wrasse to the dolphin. He wanted to save the better fishes for later, when he could give them to his friend himself. He was about to refuse angrily, but then he remembered how he had almost made her cry when he had been riding the dolphin in the water.

"Tres bien," he said. "Take one of the *bourjois*."

The girl fed the snapper to the dolphin, and she

touched it while it ate. The big fish allowed her to scratch it a little longer than it had the last time, and then suddenly it came up out of the water. It stood on its tail for a moment, its head level with her face, and then it sank back into the sea and came up beside the boy.

"Paul!" the girl cried deliriously. "Did you see what it did just now?"

"I saw it."

"Oh, Paul, I think the *marsouin* is beginning to like me a little," she said. "Do you not think so?"

"He is getting to know you, I think," the boy admitted a little reluctantly.

"Can I ride on his back now, Paul?" she asked breathlessly.

The boy bristled silently, but the resentment in him died as suddenly as it had come. "Get into the water over the stern," he said quietly. "Do it as I did, and do not splash and make a noise or you may frighten Marsouin away."

The girl snatched the mask down over her face. She slipped over the side of the stern and into the water, doing it the way she had seen the boy do it. She kicked out, swimming towards him. The dolphin darted away at her approach. It circled nervously twenty feet off, but then the boy whistled and called to it softly and it came back and nudged at him impatiently with its beak. He caressed it reassuringly, running his fingers up and down its back.

"Come round to the other side of him," he said, keeping his voice very low. "When I put my arm around his neck I will let go of the pirogue. I will hold him, and the weight of my body will take him down a little in the water. When that happens you must get upon his back quickly, and then you must hold on with your legs and with your arms because he will be moving the moment you are on his back."

The girl swam round slowly to the other side of the dolphin. She tickled it gently on its belly. To her delight and relief the fish did not dart away. The big domed head turned towards her, and she found herself being examined by a large brown eye which was barely eighteen inches from her face. It did not look at all like the eye of a fish, and it appeared enormous at that range.

"There is another thing I will tell you about," the boy went on. "If he takes you deep and stays down and you have finished your air, ease the grip of your legs and arms a little and he will rise again to the surface to allow you to breathe."

He paused for a moment, trying to assess the expression on her face. He saw the uneasiness in the eyes which stared out from behind the water-speckled plate of the mask, and he continued quickly.

"It is what I have found," he said. "And I have also found that it is possible to guide him in whichever direction you want to go by putting an arm straight out in the water."

"I do not understand, Paul," the girl whispered.

"If you wish to make him swim to the left," the boy went on patiently, "push your left arm out in the water at right angles to your body." He demonstrated quickly with his right arm and then went back to stroking the dolphin. "Marsouin will keep turning to the left while you have your arm extended, and then as soon as you remove the drag of your arm he will stop his turn and continue straight on along his new heading. In the beginning it was the drag of my arm which turned him, but I think he has now come to understand it as a signal."

"I understand," the girl said. "But what if it does not work for me?"

"Then the only thing you can do is fall off his back and swim back to the pirogue," the boy replied. "It is not much of a hardship, is it?"

"No, it is not much."

"There is one other thing I must tell you," the boy said. "Do not squeeze him too hard with your legs or your arms when you hold to his body. He does not like it, and he might throw you off or you may hurt something inside him."

The girl nodded quickly. "I will be careful."

"And be awake when you put an arm out to turn him," the boy warned her. "The drag of the water might tear you from his back if you are not careful. Lie as flat as you can along his body, and hold him firmly."

"I will remember to do it," the girl assured him.

"You are ready now?" the boy asked.

He saw her nod, and he let go of the gunwale and sank down into the water beside the big fish. He brought himself back to the surface with one kick of his legs and then he put his right arm around the neck of the dolphin.

"How can I get upon his back?" the girl asked in desperation. "I cannot jump up from where I am in the water."

"Put your arm around his neck as I am doing," the boy instructed her quietly. "And then let yourself float up beside him in the water."

He caressed the dolphin while he spoke. When he saw that she was floating in the water beside the big fish he bore down gently on the body of the dolphin, lifting himself out of the water to do it.

"Now!" he whispered urgently, and he released the fish and sank below the surface.

The girl threw her left leg across the back of the dolphin and wrapped both her arms around its neck. The big fish came alive the instant it felt the weight of her body on its back. Its great bow-shaped flukes flashed down and up. It shot away from the side of the pirogue and dived instantly, the girl clinging grimly to its back.

The boy felt the wash of the great tail and he turned under the water to follow the flight of the fish. As it turned out, he need not have gone to all the trouble of telling her how to bring the dolphin to the surface and how to turn it in the water.

He saw the big fish dive. It went down to three fathoms and leveled off, and he saw the long hair of the girl streaming out behind her as she crouched down low across the back of the dolphin. It arrowed on for another twenty feet, and then suddenly, without any warning, it arched its body and went into a vertical dive. It went straight down, and then it tucked its head in under its belly and somersaulted on its nose. The abrupt maneuver unseated the girl, and she tumbled head over heels through the water in slow motion. The dolphin swam back towards him on its back, its white belly facing up. An instant before it reached him it turned over again with a graceful roll. It came up beside him the moment he surfaced.

He thought he saw an inquisitive and mischievous gleam in its eyes, and it seemed to him that the smiling line of its mouth was even more pronounced. He grinned slyly, stroking his hand along the bulging dome of its head. He put an arm around its neck and clung to it for support. When the girl swam up beside him he kept his face grave.

"He threw me off!" she spluttered indignantly, still gasping for breath.

"Try it again," the boy said.

She mounted the dolphin, and this time she did it without his help. The big fish moved off with her on its back. She began to think she had been unjust in thinking it had thrown her off intentionally when it dived deeper and did exactly the same thing.

The boy waited for her to swim back, his face a careful blank. "Perhaps you are angering him by holding on too tightly," he said innocently.

The girl studied him skeptically for a moment, and then she slipped her right arm over the neck of the dolphin and floated her body up in the water beside it. The second she was settled across its back the big fish swam forward and dived. She hung on grimly, determined not to be unseated by the sudden somersaulting dive which had twice already broken the grip of her arms and legs.

She tensed herself, trying to anticipate it. The dolphin leveled off at five fathoms and then looped upward and turned over with a brutal swiftness. She felt herself slipping, caught by the completely unexpected reversal of tactics. She tried to hang on, but the big fish rolled and flung her off its back.

She floundered helplessly for a moment before she got her bearings, and then she kicked out for the surface, the pressure in her lungs already intolerable. She knew now without a doubt that the big fish had done it purposely. Strangely enough she felt no animosity towards it. She began to think of it with a heightened admiration and respect. She surfaced with a last frantic kick of her legs and rolled over onto her back. She floated for a few moments, getting her breath back, and then she turned over and swam back to where the boy was treading water beside the dolphin. She saw that he was doing his best not to laugh.

"Did you see what he did?" she cried, trying to pretend an indignation she did not feel.

The boy shook his head solemnly. "I was above the surface," he assured her hastily.

"You *did* see it!" the girl accused him. "I can see from the look on your face that you saw it all."

It was too much for the boy. He burst into laughter, and to his surprise and relief he saw that she also began to laugh. The dolphin swam off and began to circle them, and he heard its excited whistling and squeaking. It sounded very funny, and he began to laugh even harder. He forgot all about moving his arms and legs to stay afloat, and his laughter died abruptly as his head sank below the surface. He came up spluttering and coughing, and he struck out for the pirogue. He clung to the gunwale while he recovered, choking and laughing at the same time.

"He was playing with you," he gasped. "He was letting you know that in the water he is the one who matters."

The girl swam over to the pirogue and clung beside him. "I think he had something like that in his mind," she agreed.

"Perhaps when he knows you a little better he will not be so quick to throw you off."

"But when will that be?"

The boy shrugged. "I do not know."

"But did he throw *you* off in the beginning when you first started to ride on him?"

"No," the boy admitted. "He has never done such a thing to me."

The girl was silent for a while, pondering over what he had just said. It would be a terrible thing if the fish did not allow her to ride it properly. Perhaps it never would. It was obvious that its relationship with the boy was a very special one. It had tolerated her on its back for a short while, but that was all. She had a sudden idea.

"Why do we not both ride on its back at the same time?" she asked. "I do not think he will throw me off if you are also on his back."

The boy glanced at her. He thought about what it would be like, pressed close up against her and riding under the water. But then he thought of the great weight of both their bodies weighing down heavily on his fish. He shook his head quickly.

"It would be too much for him," he said. "I would not wish him to be hurt."

He swung around and caught hold of the gunwale with his other hand and then pulled himself out of the water. He scrambled into the pirogue and then he helped her up.

"I will give him the other fishes now," he said.

"Let me give them to him, Paul," she begged.

The boy hesitated a moment, but the look in her eyes was more than he could deny. "If you wish."

"Thank you, Paul," she said, and there was humility in her voice, because she knew from the expression on his face that the price had been high.

She fed the dolphin the four remaining fishes, the beak-nosed wrasse first and then the two fat snapper. The dolphin watched her expectantly for a moment, whistling and blowing as it churned up and down beside the boat. She made no move to feed it again, and then after a while it dived suddenly and came up right beside the boat. It rose halfway out of the water, straight up on its tail, and it cocked its head and peered inquisitively into the pirogue.

"Tout y n'fini, Marsouin," the boy murmured softly, sad for his fish.

The dolphin turned its head towards him. It regarded him curiously for a moment, and then it blinked once as if in understanding and sank back noiselessly into the water. He saw the dark speeding silhouette of its body below the surface, and he followed its flight out to sea till the shadow of its shape blended invisibly with the darkening color of the water. It came up once, surfacing in its smooth breathing roll, and then he saw it no more. He turned to the girl, a strange heaviness in his heart. He wished that there had been another fish, just one, so that he could have given it to the dolphin himself.

"It is gone," he said quietly.

"Call it!" the girl cried out. "Call it back again."

The boy shook his head. "He has gone for today. I will not see him again until tomorrow."

"But why?"

"I do not know," the boy answered. "But it is his way."

"Try to call him!" the girl pleaded.

"It would be a waste of my time," the boy said.

He moved into the bow and began hauling in the anchor. He lifted it into the boat, and he felt the effort stretch the muscles in his back. He sat down on the fore thwart and motioned her to be seated. He got the oars out and began pulling for the shore. He checked his direction once and then he bowed his head and rowed on in silence. He realized dully that there were no fish to take home, but somehow it did not seem to matter.

The girl sensed the sadness of his mood. "Will you be coming to play with him tomorrow?" she asked hesitantly.

"Yes."

"Will you take me?"

"If you want to come."

The girl was silent again for a while. "You told me that he saved your life," she said at length.

"Yes, he did."

"Tell me."

"I was spearing, and there was this *requin* which came and began to circle me in the water." He stared at her apathetically, without really seeing her, and there was a look of blindness in his eyes. "He was closing with me when from the deep water on the other side of the reef Marsouin came in and struck him like a harpoon with the beak of his head."

"He killed the *requin?*" the girl asked incredulously.

"No," the boy said, "he only drove him away, but it is sure that he saved my life, and that is why I think he loves me as he does."

He spoke without thinking, but then he thought about it and he was surprised at what he had said. But he knew it was the truth, even though it was too obscure for him.

"But that is foolish, Paul," the girl protested. "Surely it is the other way around? It is you who love him because he saved your life."

"That is true," the boy said, and then he looked up at her suddenly, searching for the words to give meaning to the thoughts in his mind. He struggled with it a little longer, his mouth working, and then it came to him.

"What you have said is true," the boy went on. "But he loves me because he knows that I have recognized with my own love the act by which he saved my life. It is a very great thing," he finished simply.

He still did not understand it very well, but he knew with an unshakable conviction that it was so. He shipped his oars and stood up, and then he picked up the bamboo pole and moved past her into the stern of the pirogue. As he stepped over the thwart he saw that the girl was staring at him with a strange, bewildered expression on her face. He shrugged mentally: he knew she did not understand, but it did not really matter.

He ran the pirogue aground. He shortened the anchor rope and threw the heavy stone out as far as he could. It landed with a splash in the shallow water, burying itself halfway into the sand.

He picked up his speargun and his mask, and after that he picked up the harpoon and jumped down out of the boat. He started off without a word or a backward glance, splashing through the ankle-deep water. The girl stared after him for a moment, a faintly puzzled expression on her face, and then she scrambled out of the pirogue and hurried to catch up with him.

"Is something the matter, Paul?" she asked.

"No," the boy said shortly. He did not look at her.

"Is it something I have said or done which makes you angry?" she went on.

"No — it is just the way I feel."

"How do you feel?"

The boy shrugged and remained silent. He could not explain it to himself, so it would be pointless in trying to tell her about it. He splashed through the last of the shallow water and continued up the sloping beach. The girl paced beside him, watching him covertly. It was a mystery to her, this shell into which he had withdrawn, and it made her feel uneasy.

"Come home with me," she said suddenly, "and I will show you my speargun."

The boy halted abruptly. He studied her, and he was wary, because he did not believe that she had meant it. Straightaway he perceived her sincerity. His eyes came alive, sparkling with excitement. He wanted to see this wonderful gun which she owned, and hold it in his hands. Suddenly he became conscious of the way he was standing, with his weight on his left foot and his body thrust awkwardly to one side. The life in his eyes went out, and he turned away from her, shaking his head.

"I must go," he said quickly. "I have work to do."

"Will I bring it tomorrow?" the girl inquired anxiously. "And the flipper feet, should I bring those also?"

"If you want to," the boy replied, and he started up the beach again.

"I will wait for you tomorrow, Paul," the girl called after him.

"All right," he said dully, and he limped on up the beach towards the low seawall, very conscious of the hard unyielding nature of the land.

The girl watched him in silence. She turned away after a while, but the retina of her mind held the picture of his funny limping walk. She felt a sudden tightness in her throat, and she wished she had not called him *jambe clopante* before.

S HE went out with him every day for the next five days. She no longer walked up and down across the lawn between the front of the house and the seawall, and she did not pretend to herself that it made no difference whether or not he came. She waited for him openly and anxiously, and she did not care about his knowing that she was waiting.

She sat on the wall now, the seventh morning she had waited for him. She sat astride the wall, her speargun and the mask and the flippers all ready on the ground beside her. She stared intently at the line of trees which swept right down to the edge of the beach, and she was oblivious to everything else as she kept her vigil. The grass on the lawn was soft and springy, and she did not hear her mother's light-footed approach.

"Danielle — " the woman said softly.

The girl spun round, startled. "Ohh — it is only you," she said with relief.

The woman laughed. "*Only* me?"

"You startled me," the girl explained quickly. "And then I find it is only my maman, and of course I have nothing to be startled about."

The brief smile she gave the woman was full of a sudden warmth and gratitude, and then she turned and once again took up her unblinking vigil.

"You are going again with Paul to fish with him and play with his dolphin?" the woman asked.

"Yes."

The woman studied the beautiful profile of her daughter's face. She bit nervously at her lip, wondering how to begin and say the things she had in her mind. It was all so difficult, especially after what she had said that first day when she heard her daughter calling the boy limpleg. For a moment she was tempted to make some innocent remark and hurry back inside the house. Her earlier determination faltered, but she forced herself to stand where she was. It was a thing which had to be done, and the knowledge that it was necessary brought her fresh strength and courage.

"Danielle," she began hesitantly, "do you think it is a good thing to go out with Paul so often?"

"Oh yes!" the girl replied enthusiastically, missing the tone of censure and apprehension in her mother's voice. "It is wonderful to be with him and play with his fish. Only yesterday I rode on him farther than I have ever ridden before. I think that today he might allow me to ride like Paul."

She spoke quickly, and she kept her eyes fixed on the line of green trees where they came down to the edge of the shining beach that glared whitely in the morning sun.

The woman drew a quick, shivery breath, and she felt sick at the thought of what she was going to say. Her heart was beating painfully, and the noise of it was so loud in her ears that she was sure her daughter would hear the pounding thunder of its beat and turn to face her in questioning amazement. She waited tensely a while longer, expecting it to happen at any moment. But the girl continued to stare at the line of trees, and the woman woke from her trance and smiled inside herself at the foolishness of her thoughts. She took another deep breath, and it steadied her a little.

"I do not think you should go out with Paul again," she said.

For a moment the girl appeared not to have heard, but then she turned slowly towards her mother, a look of shock and astonishment spreading across her face.

"I have heard you, Maman," she said quietly. "But I cannot believe that I have heard you correctly."

The woman squirmed wretchedly, but she clenched her hands and stilled the trembling inside her. She looked away, unable to bear the expression on her daughter's face.

"I will repeat it so that you may believe what I have said," she told the girl. "I do not think you should go out with Paul again."

"Do you mean from today?"

The woman hesitated, and she weakened. "Perhaps not today, but after today."

"I understand," the girl said stiffly, but the woman could see that she did not understand it at all.

"It is my wish, Danielle," she said.

"Is it that his clothes have now become too old even for you?" the girl asked, and there was a terrible hushed stillness in her voice.

"No, Danielle," the woman said quickly, and deep pain came alive in her eyes. "You know it is not that, and also that it could never be such a thing."

"What is it, then?"

"You are seeing too much of him," the woman said. "And it is not a good thing."

"Are you afraid that I am beginning to like him too

much?" the girl asked, and a note of curiosity crept into the stiff formality of her voice.

"Perhaps it is something like that," the woman said uncomfortably.

"And is that a bad thing?" the girl challenged fiercely. "Have you not told me that he is a good boy, and that his poverty is not the measure by which to judge him?"

"It is not that," the woman said, anger sharpening her voice. "I have my reasons."

"What are they?"

"You are no longer a child, Danielle," the woman said stiffly, and her eyes touched briefly on the swelling buds of her daughter's breasts. "I have watched you these last few days, and this is no longer the affair of children."

The girl glanced towards the line of palms which came down to the edge of the beach. She saw the boy climbing up onto the seawall. He stood poised for a moment, and then he jumped down and turned to stare in her direction, his face lifted up so that the light shone on it. She slipped off the wall and gathered up her equipment. She turned to her mother, and her face was cold and closed.

"I would never have thought it of you, Maman," she whispered, and the words were full of her own pain and bewilderment. "And if those are your reasons, then I will not do as you ask me."

"I will tell your father," the woman threatened, but there was no conviction in her voice.

The girl understood this, and for a moment she felt a hurting compassion for her mother. "He would only listen to me, Maman," she said softly, and then she turned and ran past the woman and down the steps which led to the beach.

The woman stared after her. There was a look of desolation on her face. But behind it all was her shame, because of the things which she had been forced to say.

The boy waited for the girl. He watched her running approach, but he did not see her really, because he was looking inward on all the troubled thoughts that were there in his mind. He had told his father about the big fish each day, and about the girl, and each time he told him about it all he saw the bitter sadness in him growing. He did not say anything, but it was there, and the boy knew he was thinking of the big killing harpoon and the dolphin all in the same thought. He felt the distress of his father as his own pain, but there was nothing that he could do about it.

He could not kill the dolphin. It was his friend, and it had given him his life, and he was afraid that the girl would no longer want to go out fishing with him if he did not have a dolphin. The thought terrified him.

The girl came panting to a stop beside him. "Come quickly, Paul," she gasped. "Let us be gone in the boat."

She started down the beach, and he fell into step beside her. There was a look of tension and strain on her face, and in his concern for her he forgot about his own troubles.

"Something is the matter?" he inquired gently.

The girl shook her head emphatically. The boy studied her a moment longer and then shrugged abruptly. He knew that something was worrying her. It was her business though, and if she did not want to tell him about it, that was also her business. When the time came, if it ever did, he would be ready to listen.

He took the pirogue out to sea in silence. Neither of them spoke. He anchored in five fathoms of water. She did not want to spear, so he took her gun, and because it hit harder and shot farther he did his work quickly and more easily. He also used her flippers. In twenty minutes he speared eight fish. He thought it was enough, and he was impatient to be with the dolphin again. He handed her the gun and then scrambled into the boat, coming in over the stern. He pulled the mask off his head and laid it down on the planking, and then he worked the flippers off his feet. He stood up, brushing the water off his face.

He called to his fish, but it did not come. He called again and again till there was no breath or strength left in his body and then in his desperation he picked up one of the oars and beat it down in the water till the last of his strength was gone. When the fish still did not come he knew then that it would not be coming to play with him. He did not believe for one moment that it would *never* come again, but he knew it would definitely not be coming today. He did not question its right to do what it pleased, but at the same time he felt an acute disappointment. He turned slowly to the girl.

"He will not come this morning, and he will not come today," the boy said. He swept his glance briefly across the still surface of the sea once more. "I think it must be that he has been far out in the night on some important matters of his own, and he is still far out at sea and too far away to swim back in time for us to play with him."

"Perhaps he will come in the afternoon if we wait for him," the girl said hopefully.

The boy shook his head doubtfully. "I do not think so."

"Why?"

"It is his way," the boy said, and though there was the same hope in him he knew that it was only a wishful dream. He moved into the bow and began hauling in the anchor.

"Where are we going?" the girl cried, and there was alarm in her voice.

"Back," the boy grunted.

"Oh no, Paul!" the girl pleaded. "Let us do some fishing for a while."

"You did not want to spear before," he pointed out.

"But I want to now," the girl protested.

The boy glanced at her across his shoulder. He said nothing, but his face broke into a grin. He pulled the last of the rope in and then swung the anchor into the boat. He straightened up and turned to face her, and the grin was still on his face.

"So you want to now?" he said.

"Yes."

"And you will be hoping all the time that Marsouin will come, eh?"

The girl's eyes widened, and then she smiled shyly. "Yes, that is what I will be hoping."

The boy shrugged. "He will not come, but I will let you have your hope. It is good to hope while it lasts."

He sat down on the bow thwart and got the oars into the water. He turned the pirogue so that the bow was once more pointing out to sea and then he turned it a little more so that the high prow was lined up with the far side of Île aux Cerf. He noticed the girl's puzzled expression.

"We will anchor on the other side of the island," he explained. "The water is less deep, and there is plenty of kelp and staghorn coral. I think the fish will be less wary over there, and in any case it is a beautiful sea under which to swim."

She nodded, and he saw the apprehension leave her

face. He settled down to his rowing, and five minutes later he backed water and shipped the oars. He threw the anchor out, and the stone disappeared among the waving stalks of kelp and moss two and a half fathoms down. The boulder-strewn beach of Cerf Island was fifty yards to their left, and past the jutting end of the island and a little farther out to sea the waves broke gently and whitely over the black teeth of the reef which reached up hungrily above the surface of the water.

"Would you like to use the flippers again?" the girl asked.

The boy shook his head. "I swim better than you do," he said simply.

Resentment flared in the girl, but it did not last. "You are right," she said. "Without the flipper feet I would not be able to keep up with you, and even with them I will have to swim hard."

The admission did not anger her as it would have done in the past: she felt grateful only that it was possible for her to make such an admission to him.

They went into the water together, and for half an hour they explored the strangeness of the world through which they moved in silence. They shot only three fish, and the boy got all of them. Most of the time they swam side by side, turning frequently to glance at each other, and when their eyes met they smiled. And sometimes the almost human expressions on the faces of the small fish made them thrash out for the surface where they spluttered and laughed, half drowning as they fought to keep their heads above the water while they gasped for breath.

On most of their dives the boy stayed down long after she had gone up for air, and when he did surface he found usually that she had already gone down again.

The boy broke through for air, and as he came up he wondered idly how many dives he had already made. He glanced round, but he did not see the girl anywhere. He rolled over onto his back, feeling a lethargic and pleasant weariness in his body. He decided that he would wait for her to surface before he went down again. He floated on his back for a time, luxuriating in the warmth of the sea. After a while he rolled over suddenly, puzzled at her long absence. He took a quick breath and pushed his head under, but he could not see her anywhere. He came up and twisted round, treading water. He saw that he was midway between the pirogue and the shore of the island, and the surface of the sea was still and empty.

Alarm prickled through him. He jackknifed quickly and went straight down, turning and twisting as he searched the water. He saw her then, ten yards in, towards the steeply sloping shelf of land which rose to the beach of Île aux Cerf.

An antler of staghorn coral had hooked and passed through under the left shoulder strap of her bathing suit. She was struggling frantically, writhing and twisting as she struggled and fought to break free. He saw the redness smoking from her shoulder where the sharp coral had torn her and let her blood out into the silent water. The strap had worked its way down eighteen inches from the point of the antler. He saw that she would never get free, not unless it broke.

He dropped his speargun, and he glanced once to see where it was falling and then he drove himself down and forward through the water. His panic and his fear for her gave him more strength than he had known he possessed. He felt the power of it surging through his legs and his arms. It did not diminish, and more of it came. He reached her with the great strength in his body still untapped. He took hold of the thick antler, hating it with all the strong power in him.

He threw his weight against it. His body swung clumsily in the water, but the coral did not break as he had expected. He did it again, and then again, and he felt the great strength in his body begin to wane.

He tried it once again, and he put all of his strength against it. He felt the coral cutting into his hands, but the great antler did not give. He realized then with a numbing despair that he would never be able to break it.

He glanced at the girl. He saw the bursting redness of her face and the popping eyes behind her mask. Air began to leak from her contorted tightly compressed lips, and as he watched the silver bubbles spitting from her mouth he knew it would not be long before she started to try to breathe the water in like air. There was no time now to try and push her up and work the strap over the end of the coral antler.

He did not know what to do. The knowledge that he was helpless paralyzed him. He was beginning to give up hope for her when he realized that there was only one way to set her free. It was so simple he did not know why he had not thought of it before.

He dragged himself down the antler hand over hand. He took hold of the strap, slipping his fingers under it. He wrenched at it with all his strength, but it held firm. He felt a hopeless despair. He had been so certain that it was the one way to free her. He jerked at it again in a sudden fury, but the material was tough and elastic. It gave, but it did not tear.

His lungs felt as if they were going to burst. He wanted to go up and breathe, and then come down and try again, but he knew that he did not have the time.

He ground his teeth together in pain and impotent rage. The idea hit him in that instant. He drew himself down a little further, and he pulled the strap against his mouth. He bit and gnawed through the double thickness of the inner hem, and then he ripped the cloth with a savage jerk of his head and bit through the other hem with a furious grinding slash of his teeth. He pushed her away from the antler of coral.

She floated free, almost unconscious, bubbles streaming from her mouth. He put his hands against her back, and then he found a platform of coral branch for his feet. He straightened his legs suddenly, pushing off with the last of his strength, and he pushed against her body and started her moving upward through the water.

She struck out for the surface, unoriented. He pushed from below, the muscles in his thrashing legs numbing from the effort and the strain. The surface film above him gradually grew brighter. He thrust against her once more, and the still film shattered. He clawed his way past her trailing legs, and with one last tremendous downward sweep of his arms he shot to the surface.

She was floundering helplessly, trying in vain to keep her head above the water. The pent-up breath exploded from his mouth in a mist of spray. He drew a gasping breath and turned to her.

"On your back!" he shouted. "Get on your back!"

She did not hear him, or she could not comprehend. He knew nothing about lifesaving, but he rolled her over onto her back and took the weight of her body on his own. He dug his fingers into her hair and then knotted them into fists. He kicked out for the shore a few yards behind him.

He swam with all his might, and it seemed to him that he had never swum so far. He felt utterly exhausted, and he did not think he could go much farther. Suddenly he felt his feet brush against something solid. For a moment he did not believe it. He turned his head and dipped his face into the water. He saw sand and rock three feet below him, and he felt a sweeping relief. He allowed his legs to sink. He put his feet flat down on the bottom. He rolled out from under her and stood up, his fingers still knotted in her hair. He hauled her upright, and then he threw her left arm across his shoulder and around his neck.

"Paul," she whispered chokingly.

"Come on," he said, and he started up the steeply sloping beach, fighting the drag of the ebbing water.

He lowered her gently to the sand, his muscles quivering with the strain. He sat her down with her back against the side of a towering granite boulder. He tore his own mask off and dropped it, and then he knelt beside her in the sand. He slipped an arm behind her neck and gently eased the mask off her head and laid it on the sand beside his own.

"How is it with you now?" he asked softly.

The girl did not open her eyes. She sat without moving, her mouth open, with only her rapidly heaving chest to indicate that there was still life within her body. The boy dropped his glance to her lacerated shoulder. He touched the skinned flesh with a great gentleness, examining it carefully. It looked worse than it was, but he knew that it would heal soon. Staghorn coral was nothing. If it had been fire coral it would have been a different matter.

His glance moved down across her chest. He stiffened suddenly, and his eyes grew round with surprise. The torn suit had slipped, and it had fallen forward in a flap across her belly. He stared in wonder and awe at the soft swelling nakedness of her bared right breast. Something came to life within him: it moved gently, without heat or passion, and it moved in his loins and near his heart.

The girl moaned softly and stirred. She opened her eyes and looked up at him. She saw the direction of his stare and glanced down. She cried out weakly and sat up a little, reaching for the sagging bathing suit.

"Wait," the boy said gently.

There was something in his voice. She paused, looking up into his eyes. They were very pale, and very gentle, and there was a light in them which she had never seen before in the eyes of any man. Her hand shook, and then it dropped back into her lap.

"You are very beautiful," the boy said.

She made no reply. She watched him silently, and she knew he was speaking of her and of her naked breast. It filled her with a sudden warmth and contentment.

"I love you," the boy said, kneeling beside her in the damp sand, staring at the secret swelling of her breast.

He had never used the word before, only to his fish, but not to another human being. He loved the man, but he had never spoken of it, because such things were understood between men without the need to speak of them. He listened in his mind to the echo of the words he had spoken. He felt a great weight in his heart, because they did not say any of the things he wanted her to hear.

He bent down suddenly, and he laid his cheek against the exquisite softness of her breast, because it was the only way he could think of to give true meaning to the feeling deep inside him. He felt her arm steal round his neck. He kept his cheek pressed lightly against her breast a little longer, and then he drew away from her.

He straightened up, looking down into her upturned face.

"You are very beautiful," he whispered again.

"You also, my Paul," she murmured. "You are also very beautiful."

He stared into her eyes, and deep down he thought he saw her soul. The message in it filled his mind and his body with a great strength and a great gladness, and in that moment he knew that it would never again matter to him that he would always walk with one leg limping. He stood up slowly, his eyes still on her face and the things that were written on it.

"Would you come with me if I did not have a dolphin?" he asked suddenly, quietly.

"I would come with you."

"But in the beginning you would not have come with me if I had not had a dolphin?"

"Perhaps not," she said simply. "But we are very far from the beginning now."

The boy nodded thoughtfully. "Yes, we are far from the beginning," he said, and he knew that it was the truth she had spoken.

He bent from the waist in a sudden swooping movement and picked up his mask. He swung it up by the strap and then turned towards the sea.

"Wait here and rest a little longer," he said. "I will go for our guns, and then I will bring the pirogue into the beach."

"I can swim to the boat, Paul," she protested, a little of her old defiance coming to life.

"It is better if you wait and rest," the boy said. "You must wait for me and promise it."

His eyes were green and fierce, but they were also gentle and full of concern for her.

"I will wait," she said. "And thank you, Paul."

The boy shook his head irritably. He swung on his heel abruptly and walked into the sea. She watched him limping into the water, and she thought that it would be strange to see him walk without a limp. She did not think he would be the same Paul, the one she had come to know so well.

THAT night the boy spoke to the man. The small lamp burned on the table between their beds, and the little flame stood up straight and fat and filled the room with its half-dark orange-colored light.

The boy sat hunched down on his bed. He kept his eyes on the floor and he did not look at the man. He told him that the big fish had not come, and right away he heard the long sharp breath of disappointment that the man drew into his body. There was the sound of resignation in it, also defeat, and it was the kind of defeat that is final and without hope. He looked up quickly.

"He will come again, Papa," the boy said. "This is something that I know."

The man brightened instantly. "Do you think it possible, Paul?"

"I am sure of it."

In his mind the man saw the harpoon going deep into the heart of the big fish, and the money that would come from the dying of its death. He thought about it for a while, and all of it was very beautiful and clear. He glanced at the boy, his eyes beginning to burn and flash. He remembered then that the boy did not share his dream. His body sagged and the light went out of his eyes.

"Then I wish you many more rides on his back," the man said, and his voice was dull once again and without life. "While you have the chance, that is," he added.

"Why do you say that?"

"In two days we will still be owing the rent, and if it is not paid you and I will have to move," the man said. "I do not think your dolphin will know of this."

"I will ride him to wherever we go," the boy said defiantly.

"You will not have time to play," the man said, and there was bitter relish in his voice. "Not while we are looking for a shack with nothing but promises in our pockets."

The boy bowed his head, and shadow hid his face. He thought about what the man had said. The knowledge that he might lose the big fish saddened him, but it did not fill him with dread as it would have done before. He would still have the girl, and she meant more to him now than the dolphin. He looked up suddenly, and the little flame of the lamp reflected steadily in his eyes as he stared at his father.

"Papa," he said softly. "In the beginning, I think the girl came with me only to play with my dolphin, but now it does not matter so much about the big fish, because I know she likes me for myself. I love her more than I love Marsouin, or perhaps it is only in a different way, and even if the fish does go away I will still be able to come and see her."

He felt a moment of remorse for what he had said, because the fish was his friend and it had saved his life. But he would always love the fish, he knew, as he would always remember it, and so there was no real betrayal of its love and friendship.

In any case, he thought, Marsouin would surely understand.

"She means that much to you?" the man asked, his eyes softening suddenly with the love that was in him for the boy.

The boy nodded with embarrassment. He did not trust himself to look at the man: he kept his face averted, watching the little flame of the lamp. He thought of the girl, and what had happened in the morning. He felt a nameless pain inside him, but there was a great sweetness in its hurting. There was a shy uncertainty in his pale eyes as he turned to face the man.

"I — I have a strange feeling in me, Papa," he began hesitantly. "When I look at her, when I am with her, and even when I think of her, it is as if a great light is on fire inside my heart. There is a strange pain mixed with it, and I do not understand why this should be so. What is it, Papa?" he went on. "Is it that I have become a man?"

The man shook his head gently. He smiled at the boy who was his son. "You have been one a long time already," he said. "A boy does not always have to grow up before he becomes a man."

"But what is it, Papa?" the boy pleaded. "This strange pain that seems to be a part of my happiness."

"There is pain in everything, mon garçon," the man said. "In every beginning, and in every end there is pain, and in between there is also pain." He paused, and his voice grew very soft. "And remember, that for every beginning, there is *always* an end."

"Why should this be so?" the boy said, frightened almost at the note of dark depression in the man's voice. "Why should something that is beautiful also hurt you?"

"I do not think I can explain such a thing," the man said.

"Try, Papa," the boy whispered.

The man looked away quickly from the groping uncertainty in the boy's eyes. He stared at the little flame, but he did not really see it. He was looking into his mind, searching for the words which would take the look of anguish from the face of his son.

"Think — think if you can of a seed pod," he began slowly, and then his voice grew firm and strong as the picture which he was translating unreeled before his eyes. "It ripens and bursts and scatters its seeds into the fertile womb of the earth. That is a beginning, and there is pain in the pod as it bursts. And so it is with a man, my Paul. When his heart is ripe with love for a woman it bursts open, and the seed of his love and his life flows from his loins into the womb of the woman, and there his seed is nourished as the seeds of the pod are nourished in the earth, and the seed of the man grows in his likeness just as the seed of the flower one day brings forth another flower. There is pain in that bursting, Paul, just as there is pain in the pod before it bursts and scatters its seeds."

That is the way it should be, the man thought, but a man being a man, it is not always what happens.

He glanced at the boy and then he looked back quickly at the little flame The room was very quiet, and it seemed darker to him now. He wanted to tell the boy

226

of the thought which had passed through his mind. But he knew it would only hurt, so he held his tongue. He stared in silence at the orange-colored flame, and he forgot about the boy and all the things of which he had spoken. He began to think of the room, and the rest of the house.

He remembered that he had lived in it for a very long time, and then he remembered that he would not be living in it for very much longer. He stifled the groan which almost burst from his mouth, and he stirred heavily on the worn mattress of his bed. He turned away from the flame and stared moodily at the boy. His was another kind of pain, but it hurt just the same. He shrugged abruptly, trying to push it away.

"Tomorrow we must begin to tie our lines together and get other little things ready," the man said, and his eyes began to move slowly round the small room.

The boy sat up straight with a start. He had been far away, thinking of the pain and the bursting which the man had told him about.

"Whaaat?" he asked plaintively.

"I said tomorrow we must begin to tie our lines together and get other little things ready," the man told him impatiently.

The interruption had broken the thread of his thoughts. Where was I, he wondered. His glance went round the room again, and he saw the nails which made a bracket on the wall for the big harpoon.

Ahhh yes, he thought, the nails.

He stared at them, and he remembered driving them into the wood, and the day he had done it came back into his mind as if it were only yesterday. His glance moved on lovingly, and there was a day and a month and a year of his life in every little thing he saw, even the knots in the rough wood.

"I have lived a long time in this house," the man murmured aloud.

The boy made no reply: there was nothing that he could say. He watched the man, and he saw the love and the pain in his eyes as they went slowly round the room. He felt a choking tightness in his throat. There would be much agony in the man, he knew, because he had said that there was pain in every ending, and this was a kind of ending for him.

He swung his legs up off the floor and onto the bed. He lay down and turned his face to the wall. He felt a desperate sad loneliness, because there was nothing he could do.

The man misinterpreted the boy's sudden move. He stared at his back for a moment, and his eyes grew suddenly misty. He cleared his throat and swallowed his pain.

"I know it is a hard thing for you to leave her, my Paul," he said, and his voice was almost breaking with compassion. "But be brave, and it will not be so hard."

The boy rolled over on the bed, every muscle in his body tensing and every nerve vibrantly taut. "But I am not leaving her, Papa!" he exclaimed incredulously.

"But you will have to leave her," the man explained patiently. "When we move from here who knows where we will find a roof for ourselves. We may even have to go to Praslin or La Digue. The people there are kinder, and they have more faith in promises, though I do not even know how we will move when my leg is as it is." He shrugged quickly. "We will find a way, because there is always a way to do things when they have to be done."

Oh my God, the boy thought.

"Praslin or La Digue?" he echoed, in a faint and shocked whisper.

"Yes," the man said quietly.

"They are many miles across the sea," the boy murmured.

"Many miles," the man agreed.

The boy turned over slowly and pushed his face as close to the wall as he could get it. He dug his fingers into the mattress and began to squeeze. His grip did not relax till his hands and his arms became quite numb, and by then there was nothing left in him with which to squeeze.

He knew then that he would have to kill the big fish. The thought of it sickened him, but what made it all so terrible to bear was the knowledge that he would be doing it for himself, and not for his father or his house. And the man had only thought of him, and that was the truth.

THE boy slept fitfully throughout the night. He woke early in the morning, when the first pink traces of dawn were staining the sky and the dark sleeping waters of the ocean. It was much earlier than he had ever awakened since the man first broke his leg.

He lit a fire outside. When the coals had started to collect he placed a breadfruit on top of them. There was still a little coffee and a little sugar left, and he filled a tin can with water from the bucket and placed it beside the breadfruit to boil. After that he walked down to the stream.

He stayed there for a long while, long after he had finished washing out his mouth and rinsing his face. He sat down on a small rock beside the edge of the stream, watching the racing water. He heard it, and he saw it, but none of it was real. He was thinking of the big fish, and of what he would have to do.

He felt a disconcerting mixture of sadness and fearful excitement. It took his breath away and tied his belly into a knot. He stared blindly at the swift flowing water a little longer, and then he sat up suddenly. His fists clenched in helpless anguish.

"I cannot do such a thing!" he cried aloud, giving tongue to his pain and his desperation.

But your father will do it, answered a whisper inside his head.

The boy stiffened. A tremor ran through his body and then he sagged. He stood up slowly, and his movements were like those of a tired old man. He turned away from the stream and began to trudge back towards the house.

There was no excitement in him now: only the sadness remained, and it was deeper and more oppressive than it had been before. He had found a way out for himself, but that was all.

He took the bucket outside for the man, and while he was washing he made the coffee. He mixed exactly half of the coarse chocolate-black grounds that were left with some of the sugar, and then he sprinkled the mixture into the boiling water in the can.

The man ate his piece of breadfruit in silence. He stared out to sea most of the time, chewing mechanically and without any enthusiasm. When he had finished his breadfruit he rubbed his fingers clean against the step on which he was sitting. He rolled and lit a cigarette, and he drank two cups of coffee while he smoked it. He began to wish again that it was the time of his son's birthday when the hesitant voice of the boy broke in on his thoughts.

"Papa —"

"Yes, my Paul?"

"I think perhaps we might kill the big fish," the boy said stonily.

The man threw the soggy stump of his cigarette away. He sat up tensely, gripping the edge of the step with both his hands.

"You do not make a joke?" he asked.

The boy felt numb. He had not wanted to say it, but he had, and now there could be no turning back. He shook his head, and he began to feel sick as he stared at the cruel eagerness which sparked in the eyes of the man.

"Do you think the fish will come back today?" the man asked.

The boy nodded mutely.

"Then take the harpoon and be gone!" the man cried. "Before it is too late."

The boy stood up without a word. He walked into the house, and into the room which he shared with his father. He lifted the big killing harpoon off its bracket on the wall and then walked out again. He halted at the bottom of the steps. He faced the man, holding the harpoon out in his hand.

"I cannot do it," he said stiffly, and then his voice rose shrilly as he went on. "You must do it!" he cried.

"Because it is you who want him dead, to pay the rent for this house!"

He felt a stab of guilt at his hypocrisy. He smothered it quickly, telling himself that he had spoken the truth after a fashion. The man *did* want the dolphin dead.

The man glanced down at the great plaster which encased his leg. Uncertainty crept into his eyes, but then suddenly his face hardened with determination.

"You will help me with the boat?" he asked.

"Can you not manage without me?" the boy pleaded.

"No — not with my leg as it is," the man replied harshly. "And in any case, it is you who will have to summon the dolphin to the boat so that I may get the harpoon into his heart."

The boy flinched. It was something he had not thought of. He wanted no part in the killing of the fish. He had almost convinced himself that by not participating actively in its death he would somehow be blameless. He wanted to refuse, but then he thought of the girl and the great stretch of water which might soon be separating them.

"I will help you," he said, and he felt a monstrous terror and disgust at his own betrayal.

"I will remember this for as long as I live, my Paul," the man said quietly. "And I will remember that you have done this for me and for my house." It never occurred to him that his son could have done it for any other reason.

The boy lowered his eyes. He began to wish that he had never been born, and that he had never met the big fish, which was the same as wishing that the shark had killed him. He went inside the house and picked up a handline, and then he collected his speargun and his mask from under the bed.

"But we will not need the line and you will have no time to shoot with your gun," the man protested.

"It is early, but the girl might be waiting for me," the boy replied dully. "I will tell her that we are going fishing. I do not wish her to think that the big fish is going to die."

"But she will know about it later," the man said. "Would it not be better to tell her the truth from the beginning?"

"No," the boy said quickly. "I will tell her about it in my own time."

His mind seethed as he thought of a way to exonerate himself. He was beginning to despair of ever thinking up an adequate explanation when it came to him suddenly. It was really very simple. He would tell her that the dolphin had surfaced while he was under the water, and that the man had put the harpoon into its heart the moment he saw it.

The man shrugged, and he pushed himself up off the step. "It is your business," he said.

He stared curiously at the boy. It was not like him, but he had no time to think about it. He felt an excitement stirring in him that was as old as the first time he had gone fishing. He hopped up the steps and walked stiffly across the veranda. He picked up the crutches which he had not used for quite a while.

It was a steep mountainside, and even with the crutches it took the man twenty-five minutes to reach the bottom. The boy limped along beside him, slowing his pace to match that of the man. When they reached the bottom of the hill the man hid his crutches under a bush and walked on. He had no need for them now, and besides, he preferred not to be seen using them to help him walk.

They crossed the road side by side and walked through the grove of coconut palms. They reached the low seawall, and the man sat down and swung his legs up and over and then over again on the other side. The boy hesitated among the palms. He did not want to see the girl. She would want to come in the boat with them, and he would have to refuse, and he could think of no explanation which would be satisfactory.

"Come on, Paul," the man urged, glancing impatiently at the boy from the other side of the wall.

The boy edged forward. He checked the sun, measuring its height above the horizon. It was early, much earlier than he had ever come before. Perhaps the girl would not be waiting.

He jumped up on the wall and then down onto the beach. He glanced quickly to his left, holding his breath, but he saw no sign of her in the place where she usually waited for him. An immense feeling of relief swept through him. The inevitable moment when he would have to face her and deceive her had been postponed. He hurried after the man, and he called out to him as he ran past him and went on down the beach.

"Wait by the edge of the water, Papa," he cried. "I will bring the boat in as far as it will come, and the plaster on your leg will remain dry."

The man nodded. Even now he thinks of me, he thought thickly.

The boy splashed into the sea and waded out to the pirogue. He tossed the line and the harpoon into the boat, and then he laid his speargun and mask down carefully. He hauled in the anchor and heaved it into the boat. He swung the pirogue and then he bent forward and threw his weight against it and started it moving towards the shore. The moment the keel scraped the bottom he stopped all way on the boat and steadied it.

"Come on, Papa," he called.

The man stepped forward unhesitatingly. He waded laboriously through the six feet of shallow water which separated him from the bow of the pirogue. He sat down on the gunwale and swung his legs over and into the boat.

The moment the man was settled the boy dug his heels in and hauled back on the pirogue with all his strength. The boat began to move, slowly at first, and then more quickly as it floated free. He pulled it into deeper water and then sprang aboard nimbly.

He took up the bamboo pole and turned the bow of the pirogue in a complete half-circle and then poled it straight out to sea. When the water became too deep he shipped the pole and sat down on the stern thwart and used the oars. He was a hundred and twenty yards out when a faint cry carried to his ears across the still water. He looked up, and there on the beach right by the edge of the water he saw Pierre Vigot waving frantically. He glanced across his shoulder at the man sitting behind him. The stroke of his oars maintained their even, driving force.

"I wonder what he wants," the boy mused.

"It cannot be anything to our advantage," the man replied bleakly.

The boy nodded in silent agreement and faced forward once again. He rowed the pirogue to within fifty yards of where the reef fell away into the deeps. He backed water with the oars and brought the boat to a halt. He stared at the big house on the high ground and grunted with satisfaction as he shipped the oars. He was a long way out now, and even if she did spot him she would never be able to see clearly anything of what was going to happen.

As he stared she came from the house and walked to the wall. She paused by it for a moment, looking out to sea, and then suddenly she began to wave. He watched her for a while, and then he lifted an arm in acknowledgment and turned away. There was a great heaviness in his heart. He wondered if she would ever think or realize that he was doing it, not because he did not love the fish, but because he loved her more. He thought about it for a while, but he did not think she would understand. How could she, when she never had to fish to pay the rent for the house in which she lived? Or worry about having to move because she did not have the money to pay it?

The man untied the coil of line from the shaft of the harpoon and flaked it down on the planking of the pirogue. He stood up, with the harpoon in his hands, testing his stiff leg and getting the feel of the boat. A faint smile of satisfaction tugged at his mouth. He turned to the boy.

"You are going to call the fish now?" he asked.

The boy shook his head. He moved past the man and into the bow of the boat. He lengthened the rope on the anchor and then threw it overboard.

"I am going to shoot some fish first," he said, picking up his mask and rinsing it over the side.

"What madness is this?" the man growled.

"I always shoot fish to feed the *marsouin* after I have played with it," the boy answered.

The dolphin was *it* now, no longer *him*, the personal friend it had been before. The boy was acutely aware of his treacherous differentiation. The burden in his heart grew heavier.

"But you will not be able to feed the *marsouin*," the man said, and his voice was suddenly gentle. "You are not here to *play* with him this time."

The boy started violently. He had known it all along, but now that it had been put into words he could not believe it. But it was the truth, and there was not a thing he could do about it. His eyes filled with blinding tears. He shook his head and fought them back.

"I am still going to shoot a few fish before I call him," he said dully. "The *marsouin* may be watching from deep down in the sea," he went on. "If I do not act as I have done in the times before, it may become suspicious. Who knows what a big fish will think?"

He did not believe that the dolphin would be watching, and even if it had been he did not think it would be alerted by any deviation from the routine which he had followed in the past. He knew in his heart that it was only an excuse to postpone that final hideous moment.

The man did not believe it either, but he understood the torment that was in the boy. "You may be right," he said gravely, pretending it for the sake of his son. "Go and shoot a few fish, but do not be too long, mon Paul."

The boy slipped the mask over his head and adjusted it quickly. He picked up his speargun and went in over the bow. In the next fifteen minutes he speared two jewel-blue wrasse and one of emerald-green, but he found no pleasure in his freedom below the surface or in the death of the fishes he had killed. He moved leadenly through the water, with the aching heaviness in his heart also in his arms and in his legs. In the end, when he could stand it no longer, he returned to the pirogue. His procrastination was only making it worse.

He pushed the mask up on his forehead. He hauled the anchor up without a word. He spat the coppery saltiness out of his mouth and took a deep breath. His tongue lifted up towards the roof of his mouth. His lips pursed and then he sent his piercing whistle out across the early morning water of the sea. In the taut silence which followed he began to hope that the dolphin would not hear him.

I am sorry, Marsouin, he told the big fish in his mind, but I have the girl and there is nothing that I can do.

"Try it again," the man whispered tensely.

The boy whistled once more, hating himself for doing it, and almost instantly the dolphin surfaced eighty yards away. It stood up on its tail for a moment, and then sank back slowly into the water. He searched for it, feeling sick, and then twenty yards out he saw the dark shape of the big fish as it swam towards the pirogue under the water.

Beside the boy the man stood up quietly. The harpoon was in his hands, and unconsciously his calloused fingers began to caress the smooth wooden shaft.

The dolphin came to the surface ten yards from the pirogue, squeaking and whistling with excitement. When it saw the man it grew silent. It watched him warily.

The boy called to it softly, but it made no move to come closer. He knelt in the boat and smacked his hand down into the water, but still the dolphin held its distance suspiciously.

"Why does it come no nearer?" the man hissed, tense with excitement and impatience. "You told me that it swam right up alongside the boat before."

"It did the same thing when the girl first came with me," the boy whispered. "It does not know you, and so it is wary."

"Do something!" the man cried softly. "Bring the big fish to me!"

The boat rocked gently as the boy stood up. "I will go into the water, and he will come to me beside the boat."

He did not want to do it, but then he thought of the girl, and he remembered the feel of her breast against his cheek. In his mind he balanced it against the knowledge that the dolphin had saved his life. He clenched his teeth and pushed the thought aside. He adjusted his mask and slipped over the bow and went down silently into the stillness under the sea.

He surfaced beside the pirogue. He reached up and caught hold of the gunwale with his right hand. He hung there in the water, and he drew his legs in and bent them at the knee and placed the soles of his feet against the hull of the boat to steady himself. He called to the fish with a soft trilling whistle.

The dolphin began to squeak and whistle again. It swam slowly towards the boy, coming closer and closer. The boy watched it, his mind and body numb. He saw the shadow of the man long and dark in front of him on the dark blue water. The shadow moved, and it seemed almost to lift off the water as the man stretched upward and lifted the harpoon high above his head.

The man waited, watching the dolphin close. He held the harpoon with a love that was almost obsessive. My sweet God, he thought, it is almost like putting the knife of your body into a woman who has never been a woman before. He felt a great hurting inside him, for himself and for this thing which he had to do, and for the big fish who was like a woman. He lifted the harpoon a little higher and then started it plunging down.

I love you, fish, he thought joyously.

The boy heard the soft explosive grunt of effort which came from behind and above him, and the shadow of the man moved on the water.

He screamed. In that moment, he realized for the first time the full extent of his treachery and betrayal. It was more than he could bear. He did not think of the girl as he lunged forward and drove the dolphin away with his flailing arms, nor was it the knowledge of her inevitable repugnance and horror which prompted him to act. He was not thinking of her, or even of the debt he owed the fish. He was thinking of himself, and of his dignity as a human being.

It was the last thought he was ever to have. He felt a gigantic blow against his back. He felt the flesh and bone under his left breast burst open as the blow on his back went right through his body, and then he felt no more.

The man stared in horror. "Jesus forgive me!" he cried suddenly. "What have I done?"

He sat down in the boat, down on the planking, and he reached over the side. He lifted his son out of the water, and he lifted him out in his arms with the pirogue listing so heavily that the gunwale was down in the water.

He turned awkwardly, holding the boy in his arms, and he rolled over on his side a little and got his right knee under him while his left leg lay stretched out straight and stiff in the bottom of the boat. He pushed himself up, searching frantically for somewhere to lay the boy. He did not want to put pressure on the harpoon and hurt him more. It was bad enough now. It had gone in through his back and the point of it was sticking out eight inches the other side of his chest.

His eyes fell on the bow thwart. He inched forward,

his face darkening with the strain of holding the boy. It never entered his head that he might be dead. That was too monstrous a thought to contemplate. He laid the boy down carefully, with his belly across the thwart and his knees on the planking supporting the weight of his body. He looked as if he were bent forward in prayer, except for the shaft of the harpoon which stuck up out of his back. There was only a little blood. It had diluted with the water on his back, and it showed pink against his golden-colored skin.

The man unfastened the line from the harpoon with great care. He snatched up the oars and began to row. He drove the pirogue as he had never driven it before, and the oars whipped and lashed under the fierce power of his stroke.

The dolphin leaped beside the boat. The man watched it lift high into the air, and in that instant when it seemed to hang suspended before crashing back into the sea he saw the big fish turn its head and peer down into the boat. It jumped again, closer this time, and it looked into the pirogue once more.

"Go away, fish," he said aloud, and then he began to think of what he could do.

Madame Morel, he thought numbly, she will take us in the car to the hospital in Victoria and the doctor will take the harpoon from his back and mend the wound I have made in him.

The pirogue ran aground with a slight jar. The man shortened the anchor rope and threw the stone into the sea. It was a waste of precious seconds, and though it distressed him, he knew that it was a thing which could not be overlooked. He would have to go fishing again.

And the boy also, his mind cried fiercely, desperately.

He scrambled out of the boat, his stiff leg making all

his movements clumsy. He lifted the boy, carrying him face down, one arm under his chest, the other supporting his legs. He splashed through the shallow water and up the beach, stumbling in his haste, the iron stirrup under his left heel digging into the sand.

The mother of the girl saw him first. For a moment she stared in shocked disbelief. She saw the harpoon in the boy's body, and the point of it sticking out below his chest. She cried out incoherently. The bubbling scream in her throat rose to a shriek. She turned and flew to the steps which led down to the beach. She took them three at a time, crying and sobbing to herself as she stumbled down them half blind with her grief. She reached the man in a last breathless spurt and halted panting in front of him.

"Oh my God!" she cried faintly.

"The hospital, Madame Morel," the man said. "We must take him in your car."

The woman stared incredulously at the man. Was he blind? Could he not see? She looked closely into his eyes, and she saw the shocked, sightless vacancy in them. She understood.

"Put him down, M'sieur," she said quietly.

The man shook his head doggedly. "The hospital —— "

The woman stepped forward and cut him off. "He is dead, you foolish man!" she screamed. "He is dead and you have killed him!"

The man shook his head ponderously. He had known it in his heart, carrying the limp weight of the boy up the beach, but even now he could not bring himself to believe that all of it was finished.

The woman reached out suddenly, and with a strength she had not known was in her she lifted the boy

242

from the arms of the man and bent and laid him down on the beach. She put him down on his side, and she kneeled beside him in the sand.

She peeled the mask gently from his face. It was half full of blood, and his sightless blue eyes were wide and staring, and blood trickled from the corner of his mouth.

The sight of it all destroyed the last of her control. She laid her face against his cheek. It was crumpled and ugly in its grief, no longer gentle and smiling as it used to be. She began to sob. There were no tears in her eyes, but the force of her grief shook her whole body.

The man watched her in growing amazement. He dropped down on one knee beside her suddenly, his left leg stretched out straight behind him. His face was stiff with disbelief, but far back in his eyes there was a look of dawning comprehension. He reached out and shook the woman gently.

She lifted her head. She saw and understood the look in his eyes. She stared back at him dully, uncaring, her shoulders sagging and limp.

The man was silent for a moment longer. "But why?" he asked. "Why did you leave him?"

The woman's eyes clouded. "There — there are things which happen, and it is too late afterwards to —"

She broke off abruptly, and both of them turned to stare up the beach in the direction from which the girl's shrieking cry had come. She was running towards them, and Pierre Vigot ran at her side.

The man turned to the woman, and their eyes met and held at the same moment. "I will tell no one," he said.

She looked at him questioningly, blankly. She knew

that his remark held some significance for her, but she was too tired to reach out and grasp it.

She stiffened a moment later, alarm leaping through her, but then it went away and left her drained and empty once more. She shrugged wearily: none of it seemed to matter now.

The man studied her a moment longer, and then he shot a glance at the girl who was now only twenty yards away and running harder than before. He noticed irrelevantly that her mouth was open. He turned back to the woman.

"He loved her very much," he said.

"Yes, I saw the change in her too," the woman admitted slowly.

"Then perhaps it is just as well," the man said quietly. "In the end it would have hurt him more than dying, because nothing could have come of it."

He stood up suddenly, pushing himself off the ground with his hands and his one good leg. He stared down at the body of his son, and there was no feeling in him now.

The girl halted in front of them in a shower of sand. "What has happened?" she screamed.

She looked down, and she saw the body of the boy. Her eyes widened in horror. She stared, and her mouth opened and closed, but the words did not come. The woman rose, and she pulled the girl against her breast, shutting out the sight of death.

"It was an accident, Danielle," she said.

She felt the girl shudder, and then an instant later she felt her begin to tremble. She held her closer as the violence of her trembling grew and her own body shook with the shock that it absorbed.

Pierre Vigot looked at the harpoon that had gone into

the back of the boy. It was very tragic, and it was very simple. Roger had put his harpoon into a tiger shark, and when the shark died it changed back into what it had been before it died. He reached out and touched the fisherman lightly on the arm.

"I am sorry, Roger," he said.

"I am also sorry, Pierre," the man replied heavily.

"I tried to call you when you were taking the pirogue out."

"We saw you, the boy and I."

"I had some good news for you."

The man nodded absently. Along the line of the beach, from both directions, and from the grove of dark green coconut trees he saw the people who came hurrying towards them. He did not want them to see his son, not as he was, not with the harpoon through his body.

He bent down low, bending from the waist, and he caught hold of the harpoon with both hands just behind the barbed head. He straightened up a little, turning the body of the boy as he did it, and then he placed the sole of his right foot gently and carefully against the chest of the boy. He strained evenly on the harpoon, but it did not give. He put a little more of his strength against it. He felt it begin to move, and then after that it came more easily and he drew the shaft of the harpoon out of the body of the boy. It came free with a small sucking sound, and blood welled quickly from the gaping hole below his breast from which he had drawn the wood.

The man straightened up. He felt strangely light-headed. He stared blindly at the harpoon in his hands, and his fingers convulsed on the blood-smeared shaft. In that instant a raging madness overcame him. He wanted to break the shaft of the harpoon over his thigh and snap it in one vicious movement of expurgation.

He raised the harpoon, holding it parallel with the ground, and he began to raise his right leg, bending it at the knee and lifting his thigh. There was the anger and rage in him to break it, but he hesitated. It was an excellent shaft, and a well-balanced harpoon, and he knew he would have to go fishing again, even if it was without the boy.

"You did not hear me, Roger?" Pierre Vigot inquired softly.

"I heard you," the man said, not taking his eyes from the harpoon.

"Then let me tell you that I spoke to M'sieur Morel late in the evening yesterday," the big Creole said. "I begged him to give you more time to find the money for your rent, and he agreed to wait until you were well and fishing once again."

The man's head snapped round. He stared at Pierre Vigot for one incredulous moment. Shock and horror twisted his face. His dark eyes filled with pain and dismay. He stared at the Creole a little longer, and then suddenly, as if he had drawn a mask over his face, it grew calm and impassive once more.

He raised the harpoon a little higher, and he brought his half-raised leg right up till the thigh was parallel with the ground. Deliberately, very deliberately, he brought the shaft smashing down across his raised thigh. It snapped in two with a report like a pistol shot.

The woman spun around, fearful and uncomprehending.

"It is only the harpoon," the man said, and he dropped the pieces on the sand.

He saw the alarm leave her face, and as he looked into

her eyes he thought he smelled the sweet scent of mountain flowers which had been warmed against the breast of a woman. It took him far back to long ago.

He glanced down at his son. He saw the dark blood on the near-white sand, and he thought of the long walk up the side of the mountain with the body of the boy in his arms. He did not know as yet how he would do it, but he knew he would find a way.

He lifted his head slowly, and he stared out to sea, and just then the dolphin leaped far out near the reef and the bright light of the sun on the spraying water hurt the man's eyes and made him squint.

He looked away. He felt very old, and there was a sadness in him that went deep down into the bones of his heart. He glanced down at the boy again.

It will be easier to carry him, he thought, without the harpoon in his back.

THE dolphin leaped again, a little farther out, and in the sky above it a frigate bird wheeled suddenly but then continued on its way as it saw the dark shadow beneath the water which fled straight out to sea.